THE
DARK
BACKWARD

THE
DARK
BACKWARD

MARIE BUCHANAN

COWARD, McCANN & GEOGHEGAN, INC.
NEW YORK

First American Edition 1975

Copyright © 1975 by Marie Buchanan

SBN: 698-10654-7

Library of Congress Catalog Card Number: 74-30601

PRINTED IN THE UNITED STATES OF AMERICA

'What seest thou else
In the dark backward and abysm of time?'

THE TEMPEST

THE
DARK
BACKWARD

1

'Why I must? I couldn't say.' She put out one hand, vaguely, palm down and fingers extended, so that it seemed to hover. ' "More things in heaven and earth...", something like that.' Brusquely she shook her head and began to turn away, leaving him huddled at the bar, his hand cupped about the tankard as though supporting its spine – whereas he, not it, was being the weakly vertebrate. And uneasily he got up and moved slowly after her.

Not because of anything she'd said, though. 'More things in heaven and earth ... Than are dreamt of in your philosophy'; mere words at the time, seeming irrelevant. Afterwards he doubted that Val knew their significance herself, heaven to her being physical sky – atmosphere, a matter of pressures and buoyancy, humidity, thermal flows. Perhaps she'd just meant that, capable and

feet-on-the-ground as she principally was, there had sometime to be an extra element to reach out for; and so her
unreasoned need for flying. But she made no conscious
attempt to grapple with the idea, nor with him. Flung it
out unregarded, left it to float or fall as it would. As, for
that matter, it was her way to leave him.

So it wasn't her words that made him get up then and
follow, but what happened as he looked after her. An
unnerving trick of the light. From congenial, brewer's
gloom she went straight out into August midday dazzle.
Motionless and black for an instant in the doorway, the
airfield reeling white behind, she flared once like the
sun's disk and then totally disappeared. There was simply nothing left of her. He was looking through where
she should have stood.

The light pulsed, with an answering vibration inside
his own skull, exploding in concentric rings like waves of
sound become locally visual. In the momentary vertigo
he was unsure whether the patterns he saw were sound, or
if he somehow heard through sight, but all his senses were
involved together in a half-awareness.

The strobe circles shimmered and droned upon his
brain, and now it seemed that they reversed direction
and he, with them, was being drawn to their common
centre; and then it struck him that the effect of which he
was a part was not one of space so much as of time, and
that some strange distortion was taking place, with himself helpless inside it, shaken out of ordered position and
then shuttled, forwards then backwards. Briefly he had a
premonition of horror and all movement seemed to cease.
He saw himself at some distance, a gaunt wedge of blackness ringed by greater mute shadows leaning in, like immense, ancient rocks; and the fear that penetrated like a
pain was almost recognition, but it just failed in defini-
tion before, in a shudder, it too was gone.

The light vortex continued to throb, but inside himself
there occurred some shift of mental axis, and with a dull
ache his eyes adjusted. He blinked and Val was instantly
reprinted, black and solid, on the noonday glare.

He turned away to count out coins and push them over
the bar counter, and Val reappeared briefly in negative,

white now on an oblong of black that floated above his knuckles.

He went out, facing bleached grass shimmering with layered mirage, his head throbbing as he ploughed after her over the stubble. Someone swerved towards him wearing overalls, held out helmet and goggles. Sarson pushed them under one arm and plodded on, still in the city suit he'd worn to drive down.

Twenty yards ahead Val was three-dimensional enough, normal in her sandy-coloured flying-suit; small, compact, capable, boyish even, with her short, dark hair blowing across one cheek. She looked up at him steadily as he came alongside the glider, her body two feet from his now, but in some non-physical way still distantly receding. It seemed to him that she was always diminishing, as though he watched her practise a free-fall, spread below him like a little, sandy, four-point star, dropping away in space before her chute could open. It was always Val who moved away, relative to him stationary.

He didn't stir, rooted there, feeling all his weight on his heels, sun burning into his shoulders through the fine wool suit, tips of fingernails scoring damp palms inside his trouser pockets. Now that she waited for him to speak he had nothing to say, had asked enough by coming here at all where he had no place. Her answer, equally unspoken, reduced him to nothing. He looked past her at the little craft she was going to fly.

She shrugged, nodded to the second seat, swung up and left him to scramble in beside her if he wished. Steve went past on the tractor and started bawling across to someone by the clubhouse door. It looked shady and comfortable back there: The Last Chance Saloon. His final drink stood barely tasted on the bar. He could feel the soft touch of foam still cool on his upper lip. He heaved himself up and strapped himself in.

The winch driver was making signals upfield. The wingtip man levelled them off and prepared to hold steady. Val looked up from checking her instruments and reached for his harness. 'Tighter,' she ordered, and rebuckled it herself. He remembered her once saying, 'You don't just get into a glider; you fit it on.'

3

He didn't have her confidence. He always felt naked up there; no engine, no carapace. And this glider was an old-type one, open cockpit, as she preferred. He crammed his buzzing skull inside the helmet and had the goggles down before she surveyed him again. Her face was expressionless, and his fear covered.

He asked himself what was he doing there, why again he'd trotted in her wake. Inertia, he supposed, once the first sense of unease had lessened. From alarm he'd started up when she flared into fire in the doorway and disappeared, but from then on he'd just continued, being already in motion. There was no point in stopping. He barely knew how to, had lost the braking mechanism.

On the ground they were checking the cable, its parachute, weak link, rope and rings. All correct, and the cable was clipped on, release rings rattled.

Val grinned over to the group logging the flight, got an 'All clear' from the signaller, shouted 'Take up slack.' The man shouted the same order back and started raising and lowering one bat, the other held low. Ahead the cable began straightening. Val had her right hand lightly on the stick, left hovering over the yellow release knob. 'All out,' and the signaller was waving both bats above his head. The winch could be clearly heard revving up over a half-mile forward and then the glider was in motion, riding rough at first and then smoothly running, the field's stubble streaming under the wings, striped as though coarsely combed; and then, accelerating, they were airborne.

The old glider held take-off attitude to a hundred feet and at that Val drew the nose up and the climb seemed to him madly steep. He would have liked to sit forward but the harness tipped him back in a helpless vee. Giddily up, and the pressure change affecting his ears.

At last the slight plucking sensation they had been waiting for, scarcely a shudder, and the nose falling a little so that the horizon again came into view ahead. Two quick pulls on the release knob and Val looking over to watch the cable drop away. It looked a good drop, well within the boundary and should fall just ahead of the winch.

4

Then he was aware of floating free, leaning on empty air, and there was that awful, abrupt realisation of having no engine, no power, upheld only by the invisible, vaguely calculable ways of atmosphere, existing merely as denser matter interpreted through surfaces. There were little, soft sounds of the fabric, and wind whining high against the vast silence around. And Val began quietly to hum to herself, as she used to years before, doing simple little things about the garden and house.

He was suddenly, violently, sick; and after that and the shaking it was better.

The ground slanted below like the side of a shallow bowl and already they were turning. He realised she was trying for a soaring flight. The launching had seemed surprisingly high for a winch one; she must have sensed the edge of a thermal. Halfway through the second circle he could feel it himself, watched her check their curved path for the space of five seconds then take it again, still banking right. One more full circle and they were at the core of strong lift, surging up on a buoyant doughnut of air, nose up to the brazen sky, with the sun, whirling copper-white, dead ahead.

He closed his eyes but the vertigo increased. It seemed an age before they were up on the cap of the thermal, feeling for a second column of upthrust. And here it came, bearing them up, for ever circling, until they were among fine wisps of haze that signalled the early build-up of cumulus cloud. And at last Val checked the wheeling, levelled and assumed a gliding tilt.

They were well upwind of the airfield, and distance flattened the terrain below, but from the colours he could tell they had crossed above a clay valley and below them the chalky plain swelled again from its chequerboard edges of blond-streaked barley and dark green potato fields to irregular, balding crowns scarred white with small quarries or close-penned flocks of sheep. On an animated map, insect traffic and a blue-green caterpillar train marked a populated fold. Across to the left, water showed like a flattened silver root deformed in places with the swellings of ponds.

This was more to his taste now, and despite the nausea

he began to react to familiar values, picking out features, interpreting light and shade into three-dimensional form, recognising geophysical traits that were as distinctive and repetitive as family characteristics – as his own Sarson nose and slanted cheekbones.

A rare excitement moved in him as, staring down, he seemed to grasp emerging pattern. Not of any one place he recalled, but it was a recognition of type. Suddenly he was sure there was something of real significance below. There was nothing he could specifically name, but a vibration started up of itself, as though he'd been idly dowsing and the twig had given a quickening leap.

'Turn her!' he shouted. 'Come about.' The wind shredded his voice but Val nodded, eyes steadily ahead. It took minutes for her to make the double turn and come back on the plain from the same angle, and they dropped some four hundred feet in making it. Val pulled down the corners of her mouth and he guessed she'd missed the thermal for ever now. It must have been a fast riser. Certainly the cloud had built up rapidly in the little time since they'd been past it. Well, that was her business. What held his own attention now was the area coming up below, no more than a colour stain on dried-out grass, but singling out an eminence that had a sort of authority over the land around.

She made an S-sweep and he had to twist, as far as the tightened harness would allow, to keep the site in view. A marked pattern of colour showed up, and with loss of height the contours were confirmed.

They sank, looping slowly down the zigzag track of an invisible mountain of air, and the markings were gone; but increasingly he recognised it was the *right kind* of place. It looked to be a certain site from a groundman's elevation.

Val was lowering her left hand, palm down, in warning. The earth approached grimly close and they were still upwind on the second leg of the landing routine. Too high for her liking though, for after the final turn she tipped a wing and sideslipped right, bringing hedgerows and the dusty lane dotted with upturned faces close under the wings as she slid into the field again, a hundred yards to the left of take-off.

Still dominated by the view over the south-west horizon, Sarson barely noticed the neat finalisation. He worked the harness release, climbed unsteadily down and stumbled in the sudden renewal of heat.

Val was there before him, turned and looked long at him with her upper-air blue eyes. 'You shouldn't fly in that condition,' she said coolly, and started walking off again.

'Maps,' he called after her. 'Can I have some local ones? Relief? Ordnance?'

She stopped and turned round. 'Plenty in the office. Ask Andy.' Not questioning his interest; completely indifferent. Moving away again, straight-backed, level-eyed. This time he let her go.

Andy was a leather-faced fifty-year-old of few words. He passed over a satchel of maps and leaned against the window frame, twisting back to watch Sarson spread them on the table. Hugh found the prominence he wanted, then rechecked it on ordnance. There was no mention of any ancient monument.

'Care to borrow them overnight? They're spares.'

'These two. Thanks.'

'You're Val Sarson's husband?'

Hugh nodded. It seemed to make him a good risk. Mr Valerie Sarson, house-trained, respectable.

'Something interest you particularly? In your line of country, I mean?'

'I don't know. I'm not entirely certain what I thought I saw . . .'

'Any time you want another look, just say. Be glad to take you up.'

'When the sun's really low?'

'Have to be evening then. Too much haze these mornings.'

Sarson nodded. That was true enough. This Andy knew he was after good shadows. He seemed, in fact, to know a lot. Where had he learnt about Sarson's profession? Perhaps from Val herself. If so, what other personal details had she given?

7

'What altitude were you thinking of?'

Sarson considered. There was a pretty good camera in the car boot. 'Low. Four hundred; five hundred feet ceiling. Something like that. For oblique shots. Can you hold at that?' It would do for the present. If these photographs showed up the right marks he would need later to go higher, get vertical colour shots.

Andy nodded, running a hand through his cropped, grizzled hair. 'We'll take the chopper. Get a good picture on hover. Be here at twenty-o hours?' he offered.

They settled on it. Simple and brief, but even at that, Val's little yellow Triumph was gone when Sarson came out to the car park. He made for the hotel he'd noticed on the ordnance map, and booked in for a couple of nights. Lunch was over, not that it bothered him. They sent up a sandwich and the bottle he ordered, and when he'd attended to them he stretched out on the chintzy little bed and got rid of the hottest hours in sleep. At about six he showered, put his clothes back on, went down for cold beef, salad and pickles. The landlord addressed him by name and at that the waiter looked interested.

'My wife gone off yet?' Sarson asked casually, when the man brought his coffee.

'About three hours back,' said the waiter uncertainly.

'Good.' No doubt soon after she'd seen him come in, or his car parked in the forecourt. Well, she didn't have to run this time, because he wasn't following. The accumulated resentment that had brought him down here had evaporated at their brief encounter. For the present he had no wish to pursue her with his personal blight.

With all I've learnt about civilisation, he thought wryly, I should know how to tackle such a commonplace situation. The Greeks had more than a word for it; they'd a cure for wayward wives. Drastic but healing to the self-esteem. Revenge, after all, is designed to serve the exactor, not the one to suffer it. Only, the simple classical solution didn't apply to his and Val's non-Olympian relationship. He couldn't react like a hero, was just left dull-witted, with a limb lopped off.

Time was, just then, nudging at seven forty. He picked

up the camera, approved the now cloudless sky and drove the six miles back to the airfield.

Andy had the helicopter out, a serviceable old West-land Scout. Apart from the pilot's there were no proper seats, but he'd provided a couple of squabs of foam rubber and put out a cotton flying suit for cover-up when crawling round the hatch manoeuvring for shots. In the pilot's seat Andy put on a pair of half-spectacles for a last check of the map, and recognising he was long-sighted, Sarson knew there'd be no difficulty getting him to pick up ground markings.

'Beacons,' he said, nodding, when Sarson pointed out the locality.

'It doesn't say so.'

'No. That's what it's called round here, though. Not Beacon Hill, just Beacons. I've never seen it written my-self, come to think of it; but ask any of the old folk. They'll tell you.'

For a moment Sarson's hopes faltered. If the name survived only by word of mouth, the beacons it referred to could hardly be earlier than the Napoleonic scare. And even the Spanish Armada was modern in his scale of history. But the word was a plural, and that gave it a ritual-istic ring. Meant not so much a message as a cult. It could be the right place, but the wrong period. Only digging was really going to settle that.

Sarson lay on his belly, with his elbows at the hatch edge. The chopper had been used for photography before and there was an adjustable frame of angle iron that fitted to the camera and gave security while he manoeuvred for shots. Andy was patience personified.

There were twenty-four shots he could use and the film was black and white, so as he varied the aspects and ele-vations, it was light that ran out first. Sarson had the feeling that some of the last shots would prove the most revealing, when the mass of the land was sombre and only little slits of brightness still lit a few west-facing rises.

'Right,' he said at last, 'that's it,' and started unscrew-ing the camera from its bracket.

'Tour of the countryside,' shouted Andy back at him.

'Hold on.' The helicopter felt to be plucked up and angled into the dying sun, and they flew over an earth that had been folded into flattened horizontals of black and tiger-orange; circled and sped over lakes of purple shadow, turned back at last over a countryside that was peat-bog black pierced with fewer stars than in the paler sky above. Down then to a lamplit signal-in, to cars towing the last of the gliders back, to a club-room where log-books were being made up, flights post-mortemed, the next day's plans being finalised. And still not a sign of Val.

Sarson wanted to settle up. Andy ran his hand again through his rough hair. 'You mean you want me to book it and all? I don't want anything. I'd have gone up anyway.'

Because I'm Val's husband, thought Sarson. Under false pretences in a way. 'Look, it takes money to run the place,' he said. And to go by the vintage stock, they did it on a shoe-string.

'Pay in kind,' said Andy. 'Come and give us a halfday handling things on the ground. Maybe the bug'll bite you too.'

'Gliding? I haven't the stomach for it. I'm not as adventurous as Val. But I'll help out sometime, come and tow or time-keep. I'll give you a ring first.'

Andy nodded. 'Do that. Glad to meet up with you at last. I'd wondered.'

During the evening as he sat in the bar, and later lay sleepless on his back staring at the angled ceiling of the hotel bedroom, Andy's voice kept coming back, the crinkly smile, the little pause and then the words, 'I'd wondered.' Kindly meant, but humiliating. No doubt wondering *why*, and what on earth sort of man . . .

He wondered too himself. He couldn't remember how it had come to be like this, where he had gone wrong, in what way he could once have been different. The longer it goes on, he told himself, the less I know. And all the time seeing the little sandy, four-point star falling away farther and farther in space, forever diminishing.

Even when the prints were in his hands, with the evidence in clear black and white, he was in no hurry to make extravagant claims. It *appeared* interesting; worth a further look. That was as far as he was prepared to commit himself officially. There were all manner of deceptions to ensnare the unwary. Circles of significant colour-change could be caused by as recent phenomena as a fertiliser-spray towed on a circling tractor, or that hoary old student-bait the cropping of a tethered goat. But not in this case, because although he had observed colour-pattern, what he had actually photographed was relief, shot obliquely, when shadows were long. And what in his most intimate thoughts on the place he now admitted possible, was an almost perfectly circular henge with from twenty to thirty shallow depressions that might mark filled-in holes where posts or megaliths had once stood. The site, in fact, appeared strongly positive.

It was no natural phenomenon – its regularity, fragmentary though the details, disproved that – but an artefact built to a pattern some four thousand years old. Nor was it just any Neolithic or Bronze Age monument left open to the sky like the giant stone circles of Wessex and Brittany, but something more special, for he sensed a secondary mystery overlying the enigma of its origin. For some reason this site, however sacred its first purpose, had later been concealed by more than the weathering of time. There was just enough of the pattern discernible to point to its greater part having been deliberately disguised. Outside the points marking alignments of solar and lunar significance, there would once have been high chalk banks and ditches crossed by one or two ceremonial causeways, and at the centre some form of focal sanctuary. Little sign of any of these here; only the merest broken traces. Natural wear of the centuries would not have destroyed so thoroughly. Why had this place, once set apart as a ritual monument, deliberately been concealed from human sight? What appalling happening had called for such total desecration? And what relic might still lie here, at depth, that required such extreme protection? – or such vehement denial?

The archaeologist in him wasn't slow to respond to the

exciting possibilities. By some means or other he had to obtain official sanction to dig. He was faced now with choice of action. A short feature offered to an archaeological glossy would at this stage be a brief firecracker attracting too wide and uninformed attention over a few weeks, especially if any of the popular newspapers, short of copy in the silly season, jumped on the waggon. Then the dry summer, combined with hikers' boots, could make a nonsense of the faint surface traces that showed at present. It might even prove one of those 'phantom' sites that show once or twice and then disappear for many years. So, no publicity until either there was conclusive external evidence or some definite commitment to excavate.

But in using the 'softly, softly' approach, with official channels open, the site would become a communal academic property. His personal link with it would be broken. At best, opening Beacons would become another enthusiasts' project with a nucleus of solid scientists restraining the ignorant amateurs, and some titular director filtering the inadequate finances until, like so many other excavations, it had to be shelved half-done, findings filed away in a museum vault, while exertions were diverted to the emergency rescue of some Roman villa threatened by the projected route of a new motorway, with bulldozers ringing the site and workmen panting to get in and destroy the fragile past.

He was being unscientific, he admitted. The sickly euphoria of last evening and now this front of defeatism. His approach was all too subjective. A site is a site is a site, that's all. Like a job is a job. No call to turn manic-depressive. Well, that, he supposed, was the Celt in him, or whatever. Best to work it out of his system, go there on foot, stay all day with sandwiches, bellyaching and stomping around until he'd had enough of this personal-link business. Take some measurements, suffer a few mathematical doubts, reduce the whole thing in scientific perspective.

Which he did, scarcely taking time off to notice the distant circling of the silent gliders or to ask himself whether Val might have come back, first checking with Andy by phone that the coast was clear.

He filled several pages of a jotter with notes, ate the lunch his hotel had packed for him, and fell asleep on his back in the shade of some whin bushes until the sun came round and burned his forehead crimson. Then he packed his stuff up, slung Andy's map satchel over one shoulder and plunged downhill again in search of water. He cancelled the second night's stay, paid up after dinner and drove straight off, dropping in Andy's maps on the way, together with a bottle of scotch.

And still on the journey back he caught himself grinning as he drove. Thinking, 'Some find. *My henge.*'

2

They sat obliquely to each other in the dining-car, the Expert (as Sarson was beginning to think of him) by the window, his famous profile static against the fleeting details of the countryside they were speeding through, long legs outthrust, so that even if Sarson had taken the opposite window-seat he would have had to turn his back on the outer world or suffer snakelike contortions. As it was, Sarson slumped from preference on the inner seat, where waiters brushed past with their loaded trays, striking his shoulder whenever the train shuddered. And it was significant, he reflected, that the other man faced forward, himself back.

'Fish?' doubted Beaumont, checking back to the menu with a little pouting of the lips that produced a corresponding grimace in the handsome, downcurved moustache. 'Species unidentifiable.'

Sarson waited for the practised performance of a single raised eyebrow, and unfailingly it came. The sharp nose and its frame of flaxen hair – so uncannily lighter in tone than the pop-star moustache and trimmed beard – bent over the inquest. Beaumont handled the fish eaters with a finicky niceness. 'Ichtyosaurus,' he pronounced. His fork probed the mound of creamed potato, prolonging the whimsy. 'Embedded in triassic marly clay.'

The buffet car lurched as it took the curved track, and the cutlery on all the tables tittered. Donald Beaumont looked up through fashionably shaped lenses, paused to acknowledge the applause and then resumed his exposé of the dish. Sarson went silently on with his British Rail cod. Half an hour had gone by, he calculated. One half-hour out of a projected seven weeks.

It was the first time he'd found himself alone with Beaumont and he'd expected some relaxation of the man's public manner.

They were, after all, colleagues with a lot of academic background in common. He wondered now whether Beaumont ever gave up projecting an image: would he still consciously put on a show after hours spent sifting a waterlogged ditch, make donlike jokes with his wife in bed, enact waggish dreams when he slept? But perhaps what seemed an irritating mask was actually the shape of the man himself, and not a barrier between. In which case it seemed that for much of their time together Sarson would be cast as audience.

He went over in his mind everything that he could remember of this man and conceded that mainly his sources were publicity ones. So far as he guessed, none of his own known contemporaries had worked with him, possibly because Beaumont's rise had been so meteoric. He'd come suddenly on to the archaeological scene with a popular book on Eastern Mediterranean sites, more of an amateur's travelogue; but this had been followed up by a television series with some very competent film, and immediately the book had become a best-seller, proliferating in paperback. Admittedly, beneath the easy line of showmanship his subject matter had been sound enough. But had that been due to the scholarship of the researchers backing him up, the little fellows whose names didn't get on to film titles? It made him in any case a team leader of some stature, and there weren't, to date, any underground whispers that might cut him down in size.

Active, energetic, enthusiastic he had certainly seemed in their early encounters round the museums and universities, and if he bounced it was to some purpose, for it wasn't until Beaumont had shown interest that the project ever seemed likely to get official sanction. But he had gone farther still, gathering specialists from this faculty, supporters from that organisation, and even – thanks to his gift for popularisation – a lordly sum as financial backing, linked with a double commission for an independent television company and a mass-circulation Sunday newspaper. In all this he'd been invaluable.

Why then should his leadership of the project feel to Sarson such an imposition? Sour grapes, because he himself had never glittered so finely in his back room of the British Museum? Perhaps. But also, protective as he felt towards this special site, he was conscious of danger. It was as though he sensed this man wasn't good enough for what would be required of him. Beaumont might be after all, not so much a digger as a dazzler, something a little spurious. What Sarson suspected in him was a failure of some essential quality – sincerity, discretion, modesty? Respect; was that it? As though the man was unworthy of the thing they'd come to find. And in that feeling might lie the reason he inwardly dubbed him 'The Expert': because on elevating oneself to that level one became in some manner a little *less* than the other men. Apart, and less human.

'This place we're booked in at,' said Beaumont suddenly, his fork raised. 'Any good, do you think? Have you tried the food there?'

'It's a pub, nothing more. It can sleep up to eight, and the landlord's wife does the catering. She's a good cook. The menus can be varied to suit us, she says, and the price accordingly. I told her we'd want plain nourishing dishes for outdoor appetites.'

'So now she's got *carte blanche* to fill us with stodge?

I'll have a word with her. I suppose there's an alternative if it's really abysmal there?'

'It's just three miles from the site. The next pub's a further four miles out. Accommodates four. Cheese and pickles sort of catering. But I don't think you'll find The Plough too bad. If you do, there's a proper hotel the other side of Farne airfield. I stayed there the weekend I stumbled on the site. Pretty good reputation for food and wine. Pricy, though.'

'Thank God for that. Somewhere to trot off to when one needs a change of faces. Smart little place, would you say?'

'My wife seems to like it. She's pretty choosy.'

'Is she, by God? Sort of place for the weekend then? Maybe Joanna would stay down and show the flag. We might make a foursome of it.'

Sarson looked away. 'Maybe. Not that Val gets much time off at the moment. She works on a women's magazine; always seems to be chasing after some feature.'

Beaumont was looking thoughtful. 'I'm sure I heard something about ... Yes, rather enterprising hobby, hasn't she? Rally driving or something.'

'Gliding. She's very keen.' Even to his own ears it sounded abrupt. He attempted to round Beaumont off the subject. 'There's this field at Farne she used to practise from last summer. I took the original aerial shots from there. They've an air-taxi service that you might find useful.'

'I might indeed. That's a good publicity angle; local co-operation and so on. Incidentally, I wired the local paper we'd be down today. They should send someone out, so lay on a little press reception when we get there, will you? There's nothing like striking while the iron's stinking hot. We shan't have the big guns down for another five days or so, when I've had a chance to weigh up possibilities and map out the story line.'

Sarson looked at him.

'Well, you don't think programmes just happen? It all has to be scripted, phased to a detail; and then inevitably the bloody weather puts its boot in and the deadlines go to blazes. There's one hell of a lot of work in directing a complex thing like this. My first concern will be to take a quick recce and decide just what the scope of the place will add up to. Once we've that fixed we can choose the slant.'

'Slant?'

'Yes. Aiming for peak viewing, we'll have to keep it light. Impressive, of course, but not ponderous. Plenty of reconstructions, some costume stuff, Neolithic ritual, build up the mystery. Romantic atmosphere's essential, but there has to be a strong story line. You can't just say, "Look chaps, this is how we start to dig, and two days later this is us a whole bloody inch deeper." Give them a glimpse of the finicky patience it takes by all means, but there has to be a pay off.'

'And if there isn't? If we don't turn up anything startling?'

'Ah, but we shall. Don't doubt it. I've always had the most enormous luck.' He sat back, delighted with himself and dabbing at his moustache with the napkin. 'And if there's no treasure trove, then it'll be a case of our ingenuity. We'll need to come up with some spectacular new theory; present it visually, a myth come to life, our own local Tutankhamen.'

Sarson's lips were a straight-drawn line. He felt a pulse beating behind the bridge of his nose. Forcing himself to breathe normally he said, in his quiet voice, 'Instant fact. Just like that?'

'Exactly. It's a challenge, but I think we can bring it off.' Beaumont leaned forward, fixed Sarson with engaging blue eyes. 'Believe me, this dig is going to be something people will talk about for years!'

And having expressed this in a voice of vibrant emotion, he gave the little intimate nod that had so endeared him to his viewers, leaned back and switched off the subject. He was away down the dining-car before Sarson could recover from his state of stunned disbelief.

'Sir?' said the attendant, presenting the bill on a thick china plate. Sarson opened it, asked for the total to be written more clearly, paid it and folded it carefully away, initialled, in his wallet. Expenses on digs were borne for a great part on one's own shoulders, but this one, he acknowledged, could be like none he'd ever known. Beaumont, he was sure, would expect a scrupulous tally kept, and the lot claimed for. Sarson, it seemed, was to be his accountant: expenses listed to the ultimate penny, applause recorded in maximum decibels.

He didn't know whether to write his resignation when he reached Farne, or sleep on it and wire London next morning. He should have known things had been going too well: there had to be a maggot in such a fine apple. And this one was right at the core.

That evening, when they had unpacked and had dinner, two reporters arrived from local newspapers. Sarson left them with Beaumont in their private sitting-room, put on his walking boots and went out on the heath.

It was cool and quite windless, the sky limpid and glowing with the softness of a small candle enclosed in a witch-bowl. Only towards the west a few thin bars of strato-cumulus striped the merging pastels and repeated the rim of the plain's dark edge. Between these bars the sky showed faintly primrose.

He walked fast, and the wiry grass, long for April, slashed at his boots. Upland scents began to reach him and he was aware that the animal reaction of anger was receding, like a dog's raised hackles slowly flattening, becoming smoothed away. But a gloom remained that was less easy to lift.

At the foot of the first low ridge he turned to look back. Across level, tussocky grassland the pub still stood out garishly vulgar, its floodlit forecourt agleam with the rounded forms of cars. Over pseudo half-timbering the fluorescent pink of the neon-framed inn sign threw a sickly flush; self-conscious little coloured lights, looped along the boundary fence, declared a special occasion. It lacked only the strident wheezing of a merry-go-round to be part of a distant fairground.

Far off he heard car doors slam and voices raised in determined enjoyment. Distance just saved the place from being offensive, made it merely quaint, even a little pathetic with its brittle, tinny brightness. He turned back to face the dark and the silence, and continued in a gentle climb towards an outline of trees.

19

He was approaching from a direction almost diametrically opposite the one he'd first arrived by over seven months before. Then it had been late Summer, the ground dried out and friable underfoot. Now, with Spring, scents and sounds as well as colours had changed. There was a resilience the turf had lost before, and a faint, bitter-honey scent of damp peat overlying the chalk. And in these same months a similar small miracle had occurred: his dream had taken on depth, acquired reality, become an official project with backers, organisation, a schedule, momentum; and he was still with it, not entirely severed from its direction. He'd be a fool to show resentment at a superior's high-handedness. Beaumont hadn't long been exposed to the idea of the site: there was a chance he might yet come to accept the concept as larger than himself.

There seemed to be a path now, or more properly a track, for it was still grass he trod on, but flattened as though once or twice a day someone took this same route across the waste ground. The trees, as he came up to them, started singly as young birches, their tips feathery in new leaf. Then there was the odd chestnut, more forward than at home, each twig-end lumpy and erect; not yet opened to fall back in split fans of green; and then, dense-packed, misshapen and dwarfish, a thicket of hawthorns, where the track merged with a path and there were stones and broken twigs beneath his feet. And after this enclosed gloom, opening out downhill, a spinney where he stood still in amazement, for the whole was aglow with an eery pallor. And then he realised it was a grove of wild cherries, with the trees in full flower. He walked on under blossom like white foam, and so he came to the edge of a crumbling bank and a tarn as sombre and smeared as ancient pewter.

> '*The sedge is wither'd from the lake,*
> *And no birds sing.*'

The words came up from some recess of his mind, and he shivered.

Perhaps there were no birds to sing, but there was some

form of life, some movement, for he caught a rustle as though quite a large creature had stirred and begun to creep away. Turning he saw branches a little above waist level sweep back into place where something had just passed through, but he could pick out no lighter shape against the shadows. Only, a few seconds later, he heard sounds of pattering steps over fallen leaves, and couldn't picture what animal would cause both them and the disturbance of the branches. He didn't think there were deer hereabouts. A runaway goat seemed more probable.

He was half inclined to follow the sounds but he had set himself a route which should bring him out in sight of Beacons. He had to set eyes on the place again. If he went ahead with his resignation, it might be his last view of it as it now stood, unopened.

When he was almost there, sitting astride the stone wall before the climb, a new wave of depression overwhelmed him. He had been prepared for a certain measure of disappointment, regret; but not for this, for it was reinforced now with a strong realisation of guilt. It was his fault, he saw, that the place was to be disturbed. The very act of excavation was at best an unholy practice, destroying what it most treasured. Even with up-to-date methods of meticulous sifting, the strata that were laid open could never be genuinely replaced. It was an act limited to one instant of time. Whatever distant past they dug into now became a loss for all future searchers. How many mysteries remained today unsolvable because of the sacrilegious haste of earlier vandals calling themselves archaeologists? He too had been guilty of the same unthinking haste, and now, faced with the man who was to undertake the operation, he was ashamed. It was he who had brought Beaumont here to strip the sanctuary. It was to be left no mystery, no dignity; even no truth if it failed of itself to yield up any sufficiently startling reward. The man's approach was one not of respectful enquiry, but of blatant self-advertisement. What had perhaps once been a temple of early civilised man was to serve a vulgarian's ambition, be converted to sterling and dollars in a chase after popular fame.

After the regret, his anger was returning, but controlled now, channelled through his own admission of responsibility. He knew he couldn't shrug off the situation and leave Beaumont free to continue unchecked, perhaps to rehash any findings in order to serve up some deliberately provocative theory of prehistory. The place had its own integrity, if the man hadn't. In case Beaumont couldn't appreciate that, being insensitive to the *manes* of a place, there had to be someone to remind him; if necessary, to prevent him. And there was no one who could stand in for the ancient dead but himself, thought Sarson. He was already linked to the place; had been so from the first moment of recognition last Summer. But now he was so much more forcibly committed, bound by his own betrayal of it, obliged to retrieve what he could of its future. Only himself could he trust to interpret.

He slid from the wall and began walking again, up the slow slope to the henge, through the circle of depressions. They were hidden from sight, but he had pored so long over the aerial shots and the sketches he'd made from them that he knew, despite the moonless evening, when he had reached the radial centre.

He had to make some act of faith, of fealty, to prove his commitment, but he could think of nothing fitting. Instead he made a promise to himself – because it embarrassed him to think of making it to a place – that he would keep an honest mind over anything they found or failed to find.

But he couldn't go on calling it 'the place' to himself; and 'the site' had destructive implications. 'Beacons' seemed an outsider's name. He needed his own word. 'Henge' came closer but there was an earlier word which he couldn't reach. In time perhaps it would come to him.

He stood there on the chalk crown and turned in a slow circle, clockwise. The ground fell away all around, stretched flat for the next few miles and then steadily rose to a low ring of downland. Perhaps just such a natural feature as this had suggested to Bronze Age men the shape of the bell- and disc-barrows distributed all over Wessex, borrowing the character of some such natural sanctuary to use in a cult of death. In imitation of just such a hill, they had cast up their inverted bowls of earth inside shallow trenched basins, labouring long days with their simple tools of bone, antler, stone and early bronze to create fitting rest-places for the noble spirits of their great men and women. Death being the passing on of spirit from the old to the new, so that nothing of the tribe's was ever lost but absorbed into soil and stone, and that the bodily continuity of birth-giving might be daemonically confirmed.

Where had all that spirit gone? What, for that matter, had become of the people themselves? Beyond their graves there was no trace left.

The land about him was now as empty and silent as the sky, and considerably darker. Apart from himself, not a single living thing had stirred on his way out here. Except the unseen creature down by the water, moving the low branches as it slid between the trees. Over to the south-west, beyond the ridge, ran a trunk road. Although he couldn't see them, there were car lights constantly passing, modern men and women going about their individual business, each preoccupied with his own life, his separate dream. As though society itself were now too complex and its disintegrated atoms split apart. But these ancient people of the sanctuary were different. He was aware of them at this moment, pressing still upon the place, massed like a silent and invisible army on the plain, looking towards this centre.

'To ἀγορά,' Sarson said aloud, the Greek word coming suddenly to him. ' ἀγορά, the gathering place, the tryst.'

The impression of solidarity was immediately so great that he found himself holding his breath, straining his eyes against the dark to make out shapes of a crowd massing outside the henge. He was conscious of their concerted gaze, and of himself alone at its centre, absorbing their single emotion. It was compounded of fear and awe and a wild frenzy of hope. And he was instantly aware of imminent danger, though whether it menaced them or himself, came from them or from something completely external, he could not tell. But it was as dire and terrible as the end of the world; total destruction; and only by their staying together was there any chance of overcoming. And then the knowledge was replaced by a purely

23

physical reaction so that he felt the heavy dragging of his shoulders and upper arms, an emptiness as though beneath his chest he had ceased to exist. His legs gave under him and he fell, rolling on one shoulder over an irregularity in the ground, his head ending up against a rock. He lay, half-conscious, and heard a tumult of shouting and a great clashing as though a battle raged about him. There were horses shrieking in fright and women screaming. Or were they children, boys? The weight of his shoulders bore him down so that he could not raise himself to look about. He knew his eyes were closed and he couldn't manage to unseal them. There was nothing but the terrible thunder and skirl of battle and the hard stone beneath his forehead, still a little warm from the afternoon sun.

There is nothing there, he told himself. No army, no sound outside myself. Only the roar of blood in my head. My head's down low, so soon I shall return to normal. It will pass. I've only to lie here a while.

Later he seemed to wake from sleep and the hillside was bare. A very long way in the distance he heard a train whistle but there was no other sound. His face was stiff and covered with a thin mask of blood. He put up one hand and rubbed away dry granules. On his forehead, above the bridge of his nose the skin was still sticky, and as he touched it, it started again to pour warm blood that ran down to the corners of his mouth and tasted salt like tears. The wound burned too as though salt were in it.

He had to get away from the henge, down into the depression, and be sick. Worse, his inside had turned to water, and even as he ran he was afraid he would be too late. But he couldn't use this place. He scuttled in shame, tearing at his trousers as he slithered on the rough grass. There was a little ditch under the hill on this side and he scrambled in, squatting among nettles and shaking with ague. Vomit burned his throat and stung the linings of his upper nostrils, so that his eyes too were filled with water. He lay still afterwards on the edge of the ditch, the warmth draining from him.

He had no warning that anyone was there. The first

24

intimation was the clink of metal against his teeth and water flowing over his tongue, running over his lips and down his chin. It was cold and tasted bitter, but it cleaned the filth from his mouth. He stared up but still the water in his eyes prevented him seeing who was there. Only a dark shape stooped over him, with the paler sky behind pricked with stars. But he knew it was a man, and the coarse hands moved gently.

He tried to speak but a wet cloth came across his mouth, wiping over tongue, teeth and gums, easing inside the cheeks and leaving a fresh, stinging sensation where it touched. It was not pure spring water as he had thought at first, but had something added. Some disinfectant he did not know.

The man went on washing his face and hands, rinsing the cloth and wringing it, then brought a fresh drink, and when Sarson lay back again, warmer and drowsy, he felt the man turn him and begin to wash his buttocks and legs. Finally he removed Sarson's boots and socks to wash his feet. He made no attempt to dry the parts he had washed but left them exposed to the air and soon Sarson felt his whole body warm and tingling from whatever the cloth had been soaked in.

All the time the man said not a word and since his own first attempt to speak Sarson had a conviction that the stranger wished him to stay silent too. He intended to thank him when he had done, but opened his eyes to find the man had gone as silently and suddenly as he had come.

Sarson's clothes and boots lay alongside, where the man had placed them, and although he still felt strange he realised he was well enough to dress himself and start walking back. If he skirted the mound of the sanctuary he should come again to the spinney and the dark pond.

But there was no need to walk, for the man was coming back from that direction now, leading a saddled horse. Seen close to, in the starlight, he looked the oldest man Sarson had even seen, his skin brown and wrinkled as a walnut. He wore a slack, shapeless suit that was either brown or grey, and from the pierced ears and the look of the skewbald pony Sarson took him for a gypsy.

He pulled out the left stirrup and angled it for Sarson's foot, then gave him a firm heave up. He left his dry, old hand on the back of the younger man's a moment and looked long at him as he sat in the saddle.

'She knows her own way back,' he said throatily. 'Knot the reins and give her a slap. She'll return.'

It was a shock at last to hear his voice. Sarson felt as though he had been startled awake. 'Thank you. I'm sorry, I . . .'

The old gypsy shook his head. 'I am happy,' he said. 'Happy.' Then before Sarson could speak again he stepped back and aimed a smart blow with the flat of his hand on the pony's flank. She quivered and danced off, heading for the spinney and the main road beyond.

As the old man had said, she knew what to do. Sarson dismounted almost opposite the inn and she turned herself, then stood cropping quietly at the grass verge. He knotted the reins and gave her a sharp slap. He heard the steady thud of her hooves some time after she had dissolved into the dark of the countryside. Then he crossed the road and entered the floodlit forecourt, seeming to step from one world into another.

3

Loud, cheerful voices sounded from the saloon bar and lounge. Sarson went past bright windows and in by the residents' door. Hearing someone cross the hall, Mrs Pyke stepped through from serving to confront him.

'Ah, Dr Sarson, you're back then? They've gone into the lounge, sir, if you'd like to join them.' She nodded and stood back. 'You can get through this way. Oh, my heavens, whatever've you done to your head?'

Sarson put up his hand to the greasy patch just above and between his eyes. 'I slipped, up at the site, and hit my head on a rock. It's nothing much.' He touched the skin exploratively. The blood had congealed into dry granules and under the grease they moved grittily. Whatever the gypsy had used seemed to stem bleeding well enough. Horse medication of some kind, he guessed.

From the mid-distance beyond Mrs Pyke, Beaumont

27

had recognised his voice. 'Sarson! Where've you been, man? Come and say your piece.'

In the passageway between the bars where he now stood, Sarson could see into all the public rooms. Above elbow-level it was a pseudo-Tudor arrangement of dark-stained timber struts and cross-beams, like the lower deck of an old sailing ship or a gallery of titivated pit-props, and every way you looked there were rows of hooks hung with brass or copper gewgaws of an unlikely lustre. The drinkers too were stagey: local yokels, seedy reps, solid citizens, hearty backslappers. Types, all of them. Beaumont was no better: craggy academic in shaggy tweeds, but spurious. Sarson looked all round him at the puppets; human underneath, but at what a depth. Effigies, with a small kernel of something live at the core.

'Are you sure you're all right?' Mrs Pyke was at his elbow again. 'Let me get you something, sir. You do look groggy.'

He smiled. 'I wouldn't say no to black coffee, upstairs.' He waved vaguely in the direction of Beaumont and the two reporters. 'Have to make a phone call. I'll be back,' and he turned on his heel, squeezing past old Pyke pulling pints at the counter.

It took some minutes to get a person-to-person call, but it was the best time of evening to catch Alan at home. He sounded relaxed, as if he might be two draws through his after-dinner cigar. But then, he was always the same on the phone, Sarson remembered. Which could account for the rich practice; all those highly-strung, opulent, South Kensington ladies needing reassurance.

'Hugh,' Alan said comfortably, 'the very chap I was thinking of. Your X-ray results are through. Nothing there at all. Clean as the proverbial whistle. How are you feeling now?'

'Better for hearing that. I've just had a repeat dose. Rather more violent this time. Almost passed out, I think.'

'M'm. When and where?'

'Half an hour, three-quarters, back. Just after dinner. It was a normal sort of meal. Lamb cutlets, potatoes, frozen peas. Then some jelly stuff with a few tinned loganberries and cream. A couple of glasses of rosé. Coffee. That's all. I'd walked out to the site, nothing energetic, though. I suppose it must be some recurring bug I've picked up.'

'Persistent little devil, if it is. How are you placed for tablets?'

'About a dozen left. Only thing is, they're back at the flat. I've nothing here. Except the horse quack's remedies.'

'What's that?'

'Joke.'

'Oh, I see. Anything rattle you? Incompatible colleagues, that sort of thing?'

Sarson hesitated, then acknowledged the pause was too long for a denial to carry conviction. 'No dig's ever a bed of roses at this stage, especially for a backroom boy like myself. But I'm not sold on this psycho diagnosis. I'm not really the nervy type.'

'Not on the surface, no. A lot goes on down under, though; or so my head-shrinking colleagues inform me. I know a very reasonable psychiatrist, if you'd like to have a chat with one.'

'Not a chance of it,' Sarson told him shortly. 'I've far too much on hand at present. But if you'd put a new prescription in the post I could carry on with the tablets. It's probably dropping them that caused tonight's attack. It was sudden and short-lived. I feel reasonably fit again now.'

'Right, but better watch the weight. Check once a week. Let me know if it drops off. I'll post the prescription tonight.'

'Thanks, Alan. All well with you and the family?'

'Flourishing. By the by, we ran into Val yesterday, in Jermyn Street. She seems to be working hard at the moment. Hadn't heard that the dig was already under way. She was quite interested, or so we thought.'

Sarson frowned into the phone. 'Well, it's near one of her gliding haunts. That's how I happened on the site originally.'

'She rather guessed so. Last autumn, was it?'

'August.' One of the last times he'd seen her. No doubt

29

Alan knew that too. He was obviously writing this marital business into his case notes, just as any Freudian psychiatrist whom he recommended would undoubtedly do, fitting the individual into a prefabricated system.

'Well, I rather envy you, if the weather holds out. At the dig, I mean. I might look in on you when I can get a genuine free day.'

'Give us a couple of weeks and then we may turn up something of interest. I'll be glad to see you any time after that. Bring your sleeping bag.'

'Perish the thought! I'm strictly for the dolce vita these days.'

He hadn't always been, Sarson remembered, laying down the receiver. They'd had some rare bohemian times as students. Not so very long ago. A decade, even less. Since then Alan had changed more than himself. He hoped that didn't mean that Alan had greater maturity. No, it was the domestic thing that made the difference. He might have changed as much himself, with a house mortgage to support and three small children. As it was he travelled light. To each his own way.

In the bathroom he carefully cleaned the edges of the gash on his forehead. If he could tone down the colour it wouldn't look too bad. The bluish purple wasn't all bruise but partly the stain of whatever the gypsy had put on. To cover it Sarson hunted an adhesive dressing out from his shaving kit. At the door of the bathroom he ran into the younger of the reporters.

'Hallo. Anybody mind if I wash here?'

Sarson waved him in. 'Go ahead. How's the interview going?'

The man was pulling off his jacket and his voice lost itself in the manoeuvre. He slumped on the edge of the bath and muttered something about not being in the same class at all. 'You not the drinking kind?' he demanded of Sarson.

'So-so. Are you getting the sort of information you wanted?'

'You must be joking. Sorry; what I meant was ... Well, I only hope I can remember tomorrow what it was all about. There've been some lovely long words going around.' He filled the basin with cold water and plunged his fore-arms in. Then he put his face down and threw handfuls of water over his head, spluttering like a sea lion.

'Trouble is,' he said through the thickness of Sarson's bath towel, 'my wise old colleague, who on the surface appears to be staying the course, went cold a good half hour back. He just hasn't the sense to fall to the floor. I must say your boss can sink his drink.'

'Can he then? I wouldn't know.'

'None better.' The young man was sitting limply on the bath again. 'I had hopes of some lineage on this. You know, potted versions for the London weeklies. They won't be sending their own men down until something big breaks. But all the routine stuff – intentions, preparations, mechanics of the organisation ... Too many long words. Now I'm talking too much.'

'Let's go down again,' Sarson suggested. 'If I gather what line Dr Beaumont's taking, I might be able to help you. Give me a ring tomorrow.'

The youngster caught up with him at the foot of the stairs, hair damply slicked back and shirt collar limp with water. He muttered his thanks as he followed Sarson through to the smoky lounge. The bars had emptied and the lights were lowered, except where Pyke still shuffled round in soft slippers emptying ash trays into a bucket and carrying back huge fistfuls of tankards. Beaumont was still expounding his theme. The old reporter sat stiffly propped against the back of an upright chair, unblinking; almost, it seemed, without breathing. His thick, waxen skin was the colour of candlegrease.

'Where the hell've you been?' Beaumont demanded of Sarson, the moment he saw him.

'I told you,' said Sarson coldly. 'At the site.'

'The site,' echoed the young reporter. 'Yes, what about the site? What's it going to turn out as?'

Beaumont seemed to change gear mentally, lifted the upper part of his body without disturbing the way he sat, and swivelled to his renewed audience. He spoke fluently, scarcely pausing for breath, and the gist of it, Sarson had grudgingly to admit, was genuine, honest scientific-observer stuff: how one didn't dare to presuppose anything, or else in following theory one might overlook, however inadvertently, some small but significant indication that the truth was other than you'd have it to be. Objectivity, integrity, meticulous check and double-check; all that.

Good Guy on White Horse, Sarson silently commented. This spiel is all White Horse, therefore he's a Good Guy. Or so we're supposed to think. And I don't, because I'm not detached like the Good Guy says we have to be. I'm prejudiced; not going by the words, but by the feeling in my bones. 'I do not like thee, Dr Fell.'

With such antipathy between the two of them, they didn't need a difference in blood alcohol to emphasise the distance.

As if he sensed this, Beaumont leaned suddenly forward and held out an almost empty bottle of brandy. There was a glass on the small table between them and Sarson pushed it across for him to fill. That was the moment that the old reporter toppled slowly out of his chair and lay without a sound, face down at their feet.

'It's all right,' said the youngster. 'It takes him that way. If someone'll give me a hand with him out to the car, we'll manage. I'm sorry, gentlemen.'

'Well, bless my soul,' said Beaumont with a perceptible hint of complacency.

When Sarson arrived back from seeing the reporters out Beaumont had removed himself, and the bottle.

And the morning and the evening, Sarson misquoted, were the first day. God help this dig and all who sink in her.

4

Shortly after eight o'clock next morning Beaumont appeared in work-like garb with rucksack, shooting stick and notebook. Mrs Pyke offered packed lunches but the suggestion was firmly turned down.

'Time enough for that sort of thing later,' Beaumont confided to Sarson. 'We'll be back for a proper meal at one. I'm expecting a lot of gear to arrive by then. Joanna's bringing it down by road. Meanwhile, a preliminary survey.'

They started off across the plain in much the same direction that Sarson had gone the night before, but skirting the trees. The almost circular depression continued round this side of the mound like a vast natural moat, but, apart from ditches and culverts, it was virtually dried out. They walked for some way along this perimeter inspecting the central terrain, and now from the north-west Sarson saw clearly something that he hadn't properly appreciated from the maps. Although the henge crowned the main eminence, the base of the mound was more of a double circle like the outline of a dumpy figure eight, the upper limb levelling off to allow the larger circle to rise a further sixteen feet or so clear of the rest. This latter was where the signs of small hollows had shown from the air. Yet neither from above nor when he visited the site before had he fully appreciated the lesser hump that lay behind and now seemed joined to it by a narrow, tilted causeway, too small to feature on the map. It struck him that the lower hillock might have had some kind of settlement, or at least a pound for the livestock of the people who'd made the marks he photographed from the helicopter. The site for excavation became immediately more complex and more promising.

He pointed this out to Beaumont who nodded and made a quick sketch of the feature in profile. Then they walked on, still circling. On the south-east side, in the lee of some scrubby thorn trees they came on a shuttered caravan: not modern and motorised, but of dark, varnished wood, with barrelled roof and wooden wheels bound with perished bands of solid rubber. It appeared to have stood there, sinking into the topsoil, for several decades. There was no answering sound from inside when Beaumont rapped on the door, and no smoke issued from its rusted stovepipe. Nevertheless Sarson assumed it was where the old gypsy had come from, for although the horse was not to be seen, there were fresh droppings in the long grass nearby. 'Derelict,' Beaumont pronounced, and they moved on, completing their circuit.

The dark tarn in its grove of flowering cherries was almost as weird by day as by night. Beaumont too seemed to feel it and stood moodily gazing into the black water, pushing at it with the end of his stick as though he expected to see some evil reflection assemble on its oily surface. Sarson heard a lark trilling somewhere outside the wood in full sunlight, and as they emerged he saw it soar, wings beating, to hang specklike above them.

They came back to the original point of the depression,

climbed the stor.e wall and went up the hill. As they passed into the arena of the henge, Sarson felt his hands clench themselves tightly inside his pockets, nails cutting into his palms, and he made a conscious effort to relax.

Beaumont seemed still affected by the sombreness of the tarn. Neither man spoke, but they moved about the hill's crown, examining the skyline all around.

'An almost perfect site for an observatory,' Beaumont agreed at last. He scratched at the surface of the ground, uprooting clods of grass with the point of his shooting stick. 'Very little topsoil.'

'It's chalk below, of course.' Sarson crouched, opening a claspknife. He probed gently into the earth. 'Four inches of soil at the most just here. Do you want the turfs preserved?'

'Good God, no. It'll grow again. No trouble with the landowner. There's ample alternative grazing.' Beaumont was looking more satisfied now, striding about the site like an actor familiarising himself with a set. Then he came across to where Sarson sat watching him, and lowered himself alongside. The morning air had whipped a high colour into his lean cheeks and the long, soft hair blew about him making him appear remarkably young. Behind their fashionable lenses his eyes were bright.

'I can't wait to get cracking. What a place! You know, I can *feel* it. I'm never wrong about that. It's all here, underground.' He struck the earth beside him. 'More than that. It's in the very air. Down in that wood, with all that white blossom ... surely even you must admit, *there's something about the place*. That pond. Black and silent. Odd. It means something. Only what?'

He expected no answer, but slid the rubber band off his notebook and began again rapidly sketching. 'You've got an inch to the mile map? Can you magnify it to wall size? Include everything we've covered this morning except the first mile from the pub, but indicate its direction.'

'Now?' asked Sarson. 'I'll need a table for that, and floor-space. Anything you want me to do while I'm here?'

'Verbal appreciation of the whole layout,' Beaumont answered without looking up. 'In a nutshell first, then aspect by aspect in more detail. Never mind the atmosphere; I'll work all that in when I knock it into shape. Just what you see. The lot.'

They worked there, with the wind lifting the edges of their papers and fluttering loose sketches that Beaumont had torn off his block and tucked under a stone. It struck Sarson then that he had missed seeing what exactly he'd cut his head on when he fell the previous night. He got up and moved about, searching. At the centre of the space was a bald expanse of chalk, but few of the fragments there seemed large enough or sufficiently sharp to have done the damage. At one point, however, the surface was less white. Over a round patch some six inches across there was a stain of lichen, and the chalk was hollowed as though an almost circular object had lain there over a period protecting it from the weather. And then he saw the black spiders that were dried splashes of his own blood guttered away between the stones. He remembered his cheek pressed against rock that still held some warmth of the afternoon sun, and he wondered who had taken the stone away.

There was a shout from Beaumont. He was standing up and waving towards a white car that was bucketing across country over the tussocky grass.

'Joanna,' Beaumont shouted. 'It's my wife. Come on, knock off for lunch.' And he was scrabbling round, packing his belongings back in the rucksack, while the car, an open Range Rover, roared to a halt down by the stone wall. Beaumont and Sarson hurried down together.

Archaeologists' wives came in all sorts and sizes, but Joanna Beaumont was like none Sarson had ever encountered. He couldn't say immediately what it was that she lacked, for she gave such an instant impression of completeness and finish that she seemed barely real. She sat quite still to watch their approach, her arms draped, one across the steering wheel, the other extended along the back of the passenger seat. Her poise was remarkable, the balance of finely modelled head on slender neck quite perfect. She gleamed with an assurance of affluence, sleek grooming and good breeding. And indeed there was something of the thoroughbred horse about her, in her air of alert detachment. She scrutinised Sarson over her husband's shoulder as he kissed her, and then reached out a long, smooth hand to shake his. 'I've heard of you, of course,' she said. 'Darling, Rudi's come along to use up some film. I left him at the pub clucking over the baggage. Someone else has turned up too. Tall, sallow, with an enormous forehead.'

'That will be Gifford. Sarson, you'll be able to put him in the picture.' He swung himself up beside his wife and covered one of her hands with his own. 'Gifford's on the technical side. Takes care of all the electronic gear. I've got the contractor coming to see me this afternoon and the volunteers are laid on for tomorrow morning. It's really getting under way. I have the feeling it's going to be something quite tremendous this time.'

'Splendid,' she said coolly, and gave a little, amused smile. She swung the truck in a semi-circle and it went bouncing back towards the road.

They were four for lunch that day and Beaumont was getting into his professional stride, socialising as a schoolmaster might who had to mix a class of new boys and was determined to supply bonhomie enough to cover any fissures in the structure. He tended to overexplain, inserting definitions as though he'd little confidence in his listeners' experience, and Sarson suspected that he might in fact be angling himself for as yet invisible cameras, selecting his own facets as he tried to sound the unseen audience. After a considerable silence Joanna came back into the conversation with a series of acute little questions that prolonged her husband's performance, but she offered no opinions of her own, nor did he appear to expect any.

How well she knows him, Sarson thought, watching; and even as he considered this she looked at him and smiled. With irony was it? She was, from any angle, a formidable woman. On reaching their communal sitting-room she had thrown off the bulky sheepskin jacket and unzipped her knee-length boots. As if the quite remarkable beauty of her body in its brief, straight tunic were not enough, she had unpinned the bright hair that had been coiled in some Grecian style on the top of her head,

37

and she stood there with it falling about her shoulders, a wanton stretching and curling her long toes in their transparent nylon sheaths in a way that was at once feline and utterly female. This was a way he had never seen Val; nor could he imagine her so, however private and alone she thought herself.

Beaumont had seized a case and gone through to the bedroom with it. Sarson, tempted to remove himself similarly, had suddenly rejected flight. 'Perhaps,' he heard himself say, 'your boots are a half-size too small.' And this reaction of his had interested her. Long after they had all met again for lunch she kept gazing his way, measuring him against future action.

'Tell me,' she asked over the coffee, while Mrs Pyke and the village girl moved glasses and crumbs from between their elbows, 'How do you spell your name? Sarsen – like the megaliths?'

'Nothing so appropriate. Just as on the vinegar bottles.'

Gifford tittered, and when all their eyes turned on him, became preoccupied with a shred of tobacco sticking to his tongue.

Joanna leaned back, draping one elegant arm across the next chair, and seemed to become aware of him now for the first time. Behind the thick lenses, his eyes blinked back once in alarm, then stared down at his huge, spatulate fingers spread wide on the tablecloth, dully saw the nicotine stains and ill-kept nails, and he remembered himself as offensively ugly. Well, he'd always been so, was used to it. But Beaumont hadn't called him in as a male model. He belonged in this group of specialists; it was this woman who didn't. Momentarily he had been able to forget himself in following the others' talk; only he shouldn't have shown his delight at Sarson's batting the woman's impudence down. Condescending cow, puffed up with her own good looks and the reflection of her husband's successes. It shouldn't matter what she thought: women were little more really than the static an active man picked up in his coming and going.

His averted face broke into a sudden grin at the passing thought, a brief, fierce rictus that he covered with one hand while a surge of red crept up his neck to the pitted, unfortunate face. Why were they all staring at him? Someone say something for God's sake.

'No doubt the derivation's the same, though,' Beaumont suggested quickly. 'Originally "Saracen", meaning "stranger", or even "nomad".'

'Outsider?' persisted Joanna, turning back to her original victim. 'Not what I'd imagined. Assuming you were Sarsen, like the stones, I thought we had a real henge-*insider*. "Saracen". Yes, I see now how that suits you. Something Syro-Arabian about your cast of features. All the time you've been reminding me of ... Darling, you remember – Damascus Museum, wasn't it? – a delightful little alabaster man. A priest. Oh, you must know who I mean. Ekhi—, Ebi—?'

'Of course. Ebikhil,' said Beaumont, beaming. 'Superintendent of the Temple to Ishtar at Mari. Yes, you're right. Sarson does have something of that statue; same large, dark eyes, wide cheekbones.'

Relieved of their attention now, Gifford raised his eyes to view Sarson sitting at right angles. The woman's mocking hadn't ruffled him in the least. If anything, he looked even smoother, more politely distant in some way. She hadn't found his pain-wavelength yet, but she would go on probing till she did. What had Sarson done to draw this on him? He was so unassuming, quite lacking in challenge. Perhaps that was in itself the provocation, Gifford thought wryly; the fact that he was capable of withdrawal. She was trying to penetrate the self-possession of the man, and it irked her that he made no response.

They were both young – he about twenty-eight to thirty, Gifford judged; she probably a few years older – both attractive to look at, with that beauty of good bones, perfect skin; but in type utterly unalike. She was fine, golden, the classical nymph. You remembered her profile, lips just parted, the tip of her tongue barely showing, moist between even, white teeth. With Sarson you were more conscious of the full-face view; the darkness of his wide almond eyes; almond shapes of high colour over slanting cheekbones marking the paleness of his flattish, almond face; the rather prominent, high-arched nose

39

casting strong shadows over the baroque mouth. Yes, as she'd said, not a very English face, though Gifford had known a Welsh family with something of the same tilted horizontals.

'Same mild, calm gaze,' Joanna went on taunting. 'A *holy* man, mark you. Do you know the figure, Dr Sarson?'

Hugh finished his coffee, put the cup back in the centre of its saucer. 'I think so. Little pudgy hands clasped on his chest, flounced kirtle, ceremonial beard, shaven head and softly rounded shoulders. I'll concede something like that might well appear in my bathroom mirror in a decade or so. He's a Semitic type. He turns up by the dozen in the Royal Standard of Ur – one of our British Museum treasures. We think it may be the sounding box of a harp. Certainly something to do with music anyway, as many of the little inlaid characters have instruments to play.'

The child helping Mrs Pyke to clear suddenly overbalanced, reaching between the two archaeologists, and Sarson caught her by one elbow and the thin little waist. 'Steady,' he said, smiling. The girl gave a sort of hiccough and trembled in his grasp. He held her until she was upright, then put his empty cup and saucer in her hand. She backed away slowly, staring at him.

'Delightful little fellows,' agreed Beaumont, waving his cigar. 'You must know the piece, Joanna. Ivory and mother-of-pearl inlaid work. Rows and rows of these cartoon characters, eating and drinking, just like Sarson here, universal uncles, smooth city gents, Savoy Grill diners.'

'I'm not that smooth,' said Sarson, tiring of the bait. 'More of a quick-pork-pie-before-closing-time sort. And, incidentally, as Mrs Pyke's out of earshot now, how do you find the food here?'

'It seems adequate,' said Joanna for them all.

Beaumont shrugged. 'I don't suppose we'd do better elsewhere locally. In any case there is nowhere else. Beds look comfortable enough. Any complaints?'

There weren't, so Sarson went off to confirm the arrangement with Mrs Pyke.

'Oh, and I'm sorry about Josie,' said Mrs Pyke when it was concluded. 'She's quite handy at table usually. Considering her handicap and that.'

'Oh, the girl. Yes, I saw something was wrong. Is she all right now?'

'As far as she can be, poor lamb. She's not like other children, you see. That's why she's allowed to help here. Otherwise she'd still be at school.'

'I hadn't realised. Is she your only one ... I mean ...'

Mrs Pyke continued to stack the dishes. Her tone was matter-of-fact. 'She's not ours. Lives hereabouts. Her parents are dead and she lives with an auntie. It's a sad story. I'll tell you about it some time.' Her hands stopped moving and she faced Sarson thoughtfully. 'No, what struck me so was that she tried to say something to you. I'm almost sure of it. When you caught her up as she fell.'

'I thought she hiccoughed.'

'Yes; she doesn't speak, you see. You were talking about some treasure at the British Museum. I happened to look her way, and it seemed to be something you said took her unawares.'

Sarson thought back. 'I said the Standard of Ur was probably the sounding box of a harp. It's in the Babylo ...'

'Yes, but then you said something more about music. Harp? I wonder, could it be that? Only it's not that she always hears what's said to her direct, let alone catch on to others' conversation.'

'I shouldn't think a child like that would have heard of harps, Mrs Pyke.'

'Ah, but she might, if she remembers that far back. Her father, you see, was Lucas Blaydon, the concert pianist. That big house you pass on the way here was where he lived when he wasn't on tour.'

'Blaydon?' Sarson considered. 'I remember. He was killed in a plane crash, about four years ago.'

'More like six now. Josie was just eight, and the only survivor. She was wandering about in Crete for three days before they found her, poor little soul.'

'And that was when she lost the power of speech?'

'Not exactly. She'd always been – well, rather like she is, but not so bad. Educationally subnormal. Only, her parents were very close to her and she went everywhere

41

with them. She'd made quite a lot of progress, and could say a few sentences even. Then this happened and they were both killed. Josie must have crawled clear before the wreck blew up, but she had awful burns. She's never spoken a word since then. Went right back inside herself.'

'Who looks after her now?'

'An aunt. Her father's sister. She's tried all sorts of specialists, and sending Josie away to school, but nothing suits her as well as just running wild about here. We all know her, you see. She'd never come to harm here. She likes to think she's helping me, so I hope you gentlemen will understand if she's a bit slow on serving.'

'I'm glad you told me,' said Sarson. 'I'll warn the others.' He was sobered by the knowledge that of such a superb musician as Blaydon nothing should remain but this speechless child. It would have been more merciful, perhaps, if she had died with her parents. And yet she was lovely, in a strange way. And it seemed there were people fond of her. Life couldn't be entirely wretched for her while she found pleasure in simple things like waiting at table for guests at a country inn.

He went back to the others and relayed Mrs Pyke's suggestions about the ordering of meals. Then, as though in an afterthought, he mentioned that the serving girl was called Josie: she was a little simple, and sensitive.

It was better, he considered, not to mention who her parents had been. There would be journalists coming here soon who might pounce on a story of such human interest. There was no need to distress the child by reviving old tragedies. Safer if she remained simply Josie, with no second name.

They went out again to the site for the afternoon. Against an impressive sky of building storm-cloud split across with ominous light, Beaumont hammered in the first marker. Rudi, an exquisite young man all hung about with photographic equipment, returned from a lunchtime sortie to restock with flash bulbs and demanded that the ritual stake should be repeatedly driven home and recorded in a number of artistically suitable positions. He also prevailed on Beaumont to remove his impeccable sheepskin jacket, the counterpart to Joanna's, and assume Sarson's sleeveless car coat which permitted unrestricted vision of the famous profile and quixotic beard.

When he was through with the photography, Beaumont set about considering which actual quadrant of the henge should first be tackled, while Sarson and the contractor went down to the depression to pick a base for the volunteers' camp. This second task was the easier because the living requirements of the diggers were known. The two men went for maximum shelter, drainage and ease of communication, and they returned to Beaumont with a semi-circle marked out on the ordnance map to the south-south-east of the site and a little closer to the old caravan than to the cherry wood. A more or less direct route to it from the main road was feasible, skirting the wood to its right. The ground was roughly level and lay a little above the depression on its outer rim.

When he trudged back with this plotted, Sarson found Beaumont still undecided. 'A circle has no end and no beginning,' he said. 'And so it's the same from any angle; only...'

'If the henge turns out to be an observatory...?' Sarson tempted.

'Exactly; then we have to decide what season to go for, and what time of day. Solstice or equinox, sunrise or sunset. Are we going to spin a coin or risk a judgment?'

'Well, we've missed the Spring equinox,' Sarson pointed out, 'so the next significant solar position is midsummer. That means that we could go for a north-easterly quadrant for sunrise, or with an extended northerly one we'd include both sunrise and sunset. But I'm not convinced that full quadrants would be the best way to tackle this site. All right for a large currant bun, to slice it in four, but our photographs show the currants on the perimeter. I favour short trenches where the marker holes would appear to have been, together with a section through from centre to outer ditch. Limited quadrants from the centre, perhaps, beginning with radials, in case there are inhumations or storage pits.'

'You sound as though you've got all this figured out in detail.'

'To some extent, going on twentieth century solar and lunar readings. But for the corrections over three or four thousand years we'll need the computer. And if we had a specialist astronomer on the spot, with a watching brief, it could be good insurance in the long run.'

'I don't want any more experts brought in at this point. If they don't visit the site they don't have to be entered into the log. Surely we can consult by telephone if queries arise? The computer should keep us safe.' Beaumont frowned at the ground.

Sarson, watching him, imagined he was drafting in advance some report: 'from our observation of solar rising and setting points at critical dates, and upon calculating the necessary adjustments over the millennia, it became evident that . . .'

'Yes, I'm certain we can keep them out for the moment. I'll leave provisional figures to you then, Sarson. Meanwhile we can establish the presumed centre, geometrically, from the aerial shots and scale them to the site, then mark out the circumference trenches. Start digging tomorrow, eh?'

'Beginning with the north-easterly arc. Yes, I think so.'

'What does all that add up to?' asked Joanna, swinging alongside Sarson as he lumped his theodolite across the grass. 'Have you both decided in advance what the henge is?'

Sarson set down the tripod and adjusted the legs. 'No. Only what the most demanding thing is that it might be. It can still prove to be a roundhouse, a temple, a bull-ring, a theatre; anything else you care to name. But where we actually dig is critical, because excavation itself is destructive, and again we could miss the biggest clue by leaving it under the baulks.'

'Which doesn't cover up the fact that Donald's jumping on with both feet to the theory that it's a conglomerate temple to the sun and moon plus an old-fangled observatory. Rather a disappointment really, because without those enormous stones it can't hope to compete in eery atmosphere with a place like Stonehenge.'

Sarson looked out at the ring of the horizon, hard and dark now as the threatened downpour began. He seemed

44

to be thinking aloud. 'It hasn't megaliths, no; though it could once have had. But it might have something even greater than Stonehenge has. Suppose that was age. A place less spectacular, perhaps; but even possibly – its original blueprint?'

5

Sarson saw little of Beaumont for the next day and a half, being mainly occupied with matters of setting up camp and allocating personnel. The volunteers straggled in, a pretty mixed bag, about half being experienced diggers, a third optimistic novices and the rest of dubious value. 'Weirdies, beardies and lunatic fringe', Pengelly the Site Assistant had quoted of them, and suggested in the same breath that a full-time security officer be appointed 'for their welfare'. He himself, Sarson recognised, was likely to prove invaluable. A sturdy, redfaced little Cornishman with close-cropped black hair, he had a formidable back-log of dig experience and a reputation for patience and the sort of impartial realism essential in this key position between organisers, contractor's men and volunteers. He showed an ability to view problems from each of these groups' viewpoints and to express them forcefully when they might otherwise be overlooked. This was likely to make heavy demands on everyone at first, but the machinery would run all the better for it. Above all he was tough, hardworking and humane.

Sarson had already put to one side certain application forms which suggested volunteers more suited to drawing office or clerical duties, and these had to be interviewed and their preferences considered. There were also several ready-made teams who preferred to dig as a group and expected some competitive structure like a football league table to be organised for the trenches.

Tents were erected as sleeping quarters. Two caravan three-holers with chemical closets, a shower and washing facilities, marked 'Women' and 'Men' were towed into cosy juxtaposition and connected to the as yet empty mains pipes laid overground from the road by the water company. A smart site hut appeared for the use of the contractor's men, and this was followed by three less impressive ones labelled 'Site Office', 'Drawing Office' and 'Store', each with an outsize padlock on the door and unsecurable windows. Pengelly at once set about providing fresh hasps for these.

A marquee was erected as a canteen for the volunteers, and a field kitchen arrived, bursting spontaneously into production with hot sausage rolls, baked beans and trifle, only fifty minutes after being set up.

Over all there was a mixed air of happy accident and practised professionalism that reminded Sarson of childhood afternoons spent watching a circus set up on the common. The roar and hum of generators, the cables snaking over grass and under wooden duckboards, the stench of blue-smoking diesel oil all added to this showground atmosphere.

'Water your elephants?' Sarson was offered by a slight, droll figure lounging at the office door when he answered a knock. 'Funny men we have our quota of,' he told the newcomer.

'MO then?'

Sarson looked at him more carefully. 'What qualifications?'

'MB, BS, London. Quite genuine. I'm issued together

with this explanatory leaflet.'

Sarson read through the letter he handed in. Peter Kent was released from Medical Staff duties at a Westminster clinic, it said, for the sabbatical period of one year. It was dated five months previously.

'Is that Dr Kent, sir?' asked Pengelly, stretching his red, round face over Sarson's shoulder. 'We've had a phone call about him. Dr. Beaumont's okayed it. I believe you've brought your own caravan, Sir? What size is it?'

'Small trailer. It has a spare bunk.'

'Let's see then. I've made a space next the First Aid tent, corner of Section C. Can you spare me, Dr Sarson, while I see if it'll fit in?'

Sarson nodded and went on checking his final measurements. The original quadrant scheme for excavation, like the round bun cut into four, had again been modified to open with a circular probe at the centre and four simultaneous trenches on the circumference, the main one on its north-east sector and curving round towards the camp. Looking up from the office window he could see the stakes connected with strings of plastic bunting that marked the excavation points. Where an initial exploration had started and the topsoil been removed, strips of exposed chalk gleamed white, but still the henge was deserted. All the swarm of human litter was down here beyond the depression. For a brief moment, standing there, Sarson remembered his odd experience alone at the site on the night of his arrival. He recalled standing at the centre of the circle and his sensation of a great crowd gathered outside, deeply concerned with whatever he might do there.

Had that in some way been a foreshadowing of the people now assembling down here in their tents and huts and trailers? He did feel for them some measure of responsibility, but not to the extent of being closely committed, as with that other invisible gathering.

Again there came a half-echo of the sounds he had heard up there, and he leaned from the window to listen, but what had at first seemed like distant cries and wailing became lost in the nearer din of a truck unloading dustbins, the chugging of the mechanical dumper and general camp turmoil.

It was perhaps only himself that was at all abnormal, an oppressive blanketing of sensation having momentarily dropped between him and his present physical surroundings. It still affected him slightly and was accompanied by a distinct nausea such as he'd felt before at the henge. He groped in his pocket for the tablets and his fingers encountered only Alan's prescription that he'd not had time to get made up. Sweat broke out on his forehead and across his shoulders. Suddenly the little hut seemed to lurch drunkenly. He looked up to see Pengelly's worried red face staring down at him.

'You very near passed out then, Dr Sarson. Here, just you lie still a minute and I'll get that young MO to give you a once over.'

'No,' he started to insist. 'I'm all right now. Or I shall be in a moment.' But the man had gone, and Sarson was still on the floor, propped against the filing cabinet, when he came hurrying back with Kent.

The doctor's earlier flippancy had disappeared. He was quite serious, examining Sarson quietly without fuss and now, close to, Sarson could appreciate that the man was older than he'd taken him to be. Deceived by the outdoor tan and his droll manner he'd previously missed the receding hair, the fine, nervous lines at the corners of eyes and mouth. His hands too, unpacking the blood-pressure gauge, were not young. He slid out of his grey jacket and now he was in a pale cyclamen shirt, with tie of dark clover.

'Your clothes,' exclaimed Sarson, astonished. 'Quick change artist.'

Kent looked at him. 'How long ago did we leave you alone?'

'I don't know. Three minutes, four?'

'How was he when you found him?' the doctor demanded of Pengelly. 'Eyes open or shut?'

'He was conscious, but – sort of glassy, I suppose.'

'I didn't pass out,' Sarson insisted.

'You lost nearly twenty minutes,' said Kent quietly. 'It doesn't matter, but I think you'd better knock off now and I'll run you back to the pub. Is your car here?'

49

'I walk.'

'Then we'll take mine. I was going across for a meal in any case.'

In the car, bumping over the rough grass, he asked almost casually, 'Are you having any treatment?'

Sarson pulled the prescription from his pocket. 'There this. I've felt this way before, several times. Sometimes worse, with vomiting and diarrhoea or abdominal cramp, but I never quite pass out. I've had all the usual tests and there's nothing wrong. Physically, I mean. Now my doctor's talking about nerves. Only I'm not the nervous type.'

'Your blood pressure's rather low. Did you know that?'

'No. It was up when Alan took it.'

'When was that?'

'Three or four times since last August. The last time would have been about ten days ago. No, a fortnight.'

'Oh well, it's the sort of thing that can happen.' He sounded almost casual. 'As you're under treatment I'll not interfere, but I can let you have something to help you relax. Until you get your doctor's prescription made up. And if you have any return of symptoms, or want to discuss it, you know where I'll be.'

'Thanks.' They drove on in silence. 'Are you interested in archaeology?' asked Sarson at length.

'Mildly. I'm more interested, frankly, in the social implications of a set up like this: what attracts the volunteers, what they've turned their backs on to come here. That sort of thing.'

'Social medicine?'

'People, and the way they live. I've had a book niggling away at the back of my mind for some time now, so when – when the chance came, I took a year's leave to get it written.'

'How's it coming along?'

Kent grunted. 'You know the saying, "Sometimes I sits and thinks, and sometimes I just sits." I'd have got more down on paper between duties at the clinic, and sneaking out of bed in the wee, small hours. But I tell myself that incubation is important.' He tapped his forehead with mock pomposity. 'When I eventually commit myself to scribbling, in the final three months or so, it'll be like the best wine, matured in the wood.' He took his eyes off the track ahead and grinned over at Sarson. 'Trouble is, I'm lazy. Never discovered it till now. I never had time to.'

Sarson considered his face, the fading tan of his skin. 'You've been abroad, I'd say.'

'New Zealand. I've a brother out there; he's a civil engineer. I spent three months watching him build a bridge, and developed this taste for camping out. They were a wonderful crowd.'

'This will be tame stuff after that.'

'Half a world away, and the object's vastly different: plumbing the past instead of spanning into the future. But I think I'll find parallels. From my work viewpoint, I mean.'

'I envy you,' said Sarson unexpectedly.

'Why that? You too are doing what you want, I take it.'

'The dig, yes. Ever since I first saw the place, it's been almost an obsession. But I wasn't prepared for the way it would all be taken over, manipulated. As the organisation grows, I lose faith somehow. The whole project begins to appear almost meretricious.'

'I'm not sure what you mean by that.'

'As though – I have the right interest, but have taken the wrong action. No, it's not even that. More as though I'm on the wrong side.'

Kent stopped the car to allow traffic to pass before turning into the main road. Behind his dark-rimmed spectacles his small eyes looked serious. 'You don't mean, surely, that you'd rather be *covering up* than excavating?'

Sarson shrugged. 'I don't really know what I mean. Not that, anyway. But I lack detachment. That's where I envy you. You're a loner. Studying a group from outside. I'm too deep by far *in* this thing of mine.' He realised he had just hit on the very source of his unease. Kent, glancing quickly sideways, saw the mask of smoothness quiver. For a moment the young archaeologist looked haggard and distraught. Then, as suddenly, the look had gone.

Externally calm and polite as before, 'You haven't met

all the dig officers yet,' Sarson said. 'Come up now and I'll introduce you.'

Kent left the car on the forecourt and followed Sarson in. He does need treatment, he admitted to himself. Alan was right: Sarson is sick. Kent thought he would probably get the chance now to give him the psychiatric treatment he'd already turned down. It was fortunate he already knew so much of Sarson's background and pressures, but any slip that revealed he was in Alan's confidence would probably alienate the patient.

They went through the hall and past the open door of the bar towards the stairs. Josie was waiting on the dark half-landing and watched the two men come up together, a new stranger and The Uncle. That was what the others had said he looked like: one of a row of uncles on a box. She didn't know what box they were talking about, but this one, The Uncle, had talked, she thought, about music. Anyway, it was about then that the music had come back. She had heard it several times since and always it was the same feeling, although different sounds. And the feeling was good. It made her feel like lying in bed and remembering nice things, and the blankets soft, and a little wisp of something silky in her hand all screwed up and when she opened her fingers it sprang out, only not right away so that she lost it, but just opened out, without any wrinkles although it had been screwed up tightly, tightly; but it came all smooth and soft again and smelling, smelling of ... something. And music stealing in, as though it was leaking round the door, the door just ajar and on the ceiling a little wedge of cheese, no, light, but shaped like cheese, and someone coming and standing ... smelling of ... and all the time music, quite close, but in another room. She wanted to be sure the music would come back, so she watched for The Uncle coming, and this evening he was early, they hadn't started the vegetables. Coming up now with another one, a new one.

When they were halfway up the first flight she softly crouched down in the dark and went on looking at him through the banisters. But he saw her just the same and smiled. He didn't speak out loud, only moved his mouth, 'hullo', and she didn't do anything back except breathe, and so they went on past.

'Who was that?' Kent asked quietly as they reached the sitting-room door.

'You saw her? That's Josie. She waits on us at table. Not one of Mrs Pyke's, but she lives nearby.' He hesitated, then decided Kent was no fool. A doctor, he'd see for himself how things were with Josie. No need to caution him.

He opened the door and stepped back for the doctor to precede him. 'Our MO,' he announced through the smoke haze, and stood aside to watch them assimilate the newcomer.

6

They were all acting slightly larger than life, as though each had learned a role and was playing it as caricature. Beaumont, in a splendidly eccentric maroon cord jacket, personified the professional performer; Joanna lounged gracefully, balancing intellect with beauty; Gifford gulped and blinked his way through the meal without notably committing himself to the conversation, and Rudi twittered pleasantly on a number of subjects which but for Joanna's ironic lead-ins would have seemed totally unrelated. His own part in the dialogue, Sarson reflected, was to caulk the fissures, much as his work as Assistant Director was with regard to dig organisation. Kent, quietly busy with knife and fork, listened and saw without appearing to watch, in the same way that he'd picked out Josie in the gloom of the turning on the stairs; and when he spoke he simply asked why this thing was and what they meant by that statement, so that everyone else, even Gifford once, enjoyed explaining themselves. And no one, Sarson realised, was fully aware of how much was revealed to that half-serious, half-droll little man, so innocent-seeming yet so intent on understanding.

As treacle tart gave way to coffee, they were trying to define civilisation, Beaumont capping the others' efforts with mocking references to the nineteenth century academics with their system of succeeding eras of Savagery and Barbarism, each neatly subdivided into Lower, Middle and Upper periods. But to sum it all, social development was, he said, a question of advancing subsistence levels. When one reached an urban level that had written language and some kind of alphabet, that was the level of civilisation. With such didactic authority he momentarily silenced the others.

Kent leaned back in his chair while the dishes were cleared from the table. 'How about you, Mrs Pyke?' he asked the woman who had just come in again. 'What do you mean by the word "civilisation"?'

She gave him a short, hard look, as though she suspected he was baiting her, and then considered it soberly. 'Well,' she said, 'if a stranger gets knocked down crossing the street and everyone there tries to do their best to help, that's what I call civilised,' and lifting the tray of wine glasses over their heads, she went defiantly out.

'Written communication,' said Kent reflectively, 'as Dr Beaumont sees it; or Mrs Pyke's selfless goodness within a community. Which better fits our case? Where does it leave us?'

No one spoke, then Joanna took out one of her honey-coloured cigarillos. 'In my case,' she said sweetly, 'matchless. Will some civilised body offer a light?'

After that the talk stayed trivial and the group began to split up. When Mrs Pyke slid in to collect the coffee cups she looked chastened. The Beaumonts having left, she addressed Sarson.

'I hope you don't think I spoke out of turn,' she ventured. 'I mean, I'm no expert like you gentlemen. But it's people I have to deal with all the time, and it's people that interest me.' She stood downcast a moment, searching for words. Then she looked at him directly. 'That's what seems so awful about that place you're going to dig up. They say there were hundreds of people living out there once. And now it's quite empty, god-forsaken. Well, where've they all gone? Whatever happened to them? It's uncanny.'

He heard the distress in her voice, and because it somehow echoed his own uneasiness he had to make some palliative reply.

'We don't know, but maybe the place has been empty too long, Mrs Pyke,' he said. 'This could be an end to it. And we are the ones to come back.'

'I'm not sure,' she said thoughtfully, 'that that's not even more scary. There's things we should let well alone.'

Peter Kent attached himself again when Sarson went out to relieve Pengelly. They drove back to the camp in the doctor's Volvo.

'From now on I think I'll get most of my meals on the site,' Sarson decided abruptly.

'Do you feel so out of tune with them?'

'They're all right. But it's better to be near where the action is.'

'Gifford seems a worthy type.'

'I believe technically he's very sound. But I don't think he'll bother with the social niceties for long either.'

Kent chuckled. 'You won't keep her at bay as easily as you think. Remove yourself from her zone of influence and she'll be popping up in the camp next.'

'I wasn't implying criticism of Mrs Beaumont,' said Sarson stiffly.

'No? I've seldom seen it more convincingly acted: The Bastions of Male Privilege Defended.'

'There are women on the site, working. Some of them are every bit as reliable as the men. More painstaking over detailed work in some cases. I'm no male chauvinist.'

'Ah, but there you have women and women. Presumably, those who've come to dig are people, not females.'

It was Sarson's turn to smile now. 'You've a lot to learn about digs. There can be General Post in the sleeping bags, according to tradition.'

'Nature red in tooth and claw?' enquired the doctor.

'M'm. Are you married?'

'Yes,' said Sarson after a marked pause. 'Are you?'

'I was. Jean died, back in September.' He spoke levelly. 'She had leukaemia. We had time enough to make plans about filling my vacuum. She used to think things up for me herself: travel here, study this, achieve that. Only it doesn't work out quite the same. The void's still there. It takes an obsession to fill it. As the book was meant to be. Do you know the most obsessional thing I've achieved? Cona coffee. Ludicrous, isn't it? I have some on all the time. Come in and try it.' He led the way into his trailer, lit the gas without a word more.

'You see?' he asked at length, crouching over the globe heating with little gasps of air, while the flask's interior filmed over and cleared continually as if it breathed. 'This is my crystal ball. I see everything through a coffee-black glass darkly. "Double, double toil and trouble..." If blank typing paper had half the allure of this coffee-maker I'd be a best-selling author by now.'

'I'm sorry,' said Sarson inadequately, putting himself in Kent's place, and he thought of Val who seemed gone but was really still there. For the first time he didn't quite evade the possibility that his future might exclude her. Has she actually left me? he asked himself. Must his life admit a void such as Kent's? Yet at least Val still lived. She could be seen and spoken with, if he went about it in a civilised enough way. It wasn't a complete void, while she was in the same world, breathing and laughing.

'You should meet Val,' he began abruptly. 'I must get her to come over.' He wasn't sure what Kent would gather from that of their relationship, and he didn't want to be deceptive. 'I suppose you'd say we're rather loosely knit; well, drifting really.' Then he had admitted too much and he wished the words unsaid.

Water shot smoothly up the central stem of the cona and the glass stopper trembled. A liquid gasp, a suck of air, and the level of the coffee grounds in the upper flask began to rise serenely in a brown circle. Kent reached for a clockwork oven-timer and meticulously set it for five minutes. His eyes on the percolating liquid already staining brown, he gave no sign of having heard what the other said.

'It gets,' he said thoughtfully, 'to be almost an end in itself.' And yet there was detachment in his voice, making no demands on anyone's sympathy. He seemed merely to state facts as he observed them. Implying that, like percolating coffee, a void took its time. The process began and one waited until it was through. He had set the timer for five minutes: he had taken a year's sabbatical leave.

'How can you be so calm?' demanded Sarson at length, his voice harsh.

'I'm not. But it's my job to know how these things usually work out. And then part of being human to get knocked off my feet just the same.'

The oven-timer began a continuous ping. 'Coffee,' Kent said and lifted the flask off the gas jet.

Sarson worked on in the drawing-office hut until almost eleven. When he left, pocketing the key, parts of the camp were in darkness, but elsewhere lamplight shone through the canvas, projecting silhouettes of the tents' occupants grouped over cards or drinks. At the southern edge of the camp there was a sing-song under way and a wood fire flickered and crackled at its centre, lighting cheery grimaces and lively gestures and the contented faces of lovers half asleep in each others' arms.

'Goodnight,' called Sarson to them as he passed, and they shouted back, one clown rising to bow over a doffed bush-hat and barely missing a fall into the flames. A dozen hands came out and heaved him back so that he dropped among a squirm of bodies and a cry went up that was part protest, part delighted squeal and had at least one version of a view halloo in it.

Sarson walked on towards the pallor of the cherry wood and the sounds grew less behind him. When he stood a moment by the water of the black tarn there was again that rustle of the undergrowth that he had heard there before. 'Who is it?' he called softly, but there was no answer. Yet he had a distinct sense of being watched and there was someone, or some creature, not far behind him all the way back to the hotel. He made no attempt to hurry and for some reason would not stop to look back.

Only when he was in his own room, before he put on the light, he went to the open window and looked across the heath in the direction he had come. So it was that he saw the dog, almost as big as a foal, waiting on the far side of the road to cross over. The figure with it was small and held on to its collar. When they moved across and the light from an uncurtained window fell on them he recognised the child Josie. He was glad then that he hadn't turned back or done anything to alarm her.

He poured a drink from the bottle of mineral water beside the bed and swallowed two of the tablets Kent had given him. Then he ran a bath, slumped beside it on a stool while the steam rolled up from the gushing taps.

Quite suddenly he heard Joanna Beaumont's voice, at first distant and then as she was passing in the corridor. With a start he caught himself on the verge of dropping asleep. It seemed he had been somewhere else completely. On a boat, was it? On a moving sea. A terrible confusion of impressions. Recovering himself he reached out to turn off the water. The level came two thirds up the bath, so he had barely slept for a minute or two. Yet he had actually dreamed, and only a few hours back he'd said to Kent, when the doctor questioned him, that he never dreamed. Dogmatically, and quite convinced that this was so. And Kent had smiled and said that everyone dreamed, but that he suppressed the memory of dreaming because his conscious mind required it of him. Well, this time he'd remembered it, perhaps because he'd been disturbed by voices in the corridor before the dream was finished, or possibly because the dream was about nothing the conscious mind objected to him experiencing (if Kent's theory of censorship was to be taken seriously). There had been a boat because of the link with water, and there was water because of the physical presence of it and he'd been thinking of his bath. He felt a little pleased with his discovery in such alien territory as psychology. Perhaps the tablets' relaxing effect had made the difference. He wondered, if now he was to remember his dreams, what it was his conscious mind had previously been cutting off from him. It might be interesting to know.

59

Acknowledging that he was far from alert, he cooled the bath and took it quickly. Then he returned to his room, put out the light and settled in bed. The last thing he was fully conscious of was the *put-put* of a two-stroke motorbike slowly making its way somewhere out on the dark roadway and gradually, taking a lifetime to do so, inexorably coming nearer.

Josie lay on her back in the dark and heard the motorbike go by. Most nights it did this, and every morning, really early, it went back the other way. And to her that meant cows. All the other reasons for getting up early allowed you to have late mornings now and again, but not cows. You couldn't keep them waiting; and so the regularity of the sound meant only this to her: cows.

She would have a picture of a dim, golden-lit byre and a slow sound of munching, the sweet scent of hay, the hiss of warm milk hitting the bucket's side in rhythmic bursts. It was comfortable, and she liked always to be in bed when the motorbike went by. There were others went past during the day, but only this one, night and early morning, that meant cows.

But the sound died and then there was nothing more. Her picture had stopped. Past the square of her window she saw only darkness. Sky and stars were clouded over. There was no moon to make the music come. She wanted it so much, coming silver, all threaded through her so that she was stitched up with soft sounds, a skeletal leaf, parts gone but their spaces alive while the sounds went breathing on. All her lost sounds. Like the porcelain knob, its soft grating on the shank of the handle, and then the drawing-room door opening, slide of brass rings as the portière rod rises, brocade curtain falling back, visitors' voices, quiet laughter, music pouring out, louder, covering her, stroking her limbs. Half-awake, half-sleeping, feeling some presence, the golden light slanting to her bed, door ajar. Warm, scented. Being lifted, pressed, held close, enfolded.

Abruptly she sat up and flung her arms out, reaching into hollow shadows. Nothing. Only empty air and darkness. She was awake now. Everything had gone. No echo of sound. Nothing but the unending screech of aloneness.

She moaned and the sound of her own voice terrified her. She flung her thin arms round herself and held on tight, but there was no relief, only fear again. She rocked to and fro, lips tight shut, but noises came through like the keening of a dog. And it went on and on, so that she thought it could never end and her back never be still and the silver moon never come back in the square of her window. Her eyes burned with a gritty fire and when she closed them all was turned red, burned red on the back of her eyelids, flickered and fed on her orangely. And she remembered frightful pain, but above all fear, and her mind ran, ran, ran through devouring redness.

A dog howling in the night, Sarson thought. Ominous. It released all manner of atavistic fears to prey on you, half-sliding into sleep. And slithering still down the incline, finding no fingerhold, no memory of the accidental present, no time at all, carrying with you only identity (and yet no name) you are utterly alone except for fear. The sound goes on but grows less, so that you know it is you, not it, that dies away. And you listen, become a total act of listening, but still you lose it and hear only yourself, the terrible sounds of your breathing, pulsing; the sound of your living, your being born, your dying. Repeated over and over. For ever alone.

7

For as long as he could remember there had always been this sound, a receding and recurring turmoil that meant to him something more than mere hearing. In his mind it was confused with physical sensations of terror and pain, as though the very sounds sucked at him, rolled him helpless over and over, lifted him, threw him but would not let go, turned him, bruised him, and crashed his pulped body brutally time and time again against booming rock. And as the sound again slipped away, so his grappling hands, straining into crevices, slipped too, and he felt himself once more being lost, as though weeds slithery as water slid through his fingers, and he himself, no more solid nor stable, was dragged away, sucked in, slobbered over, thrown off like a fish's tangled entrails upon the streaming shore.

And so he came to remember the sea.

He remembered it with all the natural loathing of a land man, but it was more than a foreign element to him. It was a trial long endured from necessity and which he must endure yet again if so the gods willed. It was his proving and his path of martyrdom, for he had not come voyaging of his own choice, but it had been laid upon him, a thing decreed.

And so, recalling the interminable, cruel ocean, and grey, foreign skies, he was almost on the verge of recalling himself. Yet, although his mind accepted there was destiny involved, he could not penetrate the dark that hung between him and the place he had lately come from. He knew as yet no name to give himself, no function to claim as his own, and no recognisable direction to his life.

His one reality was pain, dull rhythms of aching and through them now a sharp piercing of his chest and limbs. And in his skull a great pounding, as though a stone hammer smashed at the pigeon-egg shell of bone. It set his mind scuttling for some dark place it could not find, some recent refuge in black night.

As he thought of night the word exploded into bright characters that revolved and began a magic dance of wonderful significance. It seemed then that he was raised out of his body and danced along with them, the stars of evening and middle night and dawn; and when morning came he ceased dancing and came down and laid his head on a moon-white stone and stretched out on cool grass. And as the sun came up the stone's glow faded and he lay there alone at the centre of a great circle of silent, dark rocks like giants watching over him. He knew for a while he slept.

The pains returned. Now there were other seas rising and falling above the surf he had recognised before. They were like voices, the voices of men who wished not to be overheard but whose discretion became lost in the urgency of their words. Meaningless words to him, and yet their phrases had a cadence of sense. And it astonished him to be unable to understand, knowing as he did (although his own name still escaped him) that he was master of many languages and widely travelled.

Yet perhaps he deluded himself? — just as a wanderer

seeking water in the desert fancies he sees ahead the shimmer of a lake. Did he now imagine himself gifted with tongues because he was in fact a mute?

He moved his lips and the skin was splintered like old wood, his tongue a swollen leather stopper in the bottle of his mouth. A single harsh croak escaped him and at it all other sounds ceased, until somewhere nearby a breaker flung itself upon rock and a seabird cried out once like a spirit lost in the void.

Then faces appeared above him. The moon, a woman; and two sun men, wild and golden. Then hands pressed him down again among the animal smell of skins, while the pains struck again and again upon the drum of his head above the nosebridge, and a soft, warm trickle began that was blood running into his eyes.

It obscured his sight. He closed his eyes against the crimson that became black, and he smelled herbs, dry and musty, sweet and bitter, pressed into the wounds to stem the flood. Then the sea of blackness rose again about him, rocked him down to its starless depths. And yet one star, it seemed, there was. Tiny and distant like a firefly, it was coming closer, turning as it came. And it was like no star he had ever seen in all his dedication as Watcher of the Heavens, for it dulled in colour as it came, rotating slowly, alone in the vastness of space. A small, sandy, four-pointed star. Coming ever closer.

Sarson awoke suddenly, sat up in the rose-papered hotel room and pushed the hair off his throbbing forehead. He had slept heavily and gone right through to dawn. He wasn't sure but he had the feeling he had dreamed. Of what he couldn't have said, but he thought that just before he awoke Val had been in his mind.

He pushed back the blankets and went across to the window. The sun was coming up through a bank of mist. The open downland before him looked smoothed out and simplified. For some reason it brought Kent to his mind: Kent, his wife dying and his void; how he'd said it took an obsession to fill a void, and how the obsession seemed to have failed him. He wondered if the doctor was awake already, scraping away with a safety razor while he listened for the gentle plopping of coffee in the glass percolator.

Perhaps until the period of shock was through and he could reorganise his professional life the dig would help to fill Kent's void. Not necessarily the archaeological side of the project, because it was foreign ground to him, but at least the social aspect. The gathering here was as varied as any psychologist could wish for; and, considering this, Sarson realised with surprise that he actually found these people congenial himself. He hadn't expected to, but this morning he was looking forward to getting out on the site and being with them all, the grinning faces of the camp-fire, Pengelly's florid concern, Gifford and his electronic gadgets, even Beaumont with his posturings. Suddenly they had all come together and looked like a team. Because the project was at last in action. Today they would start to dig.

The barometer hand slid from Change towards Fair and stopped there when he tapped its glass in the hotel vestibule. The figures on the dial were obscured by decades of discoloration, but Sarson wanted to believe that the inner works might not have deteriorated too badly.

He could hear movements all over the hotel by now, but he hoped to get his own breakfast eaten and be out on the site before the others could delay him. He was standing by the sitting-room window, rocking on his heels and humming a tune when little Josie came in carefully carrying his bacon and scrambled eggs. She looked bloodless this morning and her thin hair hung unevenly in wisps at her neck. She fixed her huge dark eyes on Sarson and he saw how shadowed they were, as though set in bruises.

'Come along then, Josie,' Mrs Pyke had to remind her as she stood there staring.

Sarson smiled and stopped humming. 'It's going to be a lovely day,' he said. For the first time he saw the child smile, or the beginning of her smile, for it took a long while to get under way and she left before it was complete.

'Would that be your dog Josie takes for walks?' he asked Mrs Pyke later as he was leaving.

'That great old brown thing? Goodness, no. Some stray she took up with a couple of years back. Pyke's not a bit keen on having it round the place. Nor'm I for that matter, but she's fond of the animal and it's little enough bother all told. It minds what she says, and we let it sleep out in the shed, nights.'

'What she *says*?'

'She doesn't need to talk. They understand each other well enough, those two. Soon as she comes to the door it's there, and they just go off together. We're so used to it we barely see the creature, which is just as well.' He gathered from her tone that the dog must have parasites or some other social drawback. Well, they'd probably all have lice at the camp before the dig was over, but he hoped Josie's dog wouldn't have to take the blame.

Officially the volunteers worked from nine in the morning until five thirty, though with an enthusiastic and energetic crowd it was usual, at critical stages, to go on until the light gave out. The contractor's men, however, delighted in an eight-to-four-thirty schedule. One of the recurrent thorns in a Site Assistant's flesh was this initially bantering, but often subsequently tetchy, insistence on 'them' and 'us', which showed itself in every aspect of the work, be it hours, tools, accommodation, catering, or simply conditions for defecation. A watchful eye on brushes between the two parties at an early stage could do much to identify potential trouble makers and so one could draw up working schedules that would keep them apart. Pengelly was busy with this now, having checked the hired men's arrival time and set them the unnecessary task of transporting and stacking turf rolls taken from the marked ground. This cheated them of the right to complain innocently of there being nothing to get cracking on since them softies was still at their nosh, wasn't they?

Tomorrow there would be all the examined soil worked over during the volunteers' extra evening hour for the workmen to move. Meanwhile they lifted and carried and unloaded and stacked with selfconscious virtue, clucking from time to time at sight of some lounging volunteer and stoically impervious to the alluring scents of frying bacon and instant coffee wafting over from the camp. The off-duty provocants made occasional loud remarks designed to penetrate their mental defences, but the disputable hour was soon past and distinctions then almost ceased to show.

Sarson approved the way Pengelly had allocated the workers. Some were well known to the Site Assistant, being old hands at barrow excavations he'd helped to organise. These had been assigned to the 'boxes', or divisions of the trench, most likely to yield early traces of ancient workings. Three of these, two men and a stringy, middle-aged woman in faded khaki dungarees who had caught the archaeology fever during her early married life in Iran as an oilman's wife, were specially favoured with the loan of a whistle with which to signal notable finds and bring the dig officers running. Every trench was responsible for its own notebook, from which Sarson would take all entries and make up the day book, but for the present, while quite large quantities of upper strata could be removed without exposing much of interest, even the drawing and photographic volunteers were helping to sort through what the contractors' shovels and mechanical digger threw up, so all was action and optimistic enthusiasm. Sarson made the usual checks and then went back to inspect the camp. He found Kent sitting on the steps of his trailer, an open manual on his knees and a wooden chest alongside.

'It's amazing,' he marvelled, 'how easily one forgets what doesn't interest one. With reference, of course, to minor abrasions, sprains, burns and the like.'

'Yes, I imagine casualty calls aren't much in your line.'

Kent flipped over a few pages. 'No likelihood of obstetric emergencies, would you say? That's one section I don't need to go over. How did you sleep, by the way?'

'Wonderfully. Those tablets of yours sneaked up on me and laid me out for the count.'

'Good. The country air probably had a lot to do with it, but I'd carry on with the tablets for a week, if I were you. No recurrence of the nausea?'

'None. I feel really fit again. I shan't have time to be off-colour now the dig's started. Maybe Alan was right: first-night nerves.'

'Rejection,' said Peter Kent abruptly, and Sarson, looking down at him, saw the little, ironic smile twisting one corner of his mouth. 'Rejection,' Kent repeated. 'Physical voiding as a deep-source refusal to accept a mental situation. That's what the books say. That's what, a few months back, seated at my doctrinal desk and behind my horn-rims, I would have been thinking.'

'We all have our professional jargon,' Sarson said slowly, uncertain how to take him. 'And when I'm sick of something, heartily sick, I do feel like throwing up. I guess there's a grain of truth in it.'

'Some, no doubt. But you feel fit at the moment, only some thirty-six hours after a violent attack. Can the situation have changed so fundamentally? Or is it you that have changed?'

Sarson, who would have resented any prying, was left standing there, free to provide the information to himself. He wasn't *against* anything this morning, he realised. There was no longer any sense of restriction or conflict. Perhaps all he had needed was that one good night's sleep, and the feeling of well-being that lasted through till now. He had dreamed, of course. Suddenly he knew that, though the details escaped him. It had been a good dream, somehow important. While he slept his mind had contrived to sort things differently, leaving him free to go ahead. So it was himself and not the situation that had altered. But of his bodily and mental improvement, which was cause and which effect?

He looked up at the trailer's half-closed door. A small card tacked to it had a neat list of surgery hours, and underneath a phone number in case of emergencies. Kent seemed to be moving furniture about inside and whistling between his teeth. Strauss, Sarson guessed; a song from *Die Fledermaus*. And because it was a catchy little tune Sarson found himself humming it later as he went around, and twice during the day heard someone else caught up by its infection.

The initial digging went well and in Perimeter One trench they were through the first layer of decayed chalk to a harder core by evening. Sarson had samples sealed for despatch to London before he went to bed.

The local air was certainly having its effect on him, but he remembered Kent's tablets and took two. His mail had been left in his room and he read this in bed. It included the Spring number of *Antiquity* and, despite his interest in an article by Piggott, sleep caught up with him before he had read far. He fumbled for the light cord above his head, and even as he reached it he felt himself falling gently back, receding into timeless dark.

There was a sense of familiarity as though he were on the point of recapturing some half-forgotten memory. *Again* ... he thought; *I am returning*...

Wearisomely recurring, and yet never quite repeating any cadence or rhythm, the sea sounds went on, and the injured man knew that daily he was growing stronger; but still he could not walk. He lay in the cave's gloom that stank of fish guttings and stale bladderwrack, and he longed for the light that gleamed at the entrance like a cone of pale fire beyond his outstretched feet.

By day a woman cared for him, changing the packs of seaweed on his open wounds and moistening them constantly, feeding him salty broths and claylike flat cakes. At night the two men would reappear and sit in the cave mouth, lit by a fire the man could never quite see but which pulsed red on their faces and threw straddling shadows on the vaulted roof so that they mixed and dandled over him like an evil spider of monstrous proportions, while the men sat tearing at flesh with teeth and hands, spitting bones into a corner where a rough-coated dog crunched them and growled in a way that was scarcely more savage.

The tongue the men spoke made little sense to him lying there helpless, but certain words were becoming familiar, and from their gestures as they muttered together he learned when they spoke of him and he recognised that one term they used was also the sound they made when they argued over animal skins or portions of meat or fish. There was a prolonged dispute over possession of him and he watched grimly to see what the outcome would be.

One, the larger-boned, owned the cave and the woman, so his was the claim of having given shelter. The other man's right was not clear, but it seemed to go back to some earlier condition. This second claimant seemed obliged to offer some present to the first in order to retain what he held to be his own.

Both were savages, but they were not two of a kind. Each was hard and obdurate, but the one, when he was crossed, looked away and turned to other things, confident that he had already won. The other endured a blind rage that devoured him within. He was by nature a fierce man, but for some reason, at this time, he was constrained to contain his anger. He had cunning enough to know that a little lost in manoeuvre can bring a great gain in final position. For this reason he watched his opponent more warily, and his own moves with as great a caution. The injured man grew to think of him as a hunter. It was indeed from him that the skins had come. The other man returned always with fish, fresh caught from the sea, and his clothes – of a coarse fabric, not skins – were often wet and caked with a white deposit at the edges.

The sick man lay, their disputed property, throughout this time with no more human rights than a waterlogged tree trunk – or at highest level the cur they threw their waste food to – until the night they almost came to blows and with a bad grace the hunter lurched off, to return later with two further skins, one heavy and almost black, the other smooth, of a strange milky paleness. But the hunter did not easily part with them. He gestured at last towards the disputed man and then to the skins, growled some contemptuous offer and nodded to the other's woman.

The fisherman put out his hand to the smooth, creamy pelt and stroked it. The action passed a magic into him and his obduracy faded. Abruptly he laughed and beat one fist into his palm, showing big, square teeth as he rocked on his haunches. Each man bent forward and struck the other with an open hand upon the right shoulder, and so the bargain was made. The injured man was the hunter's, for the extra cost of two hides less the usage of the woman.

The hunter took her at once to the dark side of the cave and the shore man, shrugging, heaped the skins upon his knees, blowing into the pale fur and running his hand up and down the pelt with a sensuous enjoyment. The man lying watching regretted then the way the deal had gone, for this fisherman was alive to beauty in a way he had not previously suspected. But his woman meant little to him, for he seemed to close his ears while the hunter panted and laboured over his pleasures with her in the darkness behind.

Some cunning as a merchant the hunter had shown, thought the stranger; but as yet no fineness of mind. And he was to become this man's thing. When the hunter left this place of refuge he must go too.

At last the hunter had had enough of the woman and he pushed himself apart, then after only a moment of silence he came over to inspect his other merchandise. He pulled the damp seaweed from the man's skin and bent close to sniff the healing wounds. Satisfied, he replaced the remedies and then began to make swift darting movements with his hands, skimming the surface of the other's face. The man faced him steadfastly enough, but soon realising that the hunter tried merely to test his sight, nodded slightly, turning his eyes right, left, up, down, to reassure him that they functioned still despite the dark. As the hunter sat there on his heels, the other tried a word of the growling language, pointing to his own breast and making the sound he recognised as referring to possessions. He was answered by a swift and savage grin. The hunter touched himself upon the throat and uttered a new word. 'Whergh.' The bought man repeated it three or four times until satisfied he held it in his mind. He had no way of telling, so colourless was the hunter's tone, whether the word was a name or the title of Master. That he would learn when he heard other men address the man it now referred to.

The hunter's hands, as they moved over the other's body, were coarse-skinned but not brutal. Just so might he have touched a deer or a boar lately killed, valuing it for its flesh and pelt. The man enduring it required more of him: to be recognised by the other as a man. Of this there was no sign.

When the hunter motioned to him to try and rise he used his arm to raise himself and stood a brief moment upon the skins, shaken with ague and nausea, before his legs crumpled under him. The other stood looking thoughtfully down, considering the wretched body.

The injured man put out one hand towards the cave mouth where the evening sky showed pale, and in a voice of longing spoke his own word for light. Then he touched his eyes and pointed again. The man who had bought him grasped at once what was asked for, but he gave no answer, merely standing there and considering what next to do. Then abruptly he turned and left the cave.

Within a short while he was back with two other men who in build were not unlike him. One lifted the sick man while the other bound him in a sheet of sewn skins, and between them they carried him, effortlessly, slung like a bundle of cloth from their shoulders. And humped along in such a manner he left the cave.

Above him once more the sky was open and clear, with the rising moon in her middle phase shrouded and mysterious. Yet still she pointed to his star the way his journey must run, and, still, borne on these strangers' backs, he was moving northward but now with the turn of a circle's sixth part to the east. He knew no name to call himself, nor the place he had been born, but he beheld the moon as one looks upon one's god, and as he gazed marvelling, the sacred numbers came. And as they were once more revealed to him he recognised that numbers are true even when the tongues of men are forked so that their words have double meaning. To count and to measure, he knew, was divine communication.

They followed a ledge of cliff that on one side fell steeply to breaking surf, and before them circled a cove of flattish rocks ringed first with sand and then with a dark undergrowth. Here and there were bursts of deep yellow blossom with a sweet, nutty scent that perfumed all the air, so that the wood-smoke of fires and the salt smell of sea, even the animal stench of the skins he had lain in, all reached him through this other scent and softened by it, making the very night itself voluptuous. The man breathed deeply, free although bound, and leaping in his heart although his legs would not hold him. For he was again beneath the moon and his journey continued. Although carried captive, it was yet permitted him to keep faith.

So the moon sank and the day drew near and he slept, deeply, as though blanketed under aeons.

They had not in fact carried him far, for when he later awoke the smell of the sea, but no longer its sound, was still with him. Now, however, there were other scents that joined the sweet yellow blossom's; above all, the broth they held close to his mouth, rich with meaty fats and bitter with herbs, forcing strength into him. Two young men fed him from a clay bowl, dipping with their fingers for the choicest morsels and then tipping the vessel against his cracked lips so that he might drink his fill. The hunter who had bargained for him sat opposite, ankles crossed and hands dangling over his golden knees. He said nothing, but watched, and the bought man, while he ate, asked himself what this other expected of him, questioned what possible use such a debilitated body as his own might be to these splendid savages who surely saw him as nothing but debris. Had they perhaps some means of telling that there was more to this frail creature they chose to nourish than the overburdened flesh they could see? Had the goddess forewarned them, that they knew to look out for his coming?

And yet he could not entirely believe that he was safe

74

in their hands. This might be no more than the preparation for some further trial of endurance.

Mighty is Ishtar, he prayed, eyes closed above the lifted bowl; grant that in my belly an enemy's bane may be turned to wholesomeness; grant to my mind the power to see the things hidden in the hearts of all men. So shall it be done at last as is commanded.

He made an imperious gesture to the young man who had pressed the bowl once again upon him, and the boy drew back, golden brows drawn straight in a single line above his eyes. The hunter muttered some words and the two withdrew from sight. Then he rose and stood before the man who had come from afar.

The two men gazed a long while upon each other, each searching deep in the other's mind, so that the hunter recognised courage and experience and some type of dedication he had not met before, and the other saw that he was meant to be for the hunter in part a talisman, in part some kind of tally-piece employed in a contest of power.

It was of no use to tell the hunter that he would be unable to put under his own service one who had already submitted to a greater command, because they had no common language as yet to explain such a concept in. But soon, thought the traveller, I shall hear enough and know sufficient to be able to speak with him. Until then I will give no offence unless I must.

The hunter remarked the other's calm and he turned in his mind how far he dare go in stirring this strange person he had decided to use in his plans. It became clear to him, the more he observed him, that valuable as he might be to impress the superstitious, yet he might, if roused, prove a terrible danger, for there was a presence about him that warned one to caution. He was a man to win over to one's side, to impress with one's worth, before one required much of him.

The traveller watched him think. He saw the moment of doubt, the flicker of unease, the decision to stalk the prey with cunning. He too knew then how he must act. With upthrust chin he laid one hand upon his own throat, as he had seen the other do when claiming a name. He made his lips twist with powerful scorn and he spoke the word that meant a possession. Then he swept wide his arms, palms down, in utter refutation. 'The Watcher,' he said in his own tongue. 'I shall be called The Watcher.'

Something changed slightly in the hunter's eyes. Without moving, yet he seemed gathered up, like a great cat about to spring, lips and cheeks tight upon teeth, ears strained tight against skull, muscles beautifully tuned to litheness. For a moment he stayed motionless, then he rose quietly, without menace, and his feet were silent as he glided away. When he returned, in an equal silence, he held a large bundle wrapped in finest skins, and as he knelt by The Watcher to open it he took care to spread the outer cover wide, so that what was contained should at no point touch the ground, nor yet his own flesh, as the things were revealed. The Watcher observed, not missing the hesitation finally of the hands, the sudden searching of his own face, and the flicker of fear that both implied. He kept his own eyes long upon the other's and knew that whatever lay below, when he should look upon it he must in no way show emotion. He must lower his gaze and return it, unchanged, to re-encounter the other's.

He did so, and gave stare for stare. Then his hands moved of themselves, refolding the corners of the skins to cover what had been looked upon, and all the time his eyes held the other man in thrall. 'Go now,' he said, 'and tell no man.'

Without knowing a word of what had been said to him, the other rose obediently and went quickly away.

Then time, that had lately ceased, began again; and the traveller's heart, that had neither beaten nor yet grown cold while he gazed, again started up; and all that he should have felt and suffered and gloried in in that first instant came upon him those few moments late, and with such engulfing force that he seemed to die a little and then return to life a hundred times more feeling.

Shrouded again in the soft skins, the precious insignia remained still visible to him. A strange pallor seemed to leak from the closed bundle lying before his knees, and he saw once more the beauty of the white, petalled robe, the perfect craftmanship of the crescent necklace where shell and ivory and coloured stones strung on gold wires set off the central plaque of bitumen marked with the holy signs. His mind's eye passed through the thonged waist-purse and revealed the ceremonial instruments. Still he acknowledged that memory of the past was purged away from him, but yet some shifting pictures floated on a mist. He saw himself, as if a separate person, open and expectant under a sky reeling with stars, on some far distant high place, a sacred tower. And he saw himself, later, driven by his fate, attaching the insignia to a goat skin stretched with air, lashing it to his shoulders as he stood above the boiling sea and the ship broke to pieces beneath him. These pictures were himself at each end of his journey; but for what purpose and from what cause he had come he did not know, except that it was required of him and to this he must totally submit.

He bent forward and folded each hand so that it became a pronged cone, and he rested them both on the covered objects by the tips of their three longest fingers. At once he experienced a stirring within himself and knew how he should proceed, for the insignia required to be worn, that he should be acknowledged the anointed one from afar.

But first there was ceremonial cleansing. He clapped his hands and when the two young men came he pointed to the bowl from which they had earlier bathed him and he spoke the word he had heard them use for water. The ritual was clear in his mind and he followed it minutely as soon as he was again alone.

Then a second time he opened the bundle of skins and now he took out the robe and passed it over his head, securing it with the nacrine clasp. He wound about him the linen girdle and then on his bare chest he spread the necklace where gold and glittering stones were scattered, like constellations on the midnight sky of the tablet. Lastly he drew from the purse the copper knife for cleaving and the jade dagger of sacrifice, and he set the serpentine ring on his right hand, encasing the whole middle finger. Immediately he experienced such a flow of force that he could sit up, legs folded, and his back erect without any support. He arranged the knives across open palms and lap, and turned up his face to the sky.

So he sat, motionless, while the stars performed their slow rhythm upon his receptive mind, until at last the hunter crept back again and knelt to lay his hands beneath the Watcher's ankles and show himself defenceless.

Then a great peace came over the traveller and he seemed to draw all the knowledge of the skies into himself so that he walked with the stars and nothing that was of earth or the concern of men could reach him until the communion was through. All night he sat so, his upturned face reflecting the luminous bowl of heaven, and when the morning star hung pale over the dark shrubs with their sweet yellow blossom, his spirit returned and he saw that the land journey was about to be resumed and the hunters had fashioned him litter poles of willow branches, from which hung a woven hurdle spread with pelts. And so, without once having placed his foot directly upon the soil of this new land, he was lifted in and lay there, utterly strange and resplendent so that the savage men were silent in awe.

They carried him first, by the way he recognised, back to the cave where he had lain near death. The ledge this cave opened from jutted above the sea, which he heard again sucking and plashing many a man's height below, but of it he could see nothing, for between himself and the water's surface rolled a great expanse of white mist, dense but for ever moving as though some mighty cauldron boiled beneath. And all the air touching upon him hung heavy with moisture, so that he seemed to be perpetually bathed in steamy wetness. The sea from which he'd come, together with the route he had followed, were now physically quite cut off from him and joined the veiled recollections of life before he came to this place.

The man who came out to meet them trembled with fear at sight of him, and whimpering piteously the dog crouched low on its belly, eyes rolling white. And yet, the traveller saw, there was more than fear in the man's shaking: there was the beginning of anger too. As soon as they had left he would be violent, furious that such a rich prize had been tricked out from under his nose. The hunter had demonstrated too well his own cunning in hiding the insignia and the sick man's importance. But it was rash of him now to parade such a prize, for he had made an enemy of this man with whom he had commerce.

The Watcher opened the neck of the bag that hung from his waist and took a small round ball of amber between finger and thumb. Despite the veiling of the sun, light filled it with golden warmth as he held it over the other's palm. The litter was lowered as the fisherman stared at the firestone in his hand. Then The Watcher pointed to an ordinary pebble that lay among others at the cave mouth. When they had brought him the right one he placed it on a rock and struck it once with the copper knife. It flew apart, cleanly in two, and at its centre was a tiny curled sea creature wound inside just as the serpent ring spiralled about his own longest finger.

One part of the stone, that which held the petrified creature, he gave back to the man, together with the amber, and the other half, that held the creature's hollow print, he put into his own waist-purse. Then, while the man threw himself flat upon the rocky ledge, The Watcher held one hand above him, directing into him alliance and an honourable farewell. He left the man in peace, rewarded and with no more envy in his heart.

The hunters lifted the litter and now began their real departure. As the sun climbed behind them and warmed his head upon the pillow, The Watcher felt his body loosen and float free of him. All day he slept and awoke only as the first star pricked through the evening sky.

It seemed to him that in the daytime he had dreamed of being some other man in a distant, strange time where nothing was in his own world. There the men were covered over, in body and mind, so that each moved increasingly apart from the others, existing in complex hierarchical patterns that were for ever in flux, so that none spoke with authority over all but each from some small part of his experience that the others did not share; and although the words employed by all were the same, and intricate, yet each seemed to understand differently what they signified, not reaching the truth they obscured. It seemed to him a terrible world of dangers and aloneness, the people coming together and moving apart at random, seemingly unaware of peril or the need to give and share protection. But every man, he knew, had a private terror at his core, which was the more destructive because often he did not know it was there. It worked on all these people, so that although they were always striving they never knew satisfaction, since they moved one against another and thought themselves disconnected. And they lived each day as though it were the same as the day before, without progress, and as though they would live so till the end of the world, and in their dying the world would cease to be. It disturbed him that he should dream himself such a man as these, but he felt a pity for this shadow self. He knew too that he controlled him in some way, and that waking he could summon forces that would overcome any alien will to separate him from this dream part of himself. Ishtar was mighty over all things, and she had given him her special power. So, while he wondered at the strangeness of the continuing dream, yet it did not distress him when the last star had faded and he must return to sleep for the day.

In this manner they continued to travel, progressing by day while The Watcher slept, camping at night about a watch-fire, when he bathed and passed the night on vigil under the stars.

The hunters carried stores, including fish, shells, salt blocks and bundled merchandise, as well as his litter. All this, and their need to kill for meat on the way, made the journey longer. Alone at night on some high place, while the watch-fire burned and crackled and on the edge of the forests wolves slunk howling, The Watcher marvelled at the soft swelling of the hills, the natural sweet waters, the lushness of grass and dense forests. All was gently moist and dank and sweet, with an innocence as though in the breezes here the gods whispered promises to the earth, never flooding nor salting nor scorching its crust with their harsh displeasure. And such fine timber grew, and the slopes were as rich in natural stones as the valleys were with game. But there were no great rivers, and the air was cool, and such people as he had met with had no knowledge of metals, the veined stones which grow, and that, sanctified by fire, take on new forms of life. They were a simple people, he saw, and not yet to be troubled with such knowledge.

In the mornings the journey was resumed and as far as possible they avoided the densely forested valleys where wild animals abounded, and followed instead a series of upland folds that in places had been cleared and bore from time to time marks cut in the grass to expose the chalk face. These served as indications of various routes that seemed to meet and cross like a wide-meshed net flung over the ridges. Even as he slept the Watcher was a little aware of them, for they penetrated the dream he was in, and disturbed his mind with a flow of opposing and meeting forces.

The man he had become in his daytime dreams also felt their pull in diverging directions, but because he did not understand the influence exerted he could not go with any one of them, feeling merely restless and without balance. Waking at early evening, the Watcher would remember this other man and smile at his perplexity. He wished peace upon him, and as this stranger seemed in some way an unpercipient part of himself, he prayed that he might find illumination. Having requested this, at the end of his vigil the Watcher returned smoothly to sleep.

The distant sound grew closer, opened from a subdued buzz to the *pop-pop* of a two-stroke engine approaching along the Farne road, passing under the window, fading and again merging to a single tone, dying away to leave only birdsong and the vaguely personalised sounds of many people sharing a single roof and in varying states of rousing.

Sarson turned on his back, finding yielding springs where he had half expected a woven hurdle, and above him shadowed ceiling for sky. But the scent of the downland was in the room and the day was a fine one. He thought of the new white scars out on the site and the age-old secrets lying under them. He was impatient to be there and see them opened up once more to the free air.

In his haste to dress and get out to the dig, his dream itself became covered over. But not lost: his thoughts and actions lay light on it, an easily shifting fabric that would take little stirring to move apart.

9

'You're looking better,' Kent said when Sarson and he met at the staff table over lunch. He had finished his own meal but continued to sit there, leaning on his elbows, the sleeves of his bush shirt rolled up to show fine, well-muscled arms still bronzed by New Zealand sunshine.

'Yes,' agreed Sarson shortly. 'No nausea at all now.' He chased a lump of lamb stew round the plate with his fork and fielded it in, camp-fashion with a crust of bread. 'How did surgery go?'

Kent grinned. 'It's stiff joints day. Apart from that, one knife wound, accidental, from the field kitchen, a severe scalding, two hangovers and a hernia. You remain my favourite case.'

'Oh, you were right,' Sarson told him, suddenly remembering. 'I do dream. Or I have done for the last two nights.'

' "In sleep a king, but, waking, no such matter..." '
Kent's head was bowed. He seemed to be speaking to
himself. Then he looked up, blinked behind his spectacles. 'Shakespeare, of course. From his sonnets. He, if
anyone, knew what love was. It goes,

> *"Thus have I had thee, as a dream doth flatter,*
> *In sleep a king, but, waking, no such matter." '*

Sarson watched the doctor, a curiously defenceless man
for all his professional self-analysis.

'Not flattery in my case,' Sarson said lightly. 'I can't
recall much, but there were no conquests, of either kind.
I seemed to be in pretty poor shape, washed up after a
shipwreck. Yes, I remember now, the sea was in it each
time. And the dream continued from the previous night,
like a serial. Even when I dropped off for a few minutes
before the first dream, I was vaguely conscious of a boat
and heavy seas. The original shipwreck, perhaps.'

'Strange,' said Kent, turning to look at him now. 'I
should have expected you to dream of the site, because
you're obviously affected by the place.'

Sarson pushed his plate away. He frowned down at the
table, trying to fix the dream's details as they momentarily surfaced. 'No, it wasn't the site; but it was a very
long time back. Perhaps of the same period.'

'And you were there?' Kent insisted soberly.

Sarson considered. 'Yes. Travelling towards some goal.
I was different somehow. It didn't feel like me now,
but—' He stopped, embarrassed, and laughed. 'I was going to say, "as I once was, in a state of innocence".'

'Innocent,' the doctor murmured. 'You were conscious
that the you of the dream was innocent.'

'Maybe that's not the right word. A sort of holy man, a
guru. In the dream I was all of a piece, something like
that. Yes, free of time, and so in some way whole.

'All of a piece.' He repeated the phrase, but with a
wondering inflection, as though it had now, suddenly, a
new meaning. Kent watched as he covered his eyes with
one hand.

'And when you awoke you were fragmented again?'

The question barely reached Sarson. He was aware only of some immense chasm opening from which something seemed to be rising, having neither form nor sound nor substance, yet strangely affecting him. 'I —' he began, and then the word had no meaning, as though the very concept of identity had ceased to be.

Kent's eyes never left his face, and so he caught the silent transformation of the features.

'I —' said Sarson again. There was a silence and then another voice spoke, barely above a whisper. 'I am The Watcher of the Heavens, High Priest to the Holy Being. Hear me. Know that all life is one.'

Instantly the change was over. It was Sarson frowning back at him, stumbling over the phrases he had lost.

'I – the . . .' he repeated.

'All life is one,' Kent said, gently prompting. 'You said you felt all of a piece, whole; then "all life is one".'

Sarson looked uncomfortable. 'I don't know why I said that.' Clearly he'd no knowledge of that brief moment of possession.

'An inner level speaking,' Kent offered.

The words were scarcely audible and Sarson looked hard at the other hunched over the bare trestle board. The utilitarian, graceless scene about them, the crude marquee, all refuted the tenor of their present talk. It had escaped control, was out of context; and yet, despite his recall of their surroundings, Sarson felt himself in an alien state of mind. As though a new, mystic sense moved behind his normal frame of self-expression, and he had little power to control it. It was a momentary imbalance, he told himself; an equivalent in mental terms of the sickness he'd known physically before. But surely it was something he could resist. He forced himself to rise, leaning over to take Kent's empty plate and slip it under his own.

'Look,' he said, 'I'm a dirt archaeologist, not even a fancy academic one. I dig into the earth, not my psyche.'

It was meant to sound light and final, but was neither. The words were curt and the silence after them was the space for an answer the other man declined to make.

At least – Sarson thought, reflecting afterwards – Kent

doesn't lay my case at the door of frustrated sex-urge, as any Freudian would. His must be another system, a different jargon. But to be fair, the man was no psychiatrist at the moment, just a poor devil submitting to his own dose of hell, a man of grief.

Sarson turned back and searched the camp alleys for the doctor's slight form. He caught up with him just before the door of his trailer. 'If I came by in, say, twenty minutes,' he suggested, 'after I've seen Pengelly, would there be any coffee on offer?'

'Nothing more certain, friend.'

He would have gone in with him then but he wasn't ready. Too soon after the intensity earlier, he found himself with nothing to say, nothing safe to say. But he wanted to put it right with Kent, so that the little man shouldn't feel rebuffed.

Pengelly's matter-of-factness was the right corrective, and a short run through the half-day's progress effected the mental change of gear Sarson needed. He arrived back briskly factual and waded straight in by mentioning that his wife might be in the vicinity by the weekend.

Accustomed as he was to sudden manifestations of schizoid behaviour, Kent was almost tempted to believe he'd been mistaken over the brief personality change he'd witnessed some half hour back. This was Sarson completely himself again, with the touch of uncertainty customary to him whenever he spoke of his relationship with Val.

Kent asked the expected questions and was given an account of her gliding activities at Farne. 'You each go your own way,' he marvelled. 'She up, you down.'

Sarson had never seen it as a question of physical direction and this amused him. 'It doesn't sound too promising,' he agreed. 'But we do look in on the other's interests from time to time.'

It sounded feeble even to himself. He stared out of the ridiculous, net-swagged window to where a slope of the site showed between the First Aid Post and the drawing-office hut. The plastic strip bunting flickered red and white above a chalky gash in the green. He felt suddenly tired of all deceit.

'It's not the way I'd have it from choice,' he said slowly. 'I'd give a lot to go back again to our beginning.'

'Time doesn't easily reverse,' Kent reminded him.

'I know. "Perpetual change is the only constant." "We live in a time of enlightened self-expression." I'm familiar with all the trendy clichés. Only, how enlightened, for God's sake, do we have to be? I suppose you'd have me bound off elsewhere on a healthy quest for ever better sexual athletics? People seem to get sex these days like our grandparents got religion. Oh, it's there, it's tremendous while it lasts; but afterwards? What then?'

'Exactly,' Kent murmured. 'Afterwards – time for the things that matter. But it is "afterwards", and not "instead of". When all your big things are instead of sex, life's not so easy.'

'I'm not monastic,' said Sarson. 'That's excessive too. I guess it's a relationship I need, not just a mechanical mate. But that, it seems, is beyond my scope.'

'Because one person's complex enough, and two together are – incomprehensible?'

'The mind boggles.' Sarson moved his weight heavily from one foot to the other. 'How can two people ever want the same thing at precisely the same time? So, for the most part, marriage is like a pair of unequal prisoners shackled back to back, with neither hearing anything but their own interminable monologue. Better to dissolve the ties, let them try their freedom.' He turned back to find Kent's eyes inscrutably on him. At once he was aware that what he'd just said of himself had more crucial implications for the other.

'Freedom?' asked Kent. 'Or loneliness?' His voice was as calm as though the words had nothing to do with himself. He reached out one hand. 'Coffee's ready,' and he began carefully to pour the liquid, black and steaming, from glass globe to pottery mugs. And as he did so, one of the whistles sounded from the dig. Two short notes and one long.

From the caravan door Sarson could see three figures waving. One of them, he thought, was a woman. As he would have guessed, the box they were working in was the henge's centre. He knew how the layers there were

87

showing. He could almost picture the objects they had uncovered.

'Aren't you going up for a look?' Kent demanded.

Sarson didn't want to. For some reason he felt himself recoil. It was almost physical, this blocking, as though drive bands about the diaphragm and waist held him back, making it impossible to approach the site.

'In a moment,' he muttered. He couldn't offer a valid reason for this hesitation. 'We'll give Beaumont time to hear about it.'

'You don't think it's likely to be important? Nothing really old?'

'The layers are disturbed,' said Sarson. 'The hill centre has been cut off, like the top of a hard-boiled egg. Centuries back farmers ploughed there and displaced the original chalk. But also there have been excavations, possibly in the Middle Ages. The original layers have become mixed and been thrown back in anyhow. The most we can expect is to find them here and there in reverse order. In cases like this you get rubbish too. Each period unearthed contains a refuse heap of something earlier. It'll be Romano-British coins or implements, discovered and discarded as useless by the later diggers. If there are any neolithic fragments, at this high level, it will mean the vandals have been here before us. Nothing will be intact. Anyhow, we can go and take a look.'

Kent watched him closely, noting the reluctance, the brow suddenly moist as he stared against the sun. They both started moving across the corner of the camp towards the site and the plastic bunting flapping in the breeze.

In fact the finds were mainly pottery sherds. Sarson held them delicately, turning them to get light glinting on a trace of reddish glaze. He fingered what appeared to be the rim of a bowl. 'Yes,' he grunted, 'Roman, I'd say. Which end did it come from?'

He climbed down and knelt with his head in the angle of the trench where the woman indicated. Kent, leaning over, saw a spasm run through him and then a shuddering that passed up his arm at contact with the earth.

'Carbon discoloration,' he said after a few seconds.

'We'll need a sample taken here. Organic ash traces beginning. I'd say you could have struck a secondary urn cremation. We'll have to go very carefully now. Nothing bigger than a dessertspoon, please. And brush the discoloured patches separately into plastic bags. When you reach bone fragments get each one drawn and its position plotted and numbered as you go.'

He rose to his feet and Kent, reaching down to help him from the trench was struck by the livid intensity of his face. The three diggers went back into their previous positions, the woman angling into the corner for a close-up shot with her camera. Then after a pause for photographs she passed the camera back and squatted to resume probing with a soft paintbrush.

Sarson was staring down at the flat base of the trench, somewhere about its centre. 'Start digging here,' he said to one of the men. 'It's fill-in, loose chalk rubble with flints. You won't do any harm. When you come to the cap...' He stopped speaking and ran a hand over his face, rapidly as though to brush away some fine web. The movement broke his concentration and he lost the thread of what he had been saying. Then he resumed, in a tired, toneless voice. 'If you find anything, let me know.'

He began to turn away as he spoke and started again downhill, walking with a stiff, jerky gait that alerted Kent to go after him. The man's face, he saw, was utterly empty, like a somnambulist's.

They went down in silence but for the tiny whipping sounds of the stringy grass against their shoes and the perpetual singing of the upland air that was more presence than vibration and yet had just become in some indescribable way closer and more insistent. Their steps slowed as they reached the camp perimeter. Kent never took his eyes from the other, and barely voiced the question he was compelled at last to ask.

'What is it? What did you feel up there?'

Sarson halted and swayed on his feet. Still there was a complete lack of expression on his face. 'Fear,' he answered mechanically. 'Always fear, terrible fear.'

He turned abruptly to look over Kent's head and the doctor turned too. Across the scrubland, near where the old gypsy caravan stood in its hollow, was the small waiting figure of Josie from the hotel. She was looking at Sarson with the self-same glazed, cataleptic stare.

As though locked on to a mutual homing beam they started to move together, and as she took her first step there rose from the grass by her feet the lean shape of a great rough-coated dog, like a wolfhound. It stood hunched, on splayed legs. Its muzzle turned up to the sky and a sound so eery and desolate went up then that even Kent momentarily felt the horror communicate itself to him. He almost glimpsed, or seemed to remember from the primitive past some unearthly evil, and then instantly he seemed to move back into himself, in the present, standing alone on the thin grass of the downland while the two automaton figures slowly moved towards each other like a silent nightmare, and the poor beast's keening went on and on as though it had a mortal soul to lose and was suffering the torments of hell. Almost savagely Kent turned his back upon them all and went striding back towards his empty trailer.

During the long afternoon he tried to push the picture from his mind, while recognising, professional that he was, that his own reaction had been faulty. The Sarson-Josie link was a significant key-thing; it should have alerted him. Instead it had been profoundly disturbing and he had attempted flight. He found himself now regretting having come to this place, having, at Alan's request, made this first positive choice of commitment since his period of drifting had begun. Could it be something about the place itself that separated the doctor from the man in him? There was something so wrong here, and so abnormal about these people, that he doubted now his own ability to stand apart and remain uncontaminated by their strangeness. He had often before this gazed into the face of madness and, understanding a little, been able to feel compassion. But in this thing he encountered here he sensed something outside his own comprehension; unless he could make an enormous effort of imaginative sympathy, perhaps beyond all the limits of safety and sane detachment.

Now if he remained he had to contend with his own

involvement on two levels, for not only was the psychiatrist in him observing but also he was under attack in the primitive layers of his consciousness. He recognised that he had gone to earth, no better than a hunted beast. He examined himself for some reason why he should still, having lost so much, be constrained to save himself: why his reflexes should trouble to work for self-preservation when so many levels of his mind had finished with life. And he had to face up again to what had so long seemed evident but which, bound as he was by professional attitudes, he had not dared to commit himself wholly to – the belief that life was more than the interval between one personality's first- and last-drawn breaths. There was that experience Jean and he had known: what had, at certain times, been a quite sure knowledge that they had been together before in the long-ago past. Reincarnation. Was that belief utterly incompatible with his own academic competence? And if the two were irreconcilable, why should his psychiatric dogmas not be the part that was at fault? Medical learning was no absolute. His experience as a man went farther.

If he allowed himself to admit all this, where did that leave him in relationship to Sarson? At risk, his subconscious told him independently of reason. In some supernormal way he felt in peril of losing his own life, even his series of lives, because of some force let loose in this place. Kent wanted to believe this was so, if it would confirm his own experience, but could he as a doctor leave Sarson to run such a risk? It could cost the man his sanity.

Did Sarson feel the same? Wasn't that just what Sarson was presently undergoing – the recognition, even remembrance and repetition, of a previous lifetime as a member of this lost, Neolithic people? And a life, it would seem also, not in any way an ordinary one; for the man seemed caught up and enmeshed by some terrible, immeasurable influence that had reached out for him through the space of four thousand years, to claim him back and finish what was then left undone.

This was no occasion for careful casenotes, he saw intuitively; but for action. The link had to be broken and Sarson separated from his earlier persona before its insidious powers could feed on his present life and grow in strength. And the most sure way to break the place's obsessive hold upon the man was to restore what had caused his mental void. The power of the present lay in Sarson's wife.

Kent fetched his jacket and went round to where the cars were all parked, on the road side of the camp, and on the way he stayed alert for any sign of Sarson or the girl. Where Josie came into the phenomenon he could not figure, but he was convinced the connection was a morbid feature. She was herself autistic, or so he diagnosed from watching her. In such a state she was charged with psychic high explosive. Reacting on each other in this dangerous phase, she and Sarson might create such a field of force that unimaginable horrors could burst into existence and engulf them all.

He went up again to the opened trench at the henge's centre. There were half a dozen people standing about and Beaumont was being photographed, the shots angled up, showing him astride the piled earth, from below a Goliath, profile against the sky, Viking fluff of beard lifted by the wind.

Something familiar in the stance nudged at Kent's memory. Of course; as though the trench were some poor bloody rhinoceros the barbarian had shot down on safari.

But the two he was looking for were nowhere to be seen, although Kent swept the surrounding downland with his field glasses and made a complete circuit of the camp before setting off by road to Farne. What he had to say could not be telephoned from the pub. It was essential he should contact Alan at once and get him to bring Sarson's wife with him as a matter of the most immediate urgency. It would be better for Alan and himself to seem to meet accidentally and for the first time. Any hint of collusion between them could alienate Sarson at a critical time for his own safety. The meeting would be a delicate one, but he needed to see Val for himself and to appreciate the relationship she had with her husband.

When his call from Farne was put through, Alan was out on a case, but Kent left a request that on contact Alan should immediately ring him back at The Plough, although privacy couldn't be guaranteed there. The receptionist seemed to take it seriously enough and Kent felt he had done all for the moment that was possible. He drove back to the inn and was relieved, on looking in at the kitchen window, to see Josie quietly at work with a little pick smashing ice to fill the buckets for the bars and dining-room. Of Sarson there was no sign, nor did he turn up for their evening meal.

Pengelly came in late to say there had been a slight case of vandalism reported and Dr Sarson had elected to stay on at the site in case of damage to the workings. He'd get his supper at the canteen marquee and Pengelly was to take his sleeping-bag across later.

Kent enquired where the vandalism had been, and was shortly told it concerned the old gypsy caravan. Apparently one of the youngsters had broken in. Beyond that Pengelly declined to discuss the matter.

After their meal Kent went through to show Pengelly where Sarson's things were, and in looking for the sleeping-bag he came across the remaining tablets he'd prescribed. Immediately he recalled Sarson's words about the continuous dream and in retrospect it now had an alarming significance. It seemed likely that Kent himself had been instrumental in intensifying Sarson's predicament, for in relaxing his outer awareness he had allowed the subconscious levels of the man's mind to function with greater ease. Distant memories – whether of actual experiences or imagined ones – were more able to penetrate and take him over.

Drugs might still be the rational treatment, but part of Kent's own mind insisted that in this case they had already activated the danger. They had relaxed the controlling conscious, allowing the dream to emerge, and the dream, once begun, had established its own pattern of compulsion. Even if the tablets were switched now for a neutral substitute, the effect might well continue. And Sarson was choosing to sleep actually within the area where he imagined some significant happening had occurred to his other, now emergent, self.

Imagined? Believed, anyway. More now than ever Kent was aware of the division in his own mind. In one of

93

its compartments Sarson was diagnosed a very sick man. In the other – and this was the conclusion he was having to will himself to restrain – Sarson was something more. Something Kent was not yet prepared, even to himself, to define.

Yet one common need sprang from both conceptions of the man's state. Whatever the cost, Sarson must be protected.

Kent gave Pengelly the keys to his trailer and directed him to spread Sarson's bedroll on the spare bunk there. In this way at least he'd be on hand if anything untoward happened to the man that night. He also made it quite clear that Dr Sarson's responsibilities were far too great for him to be allowed to take a watch unaccompanied, even if he should insist on this, and Pengelly agreed. He too was a little uneasy, it appeared, since Sarson had been taken ill on the day of Kent's arrival. He expressed the opinion that duties were far from evenly distributed among the dig officers, and that although it wasn't his business to say so he'd be glad to back up any suggestions of Dr Kent's to spread the load more fairly.

When Pengelly had gone off with the bedroll, Kent was free to wait for his phone call. It came through a little after nine and Alan seemed to grasp quite a good part of the situation from Kent's guarded remarks.

'If it's a matter of Hugh's health,' said his friend, 'I'm sure Val will see fit to come down. In any case, given good weather, she's arranged to be at Farne for the gliding this weekend. I can run her down myself without having to alarm her with too many details. Of course, she's no idea how serious a view I take myself of Hugh's condition. Thank you for taking this on, Peter. It's good to know you're on the spot if there's trouble.'

' "Trouble"?' Kent repeated to himself when the call was over. Alan had such a way of understating the momentous that for an instant it seemed unlikely he understood the implications of his friend's crisis. Yet he had been so insistent that Peter should take on the case, even when Sarson himself had refused to see a specialist. Certainly then he recognised the need for psychiatric appraisal; but could Alan ever admit, Kent wondered, that it might prove a case where conventional medical systems were not enough?

Soberly he drove back to the site, made coffee and hoped that in some way this would ensure Sarson's turning up from whatever corner he had concealed himself. Not long after midnight he appeared at the trailer, very pale but calm and a little abstracted. He answered Kent's queries patiently, having to make some visible effort of concentration to find the right information, and this in itself, Kent considered, could be viewed as either a favourable or an ominous sign. On being asked where he had spent the past hour or so, he mentioned 'the grove' and Kent then discovered he meant the little cluster of cherry trees with a stagnant pond at its centre.

There was an arrangement that the security officer should call Sarson only in case of emergency, but still he would remove no more than his top clothes and left a raincoat near at hand in case he had to slip out.

'What are you expecting to happen?' Kent insisted.

Sarson shook his head. 'Who knows how it may come out? There are strange influences at work.' He was silent a moment. 'We are all acting differently. Can't you feel it?'

Kent was startled. 'There are tensions, yes.' He hadn't realised that Sarson, immersed in his own affairs, had noticed the outbreak of tetchiness among the volunteers. There was a claustrophobic intensity now about their squabbles that threatened to flare into ugly aggression. Possessiveness was at the root of it, he thought, and the women weren't helping, setting the boys against each other whenever it suited their vanity. In such a prevailing mood the little pricks of minor thieving and social clumsiness acquired a new perspective of importance. Tempers grew short and fists took over from reason.

'We're too close on top of each other,' he commented. 'But things will cool down over the weekend. Everyone seems bent on clearing out to town. The Beaumonts have booked in for Saturday and Sunday at that hotel you recommended. They're hoping we'll join them tomorrow for dinner.'

Sarson shook his head again but said nothing. Kent got

up from his bunk and moved between the other man and the blank window on which his eyes were fixed. It caused no interruption of the sombre stare.

'What happened about the gypsy caravan?' he probed, trying a new line.

At last there was some movement of Sarson's features. He turned slowly to Kent in surprise. 'Pengelly didn't tell you? No. He was upset, of course. And you were away this afternoon when it happened.'

'He said that one of the students broke into it. That's all. Was there more to it?'

Sarson moved stiffly. He took time to answer and then his voice sounded over-controlled. 'There was an old man there, dead. A gypsy. It seemed as though he'd been embalmed in some way.'

'How strange. And no one else there?'

'No. The police came out and took him away. But he had a pony. She's run wild. They say she's been coming to the trash cans at night for food.'

'But no other gypsies? Why should they embalm him, for God's sake, and then go off and leave the place? The caravan was locked up, I thought.'

'The door had been forced. It was the only way, because the lock was so – rusted.'

'How long then do they think he lay there like that?'

Sarson's lips twisted. He thought of the very old man who had taken care of him that first night of the project, less than a week ago. He remembered his voice and the gentle way of the coarse-skinned hands.

'Some time. At least a few months, they think. There were wild apple twigs in a jam jar, and underneath them a rotted sort of mess where the young fruit had dropped off and decomposed. But the twigs were in a state of perfect preservation. Like the old man. He'd lain there all that time, maybe was dead when I flew over last summer and noticed the site for the very first time.'

'Macabre enough,' agreed Kent, still watching him, 'but why should it affect you so?'

'I knew him,' said Sarson. 'It was the same man. I spoke with him only last week.'

10

A wolf howled nearby and was answered from two separate directions. The Watcher of the Heavens lowered his
eyes and scanned the ring of black beyond the firelight.
Something flickering on the edge of the forest hesitated
palely, then changed position, but without any sound.
He felt, rather than saw, human eyes encountering his
own. At once he put out his right arm in a gesture of
bidding.

Again the howl of wolves, closer. Bushes rustled, a
bramble swore, tearing at flesh and fabric as the last
undergrowth was thrust apart, and now he heard feet
pounding, frenzied breathing as the figure came stumbling up the clearing towards him and the security of fire.

White-limbed in the starlight, the woman ran across
the open space to throw herself at his feet. He had drawn
a brand from the watchfire. Now he circled it about his

head and let it fly towards where the red eyes burned at knee-height in the dark beyond.

At once the hunters roused, leapt to their feet and began to prance, weighing their flint-tipped spears longingly on upthrust palms. But their eyes had not the night-skill of The Watcher and he saw the slinking beasts melt back into the gloom of the great trees.

Whergh came swaggering forward and wound the fallen woman's hair about his fist, dragging her face up towards his own. It was the shoreman's woman he had taken once in the cave, and he crowed with laughter at the sight of her.

She half-crouched, half-hung, contorted while he shook her, but she made no cry, only reaching out desperately with one hand in the direction of The Watcher. He avoided the profane touch and again scanned the sky while the hunters gabbled and Whergh twisted her to display her charms, boasting of how he'd once had pleasure of her.

Ishtar had risen early in the evening star and now reigned calm and mature above the moon. She was in middle phase, neither maiden nor crone, but nymph, and that surely indicated the woman here before them. The Watcher reached into his waist-bag and drew the copper knife. He retracted his legs that they might not be fouled, and struck forward with the blade. It hissed into the thick rope of straining hair and with a little moan the woman fell heavily and lay still.

The men's babble was cut through. Whergh's hand flew up, relieved of its burden, and the fire-bright strands writhed like serpents about his wrist. He drew a quivering breath of fury and male challenge.

His eyes burning coldly into the hunter's, The Watcher sat cross-legged, the knife reversed in his palm. In the corner of his vision the woman put out a hand to touch him and he spoke a quiet word of denial.

At this the hunter seemed instantly to understand and his anger cooled. Almost without passion he pushed the woman aside with his foot, so that she could not profane the other. He looked curiously down at her, and the shorn head was like a tuskless boar's to him then, with no more power to fire his lust. In his thick language he ordered her to withdraw and she crawled a few paces off towards the shadows.

But by the light of Ishtar she must be held in honour, and The Watcher signalled the men to provide food, and cover her travel-torn body against the winds of night. One brought a piece of deer meat, charred and cooled again after their own meal, and the other made it clear that it was his own sleeping-skin he gave up for her, mistakenly thinking it might buy favours later for himself.

The Watcher regretted he had no words to warn the men how the woman was now protected and set apart, but he believed that somehow Whergh had perceived it. Savage as he was, he had a gift that was denied the others. He sat now, across the fire from The Watcher, arms loosely crossed on his knees, but despite the casual disposition of his limbs he burned redly within, redder than the firelight on his stone-set face, redder than the vulpine shine of his hot eyes.

Within himself The Watcher felt his heart restive, longing for the man who now resented him so bitterly. In a moment of revelation he saw the years stretching out ahead with the two of them face to face, locked in opposition, and he knew that in some way this man was his soul's heaviness, his own dark side. He desired then no more than to rest his hand on the other's and to pass peace into him, but it was not permitted and he must not dissipate his power. Their ordained path was conflict, each like flints striking fire from the other. Never in life could there be peace between them and open love, but each required the other as vitally as he needed his own blood, his own dreams. Each, to fulfil his separate destiny, was, in some obscure way, a part of the other.

He hooded his eyes lest Whergh should see the thoughts behind them, and his gaze rested again on the copper knife lying reversed across his palm. He was ashamed then that for a space in time he had felt as a man about another. He was reminded now of his sacred duty and of the stars that had moved for minutes unregarded. He had no cause to regret what was ordained, nor to fear for any future under the bowl of heaven. He

99

raised his face again to the sky and retraced the age-old dance of the stars upon the midnight of his mind.

Sarson awoke suddenly, every sense alerted. The fire had burnt out and there were no stars. Darkness pressed upon him as though he were in some closely confined space. He could hear breathing nearby and then a curious scratching sound. Immediate upon it came the eery howl of a wolf. His hand, reaching out in the blackness, encountered his raincoat thrown across the sleeping-bag. He pulled it about him and groped his way to the door. Not a wolf at all, but the girl's dog. It should have been shut up in the outbuildings of The Plough, not roaming the camp by night. He unlatched the trailer door and opened it slowly, trying not to disturb Kent who lay to one side of it. At once a wet muzzle was thrust into his hand and he stopped short. Two steps below, Josie was curled up asleep. Awkwardly he stepped over her, and the dog came about behind, cowering and slobbering on his feet.

There was no sound from inside the trailer, though the doctor had been alerted and lay silent, listening for what would next happen. Had Kent stirred then Sarson would have called him to come out and look to the girl. If there had been no one else in there he might have carried her in and let her sleep on till dawn on the second bunk. As it was, she must either be wakened or left to risk exposure. He experienced a curious reluctance to touch her, as though to do so were to violate some taboo. Also there lingered in his mind some echo of the situation, or some hint that what happened now had already occurred some little time before. He even thought he recalled someone having covered the girl's sleeping form with a fur rug. He brushed one hand across his eyes and shook his head to clear it. When he looked down at her again she was awake and gazing up with her strange, vacant eyes.

He knelt and took her hands between his own. They were very cold. 'Why did you come all this way in the dark, Josie? You should be tucked up in bed, in the warm.'

She said nothing but continued her disconcerting stare.

'What is it? You couldn't sleep? Is something wrong?'

Her fingers slid out from between his hands and wound themselves about his lower arms, searching in under the raincoat sleeves. She gripped him hard, demandingly, and her face screwed with the effort of communication, but still no words came.

'Never mind, love,' he said softly. 'We'd better walk back now. They may miss you and worry.'

The dog pushed its rough muzzle on to her lap and growled uncertainly, rolling its eyes back to show their whites as it watched what Sarson would do.

'Come on then, both of you. Let's move.' He shook off her straining hands and lifted her from the armpits, and as he did so a tremor went through her and she gave a little animal cry. Then she was pressing herself against him, forcing him to hold on hard or be pushed over. For a moment they stayed locked together and he felt her heart leaping against his chest. He was appalled: first that she could be so lonely and have such need, but then that he had almost shown himself incapable of response. He bent and kissed her forehead, as a father might, and hugged her tightly an instant. 'There's a dear girl. Now, off we go back home.'

She looked up at him and the slow smile began transforming her face. She moved backwards a few feet over the grass, made a little sign to the dog, then turned and ran. She went so swiftly and was so immediately lost among the shadows of the tents and huts that he had no chance to follow. But the dog was with her. It was almost sure they would make for The Plough.

Sarson stood uncertain at the foot of the steps and from alongside a spotlight was flashed on his face.

'Oh, is that you, Dr Sarson? Everything all right?'

'I – yes. Quite all right, thanks. Anything to report?'

The watchman hesitated. 'Been fairly quiet for the last two hours,' he said.

'What time is it?'

Another pause while the man pushed back his sleeve and consulted the illuminated dial. 'A bit after three. About four minutes past.' He waited for Sarson to explain himself, perhaps laugh off the incident with the girl, but he didn't seem to think it necessary. He was turning now to go back into the trailer. 'Oh,' he said at the door, 'that pony, the gypsy's, did it come for food tonight?'

'Hasn't so far. Shouldn't think it would now. Funny, that, because the cook had left a nosebag out, special.'

Sarson stared out over the camp. 'Maybe she won't come any more,' he said slowly. 'She may know they've taken him away. Animals sometimes sense these things.'

'More likely one of his gypsy pals has caught up with the beast,' said the man. 'It's not like that lot to let a free gift go begging. Not that I've seen anyone about on my watch. Except yourself and your girl, like.'

'No, I see. Well, goodnight then.'

He let himself in quietly. When he'd taken off the raincoat, Kent spoke to him through the dark. 'What was all that?'

'Just the man on watch. I heard a sound outside and went to see. Everything's all right.'

'Good. Let's get back to sleep.'

Sarson kicked off his shoes and lay down again. Morning, he thought. There'd be plenty to do once the sun was up.

He read in the stars that their journey was almost over. The place he had been directed to was now less than a day's slow walking away. For this reason the hunters were in no hurry when they woke but spent some time redistributing their loads and making preparations for a final killing of game.

When they had drunk water and he had cleansed himself, he signed to Whergh to come and sit near him and then to call the woman over to be questioned.

She told them that her name was Alsleth and she had been born within sound of the sea. Her father had counted thirteen summers before he gave her to Mordui and she had been in the cave ten moons before Whergh had brought The Watcher there.

Was she with child? The Watcher asked, rocking his arms and pointing to her belly. She denied this vehemently and his eyes narrowed as she answered. Grinning, Whergh went across, pushed her flat on her back and leaned his weight upon his hands that were pressed, thumbs locked, across her navel. She endured this, making no move to protect any small creature within.

Whergh put further questions to her, but she turned from him and held up her hands before The Watcher. She made a single finger stand and spoke her husband's name. Of the other hand she made a circle with finger and thumb. This she called by some other word and stabbed through and through it vigorously with the finger Mordui. Her face showed determination, desperation, then despair. At last she wiped the circle away with a single sweep of the other hand. Then she made a second circle and spoke another word. The movements were repeated with increasing desperation. That circle was in turn destroyed and a third one formed. With this she spoke her own name and pointed to her breast. She was, she said, the third wife to Mordui and he had served her as he had the other two, but she was as childless as they. She held the circle still before them, with the other hand raised to wipe it away. The Watcher nodded sombrely and signed to her to withdraw. Fearfully she looked from him to her own hands and he saw her tremble. Death was to her, he recognised, a most terrible thing. He raised his own hands before her, shaped in the same way. Then the finger Mordui he moved apart and closed. The circle remained.

'Live on,' Whergh translated for her, shrugging, 'barren one.'

When they had gone The Watcher lay alone pondering what this should mean. Ishtar had seemed to protect her as she fled alone behind them from the cave. The moon star marked her as chosen, but she was seemingly forbidden priestess rank, not being a virgin, nor was she worthy of any man, being unable to produce a child. How could this woman, abjectly shorn, barren, bartered as part value of skin rugs, already despised by these profane and barbaric hunters, ever be preferred in the divine image? Yet it was not his place to doubt. In time revelation would come, the pattern emerge and he would discern it. Until then she must be put apart and a careful overseeing be maintained.

He drank water himself when the sun had come up, and the men came to turn the litter and hang skins so that light should not disturb his sleep. Within himself he felt a warmth move as though wine and good meat were satisfying his stomach, and he closed his eyes knowing that when they opened he would be at the chosen place and among his new people.

11

Sarson was roused by the pounding of rain on the trailer roof and at once he remembered the trenches. There was no peace for him until he had been out and seen to it that the tarpaulins were secure.

His rubber boots were over in the site hut and he went there first, to find Pengelly was already up and drinking sweet black tea that he'd brewed on his primus stove. He had done the rounds a half-hour back, he told Sarson, but at this rate there'd be no harm in taking another look soon. The stays were holding well enough, but they might need to bail out the covers.

Sarson was impatient to see for himself but he let the man press a mug of tea on him. He drank it steaming beside the grey-lit window over which water poured as though from an invisible bucket.

'The guttering's gone,' grunted Pengelly between sips.

'I'll have a bit of zinc put over, or the wet'll be in down that corner in no time. Radio says it'll clear by midday. It'll need to, with Mr Beaumont planning to have those photographs taken.'

'What photographs are they?'

'Oh, publicity stuff, I gathered. Him and his lady up on the site. They're planning a bit of a party here for the evening. I thought you were in on it.'

'I haven't seen Beaumont,' said Sarson vaguely. 'I understood they were dining at Farne tonight, at the hotel.'

'Couldn't say about that, but there's a whole lot of stuff to be delivered for tonight. Floodlights, the lot.'

'Let's hope it's not a damp squib then.' He stood staring out at the monochrome camp. The sun must have risen by now, but through such a felty thickness of cloud there was no seeing in which direction it lay. Poor Josie's cherry trees, he thought: all the blossom will be finished.

They made their way round the site checking on the workings, and the frames were firmly in place. A considerable weight of water had accumulated since Pengelly's last visit but they cleared most of this and already the downpour had settled to a trickle by the time they arrived back. The wet chalk, however, was appallingly slippery and any further work until the surface dried was out of the question. Sarson went straight back to Kent's trailer to beg a lift to The Plough.

'Sure,' said the doctor, busy with his battery shaver. 'Civilised breakfast for once. Pencil a note on the door, will you, that surgery will be forty minutes late.'

They skirted all depressions on the way across the downland. Most of the track had worn hard by now but there were pockets of surface peat over clay where the car might have lodged indefinitely.

'Have you heard anything about a publicity party at the camp tonight?' asked Sarson.

'Vaguely. Some personal arrangement of Beaumont's, I gathered. We're all having dinner at Farne, you remember. This other business is for later.'

Sarson seemed barely to register what he said, but Kent wasn't bothered. When they reached The Plough there'd be a telegram waiting from Alan and Val. He wanted to be there when Sarson opened it.

In the residents' lounge they ran into Joanna looking through the post. She greeted them like intimates she'd been forcibly restrained from meeting. Kent gathered that boredom was eating its way into her affected coolness. 'Hugh dear,' she cried, 'and Peter! This blessed rain, to send you both trooping back! You're such gluttons for work, the pair of you.'

'And socially a dead loss,' grinned Kent. 'It was only hunger drove us home.'

'There are a couple of letters for you Hugh, and a wire. My guess is the British Museum feels the strain without you.'

'I shouldn't think that's the case,' said Sarson. 'More likely they can't lay their hands on something I've put away.' He ripped open the envelope and scanned the wire. 'Actually it's nothing of the sort. Just some friends who're coming down. This afternoon.'

Kent looked at him quickly. *Friends?* Surely he meant 'my wife and a friend'? And he'd read the time wrong.

'When?' he asked innocently.

Sarson opened the envelope again and read the wire a second time. 'Oh no, it says for lunch. At Farne.'

'Fine,' said Kent quickly, 'I'll drop you off there. I have to go that way myself.'

He took a seat opposite Sarson and watched him from time to time as he ate. He seemed abstracted but Kent didn't associate this with the telegram, for that appeared not to have affected him at all. At the narrow end of the table Joanna observed them both, an ironic little smile on her lips. She was hooked, he observed, on the grapefruit and black coffee routine. The little eating she permitted herself involved much throwing back of the elaborate sleeves of the filmy peignoir she wore. Not designed, he noted, for anyone chronically bronchial. But she was well made. He had to admit that much.

When they were almost through with the meal Beaumont came groggily in and stared sourly at the two men.

'Yes,' said Joanna with a touch of malice, 'see how honoured we are today.'

Beaumont grunted good morning and went over to ring for more coffee. He ran his handsome, big-boned hands over rumpled hair. His neck and the matted vee of his chest at the opening of his dressing-gown were stained with a dark mottling like angry nettle-rash. His puffy eyes watered as he yawned.

'For God's sake, what a day,' he complained. Kent doubted if he'd got as far as noticing the rain.

When Mrs Pyke came in again Sarson looked up and enquired, 'Where's Josie? Is she all right?'

'Still in bed,' said the woman. 'She's sleeping so sweetly I hadn't the heart to disturb her. It's not often she'll lie in of a morning. She's not a good sleeper at all, poor little thing. Tonight her auntie's taking her off to Bristol for a few days, but we've got another girl coming in from the village. Older, like, and happen she'll prove a bit quicker.'

That was very convenient, Kent thought. The night-wandering Josie out of the way and everything set for a reunion between Sarson and his wife. The outcome would depend a great deal on what sort of girl Val turned out to be; but Alan thought a lot of her and he would have been very careful how he briefed her on her husband's condition.

Kent had to get back at once for surgery, so, as the other two men had business to discuss, Sarson and he split up on the understanding that they'd have a drink together at noon before setting off for Farne.

Nothing, thought Kent, could have worked out better. He wasn't prepared to find Joanna sitting behind the driving wheel of his Volvo when he arrived outside.

'I've shaken you,' she claimed.

'I've met quick change artists in my time, but that must be a record.' He looked coolly across at her. 'But your makeup was already on, of course.'

'Waspish today, my dear. Yes, it takes no time to fling a dress on. It's women who shed their clothes fast you should be frightened of. But then you're a doctor of sorts, so you know.'

'Tell me where I can drop you.'

She laughed aloud. 'Do I have to frisk you for your keys? If it had been Hugh Sarson here we wouldn't need any. He could give the ignition a touch of the influence.'

Kent reached in his breast pocket and dangled the keyring just out of her reach. She pressed across him to take it and her hair, with its creamy fragrance, touched his cheek. 'What was that supposed to mean?' he demanded.

The car roared into life and she played with the accelerator, feeling the power of the engine. Kent pushed the choke back in.

'Oh come now, let's not pretend. I'm not blind, nor is Donald entirely. This place does something to Hugh. It's got hold of him in a strange way. I've been following things pretty closely on the site, and Hugh's reactions are to my mind the most significant discoveries to date. I'm not the only observant one either. The volunteers are talking. They think he's heading for a nervous breakdown, but I think there's more to it. He's fey, isn't he? Or do you psychiatrists have some special, devious way of stating the obvious in these matters? Has he delusions? Or does he really get the vibrations?'

Kent stared ahead and said nothing. When she had cleared the main road and they were bumping and slathering across open country he looked at her again. 'What's your opinion?'

'What's it worth – a mere lay opinion?' But her eyes became serious, almost wary. 'I've been around the world some,' she said, 'and I have seen one or two very curious things. Even in this neck of the woods. There are happenings I find it very hard to explain away. One shrugs them off, of course. Things like dowsing, pendulum siting, precognition, déjà vu ...'

'Clever girl. You're well versed in the jargon.'

'Technical terms. They have their uses, like doctors' Latin; they keep the problems at a distance. One feels safer that way.' There was no disputing the seriousness now behind her words. 'I think,' she said slowly, 'I have a respect for the occult.'

'Which pays it a unique honour, it would seem.'

Her beautiful mouth twisted wryly. 'I am enjoying you in a weirdly painful way, Doctor Kent,' she told him. 'Be careful or I could find myself respecting you too.'

He slumped in the passenger seat, prepared to travel

the rest of the way in silence. He needed to ask himself some questions and be very cautious about evaluating his answers. To be called 'Doctor Kent' in that tone she had used; should it strike him as so much more intimate than her usual familiarities?

'You're right, of course,' she reflected. 'Or very nearly so. I respect *myself*, and that's about the sum total.'

'And your husband?' he dared to ask.

She changed gear and did it badly, stabbing too briefly at the clutch so that the gearbox growled fiercely. 'I used to think,' she said a moment later, 'that Donald was God. Perhaps that's why I married him. No, that's not true. By then I knew better, only I'd gone too far to withdraw and admit I'd been wrong.' She glanced defiantly at him. 'And I don't admit it now.'

'So you go along with the act, helping him to fool all the others.'

'That's right.' She sounded gay again.

'And do you ever find time to ask yourself whose fault it was that you were mistaken?'

He had touched her on the raw again. He, who could be so patient, had no need to bait her like this, and he was sorry at once. But her anger when it flared was not against him.

'How dare he,' she asked in cold fury, 'how *dare* he pretend to be what he's looking for in me?'

And that, Kent told himself marvelling, is Eve for all time. Heaven help any man who tried to make sense of it.

'Look,' Joanna said suddenly, 'all the cherry bloom's gone. The rain's ruined it. You know, it must be very mild down here; that was the first I've seen this Spring. Why should that be?'

'The hollow's sheltered, that's all.' He remembered as he said it that this was a favourite gliding area. That meant good thermals. There must be something about the composition of the soil itself that warmed the air and set it rising. Well, he was no geologist, but obviously there was a simple explanation, a physical sequence.

He showed her where to leave the car. 'What now?' he asked. 'I hold surgery in the First Aid hut. If you want somewhere to go when you've been round the camp, you know where my trailer is.'

She gave her deep-throated laugh, exposing perfect teeth. 'When I've "been round the camp". That's the phrase Donald would have used, considering my interest quite useless except as a constitutional. Or would you take me for some kind of Health Visitor, do-gooding as I go?'

'I assume you socialise for pleasure. You seem to know everyone here and everyone knows you.'

'People interest me, and it helps that I haven't a specific job. The diggers like to sit and talk to me, because I'm a woman.'

He smiled. 'You make it sound like a qualification, not a divisive physical factor.'

'And so it is. It's taken me a lifetime to become one. Do say I've done rather well. In Donald's eyes at least I'm Woman, capital W. And so I don't need to be a person as well. That he might find too demanding. No, a female woman is about the size of his requirement – a creature purely of sensation and no censure. Someone to indulge *de haut en bas.*'

'It's rare enough to be all that another person expects. I hope he's appreciative.'

She looked at him squarely, suspecting mockery, but his face betrayed nothing.

She grimaced. 'He hasn't enough imagination to see me in any other way. That's why I've diminished to what he thinks me. And the sick thing is that to him that's quite enough. He never looks at other women, do you know that? I'm part of his equipment; wives, one, de luxe. Therefore, like his car, his hi-fi, his camera, it's automatically the best model one could obtain. Why admit it might need replacing?'

'Some regard wives as for all time in any case.'

'But they can still see other women. Like I see other men, look at them and wonder.'

'They interest you. Like Hugh Sarson?'

'Like you, even. But like Hugh, yes; only, Hugh's different. Someone all-woman wouldn't be enough for him.'

'What gives you that idea?'

'I feel it in my bones. Something in the way he looks past me. Not deliberately; no, he's always calmly polite.

But if I provoke him and he turns back to speak to me, I know I've interrupted. He makes me feel small.'

'Contrary Mary, wanting the green grass from the other side of the hedge. Believe me, if he ever reached for you, as for example I well might, you'd walk the other way.'

She thanked him for her dismissal and as she went off there was an irony in her smile that he found provocative. He told himself that it meant nothing, was part of the front she put up against the world, setting her apart in a special mystique; a piece of technique, a stage prop. Just the same, he would like to know what she thought of himself.

He had chosen the wrong morning to start surgery late. Pengelly had been so concerned about the size of the queue forming that he'd taken names and made out an appointment roster, sending all but the first two patients away.

'I know it's none of my business,' he excused himself, and it struck Kent that the phrase was becoming familiar, 'but they'll not improve, waiting in the drizzle. There's a troublemaker or two among them. We had to break up quite a shindig last night. It wouldn't take much to have them at each other's throats again.'

'Thanks,' Kent told him. 'I'll know not to waste sympathy on black eyes.'

The first boy he saw looked pretty sick. He had strips torn off a grubby shirt wadding a three-inch gash on the upper arm. The edges of the wound were firm and the oblique slit went cleanly back into the fleshy cover of the flexor. Three inches to the right and the knife could have sliced in between his ribs. The opening was beginning to bleed again.

'And what story have you dreamed up to cover this?' Kent asked him, but the boy had nothing to say.

'Lose much blood?'

'Bloody buckets.' He didn't look a roughneck. Kent had noticed him two nights back, sitting at the edge of the firelight, strumming quietly at his guitar. There had been a rather pretty plump girl with him.

'Had an anti-tetanus jab recently?'

He didn't think so, and Kent made sure of that now,

then put six neat stitches in. He would have liked to prescribe some iron for the blood loss, but guessed that a normal GP wouldn't bother, and he didn't want to fuss. The boy seemed strong enough and should make up the deficiency on normal diet.

Three patients later, and separated from the boy by a twisted ankle and a fresh dressing of the previous day's scald, came the girl he remembered. One side of her face was badly bruised, with swelling and discoloration on the lip and cheekbone. She had spread some cream over the marks and although the general effect was unsightly for the moment, there was no permanent damage. Her hands were different. Kent opened them gently, cleaned them as best he could and wrote a note for the hospital.

'Oh no,' she insisted, 'I don't want any bother, really.'

'Nor do I,' he said drily. 'Have you tried using them since? What's your job?'

A hairdresser, she told him. Well, that was bad enough, in view of the ligament damage. He supposed it would have been worse for her if she'd been a typist or played the violin.

'I'm afraid you'll have to tell me about it.' He tried the soft approach but still she wanted to brush the injuries off as unimportant. 'Look,' he said finally, 'the only other time I saw a woman with hands like that, she was on a mortuary slab. With her throat cut as well. Do you see what I mean?' She gave in then, because clearly she'd been really scared at the time and still felt out of her depth. He didn't think anyone had threatened her to stay quiet about what happened; she did so because it embarrassed her. She'd behaved out of character, so she assumed the others had too.

She blamed the cigarettes they'd been smoking. No one had meant to get that wild, she said. Only one of the boys had had a knife. The other had used his fists. Luckily she'd been sick and that made them stop, but not before she'd got her hands cut when they started on her friend.

What did she want to do now, he asked her: go home or stay on?

She couldn't go home in this state, and anyway she'd told her father she'd be away for ten days. She'd nowhere else to stay. She wouldn't be much good at digging, but there must be something she could manage. Then when she did go home she could say she'd torn her fingers opening a tin.

'I think you overrate the hospital,' he said. 'I'll see what Dr Beaumont and Dr Sarson say. They may not want to be responsible for you.'

'I'm over the age of consent.'

'You were last night, and look where it got you.'

She started to cry then, not aloud but miserably, and he inwardly damned Pengelly for his interfering allocation of a bare ten minutes to each patient. The queue was straggling along the side of the hut again.

'There,' he offered,' 'take this note to Casualty. Get your boy friend to see Mr Pengelly about transport. There's a truck going in soon for provisions. And cheer up, or you'll make my other patients panic.'

In the event there were only four more to see, the queue having been swelled by supporters and hangers-on. All the same, it was a sick parade out of all proportion to the size of the camp, and only two of the complaints really negligible. When he reached the end of the line he stowed his things back in his case, picked up his notes and went back to the trailer.

He had completely forgotten Joanna. She was lounging on his bunk and thumbing through some textbooks. He raised one eyebrow in a supercilious way and started straight in on making coffee.

She watched him with amusement, and when they were sitting side by side with the tray before them, she asked, 'So this is where Hugh was last night? I hadn't realised that.'

'Where else would you expect him to be?'

'I wondered. When I found he wasn't . . .'

'You were looking for him? In his room at The Plough?'

'You make it sound positively clandestine.'

He didn't rise to that. Instead he glanced at her hands, and they betrayed a tension her voice belied. He weighed the words before he spoke again. 'Have you met Val? His wife?'

She stretched out her fine, beautiful legs and appeared to examine them critically. 'No. Am I supposed to?' The question sounded artless but Kent had the impression that nothing about her was entirely without guile; that everything she did and said led towards some end that was of importance to her. Under the sophistication and the ironic humour was a quite different, even vulnerable, creature.

As though she sensed then a change in his appraisal of her, she looked up at him and asked quickly, 'Has Hugh said much to you about the site?'

He went on steadily pouring the coffee. 'No. But then I'm not very knowledgeable in such matters. You don't waste Greek on a barbarian.'

'Perhaps he regards us all as barbarians.'

Kent pushed the sugar bowl across. 'He's been working pretty hard. It hasn't left him much time for chat.'

'Well, let's hope he's making up for it now, or Donald will be intolerable for the rest of the day. This is the moment he's picked for getting the story line settled.'

'Do you mean he's trying to pump Sarson?'

'What an expression! "Lead him out" is the genteel way of putting it.'

'To what purpose?'

'Peter, how infuriating you are. Surely it's normal for Director and Assistant Director to discuss the progress of a dig? They've seen very little of each other these past two days.'

'But the reports have been detailed enough. Surely your husband keeps up with the daybook?'

'Oh that, of course; bits of bone and pottery and ashes. But what does it all add up to? What interpretation are they going to put on the place? What was its true purpose? We've been here nearly a whole week now and there's no story line prepared. Donald isn't used to not knowing where he stands.'

'Why wait for Sarson to produce the theory? I wouldn't have accused the famous Dr Beaumont of timidity.'

Joanna gave her rich, deep laugh. 'Depend on it, whatever stand he eventually takes, it will carry conviction. He has a nose for finding the pay-off line, but first he has to move aside and sound the market out. Once Hugh declares himself Donald will know at a stroke whether to go along with what he says or to hold it up to ridicule. He hasn't had the opportunity yet to decide, because he thinks Hugh's playing his cards very close to his chest, and it leaves Donald rather jumpy.

'I see. Only, "going along with it" isn't quite what happens, is it? If he likes a theory he takes it over. His site, his solution to the mystery; isn't that so? And Sarson with as much recognition as a sucked-out orange. I can't help hoping they meet at loggerheads.'

Joanna still wore the sardonic smile, but there was a degree of speculation in the way she faced him. 'And your money would be on Hugh Sarson? You think that whatever he has discovered about the people here all those millennia ago will prove to be right.'

'I wouldn't go so far as that,' said Kent and shook his head. By "proving something right" she really meant only convincing the public it was right. Sarson could still light on the truth, yet Beaumont, opposing him, be the more persuasive.

'I think,' he said, half to himself, 'Sarson's very close to the place, very likely to perceive the truth.'

'So do I,' she agreed, utterly serious. 'Hugh Sarson is a most remarkable man. And he doesn't yet realize himself how remarkable.'

The veneration in her voice startled him, and suddenly he knew the reason for his earlier uneasiness. She married Beaumont, she had claimed, "thinking he was God"; and now she thought she recognised something supernatural in another man. Somehow, in her direct, sensual way, that she covered with shifting, intellectual surfaces, she had become aware of the numinous in Sarson, and the woman in her was reaching out, demanding to be taken along with him wherever his strange path should lead.

Did Beaumont have any idea, he wondered, that if he ridiculed a psychic function for this ancient site he stood in peril of losing his wife? As postulant to a holy man? For wasn't that what Sarson's earlier identity increasingly appeared to be? – the celebrant of a High Place of some ancient god.

12

Although he knew she would be there, it was a shock when the small, dark-haired girl by the bar turned her head and it was Val looking at him. Not that anyone else had quite her way of standing, straight and sturdy like a boy being carpeted for some school misdemeanour. That had been part of Val's lovableness, that she never used her femininity against him, but met him on an honest level, was all woman only when he'd needed it.

'It's good to see you,' he said and slid a hand under her elbow. He wasn't sure whether to kiss her, but she stood on tiptoe and pressed her lips coolly to his cheek.

'Hugh, hullo. How are you?'

He was reaching across to pat Alan's shoulder. 'Oh, fine. Yes, fine. No need to ask you. You look marvellous.'

'D'you want to stay in here, or shall we go through to our table? Alan's ordered one over by the window.'

It struck him that she was bungling something. Hurrying him on. Away from the bar? Then he remembered the last time he'd followed her to Farne, and how he'd been feeling ill and she'd thought he was tight. It was the day he'd flown over Beacons, and been sick. Well, he'd not felt like that for almost a week now, thanks in part to Kent.

'We can go through,' he said. 'Hope you don't mind, but I've brought a friend along. Colleague of yours, Alan. Peter Kent. He's acting as MO for the dig and drove me across.'

'I guess I can bear up,' said Alan mildly, 'if Val can.'

'He's coming now. Over here, Peter.' He briefly introduced them.

'You probably won't remember,' said Alan, 'but we did meet once.' He was staring fixedly at Kent. 'I've referred one or two patients to your clinic over the past five years.'

Kent looked at him assessingly. 'Yes,' he said, and it wasn't clearly statement or question. 'London practice?' he asked cautiously. The two doctors walked ahead and Sarson found himself alongside Val. She was looking up at him, a little pucker between her brows.

'You don't look all that fine,' she told him.

'I've had a digestive upset, but it's over now.'

'I suppose you miss meals and then eat all the wrong things.'

'Oh, no ulcer or anything like that. Kent says it's just nervous reaction, tension due to the job.'

'You wouldn't take that from me,' said Alan over one shoulder. 'It's more than you deserve, happening on Dr Kent.'

'What about the dig?' Val asked, when they were all seated together. 'This must be quite different from the other ones. Shall we get a chance to meet Professor Beaumont?'

'Not Professor; Dr,' Sarson corrected. 'That's a mistake the TV people and journalists perpetuate. He's freelance. As for meeting him, it depends how long you'll be around. They're coming here tonight and there's some kind of party afterwards at the site. You've been invited.'

Val and Alan exchanged glances. 'Sorry, I have to get

back,' said the doctor, 'but Val's staying over for flying tomorrow.'

'I'd like to come,' she said promptly.

For a moment Sarson was uncertain. He had the sensation of some three-dimensional puzzle clicking neatly into place, and of himself somehow pinned down because of it. He wanted Val there, of course. For such a long time he'd been wanting her that there could be no question of that. But just now, with the excavation at its present juncture, he wasn't able to think clearly about what it might mean and how he should behave towards her. He just wasn't free in his mind and it induced a mild sort of panic in him.

Alan started talking about gliders, and remembering Andy who'd taken him up, Sarson asked after the club members he'd known. Then Alan and Kent broached medical matters, leaving Sarson to find out from Val how her work was going.

She wasn't entirely satisfied with how things were, he could see. Over the years he'd come to recognise and interpret the slight lifting of her shoulders, the slant of her brows that indicated impatience. But her voice was level, her comments controlled. He received then the impression that Val was at present earnestly involved in being fair-minded to everyone about all matters equally, and this struck him as untypical. Her strong line of logic had always been her ability to select priorities and grade other considerations in order behind. It had simplified life for her and made her credible. This new caution somehow blurred her edges, and he regretted again the preoccupations that made him feel his mind was no longer his own for considering personal problems. At present he was inadequate for coping simultaneously with both his marriage and the enormous involvement with the henge. He must concern himself with the one or the other. Whichever way he chose, the choice diminished him.

'Eat up, Hugh,' said Kent. 'You won't get anything like this at the camp.'

He wasn't hungry. It had been a mistake to come here. If he was to meet Val again it should have been on his own ground. They could have wandered round the camp and looked at the finds. For a while she would have been part of his life, drawn into the things he identified with. Even if he had gone with her to the flying club it would have been a restatement of their link with the site, because while gliding he'd first come upon it. What he couldn't stand now was this dichotomy of himself, torn between two forces.

'After lunch,' he said abruptly, 'I'd like to show you the camp, Val.'

'I'd like to see it.' Again this submissiveness, as though she were acting with deliberate caution, or been rehearsed. It was untypical and a little sinister; but the important thing was that she would come. If they could be there together – he didn't know what he wanted of her there; perhaps just to sit and gaze at her, or more likely to see her in the frame of the site – the tension would be less. His mind would settle.

They had reached the dessert when a phone call came for him. He excused himself and went out to take it in the hall. Kent followed him with his eyes, then looked down at the table. 'Well,' he asked Val, 'how do you find him?'

She took her time to answer. 'We've gone a long way apart,' she said then, in a small voice. 'I know that's been happening over two years or more, but I can't properly – find him any more.'

'Do you mean he's not himself?' asked Alan.

She hesitated.

'But he's not anyone else?' Kent tempted.

'Oh no, he's himself; but he's a long way off. He's withdrawn. Perhaps I'll get through to him when we're alone. I'll try. I know a lot of this is my fault, but I didn't understand how he was affected. I do want to try and put things right. I couldn't bear him to be ill because of anything I'd done.'

'You don't have to sacrifice yourself,' said Kent gently. 'Being fond will be enough. Don't worry.'

Her lips were tightly together and a vertical line appeared between her brows. 'How ill is he?' she demanded. 'Is he likely to have a mental breakdown? Alan says he's obsessive, but I don't know how much that implies. Can he get over it, or will there always be some risk?'

Kent smiled at her. 'Have you ever been in shock? After an accident, or when someone you loved had just died? Think of it like that. You can't get away from what's happened; it almost takes you over. You escape momentarily and then suddenly without warning it wells up and overwhelms you again.'

'I had a crash once at take-off. The towrope wouldn't release. Yes, it still comes back in nightmares and I go hot and cold.'

'Remember how you felt just after. Not while it happened, but, say, a few days later.'

'I couldn't concentrate on anything. I had to talk to everyone about it, talk it out of me. When I shut my eyes to get away, it would start happening all over again.'

'What Hugh is going through is a form of shock. Love is too, a positive form. That's why we think you can help him. That you can slip back into his mind, in centre, and distract him from this other.'

'Yes. I think I see. Only, what is "this other"?'

No one answered her. Then Kent moved his hands apart. He spoke slowly. 'We don't know. I doubt if Hugh does yet, clearly. But he is strongly perceptive, which opens him to many dangers. I can only recognise a disturbance of the psyche. What causes it is uncertain. But the dig site has a strong influence over his mind. I think something happened there once that is powerfully bound up with his identity.'

She stared at him wide-eyed. 'But you speak as though it's real. As though it's not just something in his mind . . .'

'Oh, it is real,' he said soberly. 'Everything in one's mind is real. That's where it's happening. But talk to him. Get him to talk to you, tell you what he dreams about, what he's thinking when he's alone. Let him talk it outwards, as you feel you had to after the crash.'

She sat with head bent, her flexing fingers worrying at crumbs beside her plate, and she seemed to be hearing his words over again and examining their logic. She still had not broken the silence when Hugh returned, outwardly calm but with a new alertness in his eyes.

'That was Beaumont,' he said, 'with news of a fresh development. Mrs Morrison, the woman from Iran, insisted on starting up at her trench when the rain let up. She's deepened the central box and unearthed a child's charred bones in a Roman urn. And there's a large stone slab, possibly with a chamber beneath. At some time, they think, it rested horizontal, balanced on stone uprights, but the earth has shifted and one end has collapsed.'

He stopped, then resumed in a more casual tone. 'The find coincides nicely with Beaumont's publicity party, and he wants a floodlit excavation of the chamber, later tonight.'

In the event the afternoon was quite unlike what either he or Val had envisaged. On reaching camp Sarson found Beaumont in active command out on the site and Joanna, planning refinements to the projected entertainment, spreading dissent and open rebellion in her wake. He went straight to the site hut and found Pengelly in mid-argument with the contractor's foreman.

'Well, you can take this,' the man shouted. 'We'll not be buggered about by Madam Tartyboots. If you want it, you say so and I'll ask the lads. But it's double pay, and they've a right to a free meal thrown in, the way I see it.'

Pengelly stood square on wide-planted feet and his eyes had the dull, flattened look of a bullock. 'I'll need eight men on standby,' he said tonelessly as though the other hadn't spoken, 'and lifting gear up to twenty tons for three hours, nine to midnight. Double pay subject to a timekeeping check. And no guarantee about photography. If your blokes get on with their own work we can leave the cameramen to theirs. See yourselves as film extras and you'll be having trouble with Equity. Now tell them what I say. Hot dogs and a couple of pints apiece at the end of it. That's all we're offering.'

'Time was,' he said ruefully after the man had left, 'when they'd have done it for a set sum and the fun of the thing.'

'Not with volunteer diggers around,' Sarson reminded him. 'It's put them on their mettle as good union men. What started them off though? What did Mrs Beaumont do to upset them?'

Pengelly grunted. 'A midnight barbecue, would you believe it? And she's got some go-go girls coming down from the TV studios. I wonder she's not thrown in a fashion parade for good measure.'

'I take it the lifting gear is for the capstone?'

'Dr Beaumont wants it done at night.' Pengelly's voice was serious. 'They're going to fake it to look like a full moon. I'd a damn sight rather tackle it by daylight, the way the stone's lying. One small slip and anything lying underneath could be crushed to powder.'

Without a word, Sarson turned on his heel and began striding up the incline to where the henge's centre lay uncovered. Behind him Val scrabbled over tough grass slippery with scatterings of chalk and marl. 'Hugh,' she called after him but he didn't seem to hear. When they reached the open workings she came carefully up to the edge behind him and slid her hand into the crook of his arm. Then he turned to look briefly at her and she saw him blink.

About three and a half feet below the level they stood on, and protruding only two inches or so from the wall of the trench was a slab of greyish stone some two feet deep. The projection was oblique, with the outer edge higher. In the irregular cavity tunnelled beneath it Val could make out the side of another slab standing almost vertically. Two volunteers were at present occupied in extending the trench at that point to reveal more of the erection.

'They've found the pit,' said Sarson, barely aloud.

'It looks more like a vault.'

'It was the chief's burial place, but first they...' He stopped and rubbed a hand across his eyes.

Beaumont, who had been kneeling a little to one side of the stonework, looked up at his voice. 'Ah, Sarson. Come to see our little find? What do you make of it?'

'I had to go farther in,' explained Mrs Morrison, pointing with her trowel, 'to follow the carbon marks, and I found the urn with charred bones, as you said. Then this. What do you think we've got?'

'It's marvellously preserved,' Beaumont went on. 'Recognise the stone?'

Sarson seemed to take a grip on himself. 'Probably from Marlborough Downs,' he said quietly.

'I'd say so myself. Not a sign anywhere of splintering or stress.'

'Something's given way at the other end. The cap-stone's fallen in.'

'Delicate business to raise it, yes. Would you like to hazard a guess where the far end lies?'

Slowly Sarson walked round the edge of the trench and a step or two farther. Then he stopped and looked at the ground.

'As short as that?' demanded Beaumont, sitting up on his heels. 'You don't think it's a gallery then? But even a single chamber would reach farther than that.'

Sarson didn't answer, but Mrs Morrison plucked up courage to voice an opinion.

'Going by the angle of the roof stone,' she suggested, 'and assuming it's only slipped, and not fallen apart in the middle, the other end of a single slab could be just about where Dr Sarson's standing.'

Beaumont stood a moment undecided, then he went over to the spot. 'Well, let's dig down at this point and see who's right. With two points being opened at once it will be quicker in any case.'

They sent for two of the workmen with shovels, and each load as it came out was spread on a tarpaulin sheet and examined closely. The only sizeable finds were debris flints and an antler tine about eighteen inches down. The digging went on past the level where the first stone slab had been found and still there was nothing.

'It's loosely packed,' said one of the men. 'There's been subsidence below.'

'Go carefully now towards the inner end,' cautioned Sarson. 'The far wall has caved in over the fallen roof. You must be just above it.' He motioned them to take away the shovels and felt about with the tips of his fingers. Then with a little grunt of satisfaction he slid one hand in and rubbed at a solid surface. 'Yes, it's here all right. Now you'll need to clear a triangular space outside and lever it back almost upright. Not completely vertical, though, or the roof won't fit back on.'

They went on clearing and sifting, far more slowly now for Beaumont was putting aside samples of soil for analysis and stone fragments of different colours, small snail shells, fine granules of a solid that might prove to be mineral or vegetable in origin. When the earth was removed sufficiently they all knocked off for a while and straightened their backs. Beaumont sent for the lifting gear and Pengelly. At that point he noticed Val for the first time.

'My dear girl,' he exclaimed, opening his arms, 'how can you forgive me? I've been unforgivably rude. You must pardon an inveterate enthusiast. When I'm on the trail I lose all sense for anything else. You're Hugh's wife, of course.'

'Valerie,' she told him.

'And I'm Donald Beaumont. Now do let me make amends by taking you down to the camp for a cup of tea. It's the best we can offer for the moment, but I've a feeling there may be an occasion for champagne before we're through. Hugh, old man, you can spare her for half an hour, I hope? Just see our thick friends don't put their great boots on anything of value when they get here. I'll be back before they have their tackle set up.' And, every inch the personality of the small square screen, Beaumont set about commandeering and charming the new arrival.

Val looked to Hugh for a lead, but he was frowning into the trench and seemed hardly to have noticed what Beaumont said. She would so much rather have stayed up here with Hugh but feared to offend his senior dig officer.

'That's very kind of you,' she said. 'I'm not very thirsty myself, but you must be, after all that effort. I don't know anything about digs, but I suppose that's a very important find?'

'Immensely,' he agreed, 'even if the chamber's empty – and I hope to heaven it's not! I rather think you must be our lucky mascot, my dear. We haven't had any luck to speak of until you came.'

She followed him down, allowing him to reach up and steady her on the slippery stretches of wet chalk, and she wondered how you possibly conversed with such a man, or whether, as it seemed, he could go on for ever mono-loguing, just turning to his listeners now and then for an approving smile.

In the caravan he used as his office, sitting listening, she learned the answer from Joanna, her eyes going from the one to the other while they put on their double act with the wife sardonically casting herself as feed man. Careful not to queer Hugh's pitch, Val smiled when she felt it would be appreciated. It wasn't difficult when you only heard Beaumont's voice, for he spoke well and with a practised sort of diffidence. It was when you watched him too, she thought, that you resisted the contrived charm; for then you caught the quick gleam of self-satisfaction in his eyes and recognised the phoney.

After some twenty minutes of reminiscence on earlier digs he was suddenly off again to supervise the raising of the collapsed wall stone, and Val confronted Joanna's mocking eyes.

'You are just the sort of woman Donald most admires,' she told her. 'He'll be singing your praises for days on end. How charming, how feminine, how modest, etcetera.'

'Whereas?' demanded Val with some spirit.

'Whereas,' said Joanna appraisingly, 'you're a pretty formidable person.'

'I hope so,' admitted Val. 'I used to think so myself.' She looked levelly at the other woman and felt a momentary envy. It seemed unlikely that Joanna could ever feel as out of her depth as Val now did faced with Hugh's dilemma.

'What do you think of my husband?' she found herself asking.

'Hugh?' Joanna didn't answer for a moment. 'It's very hard to say. He's such a complex person.'

'Very private,' said Val. They both considered this.

'Perceptive,' Joanna offered. 'And sensitive. How long have you been married?'

'Eight years. And you?'

'Twelve.'

'Eight years is a long time,' said Val in her small voice. 'Long enough to know someone too well. As I think he does me. He finds me predictable.'

'But prediction's impossible. There are always surprises left.'

'I can *do things* he doesn't expect. But then once he's observed that, he assumes the new thing's done for old, familiar reasons.'

'You still mind what he makes of your motivation? It sounds a positively robust relationship.'

'But it's not just what he thinks that I mind. Suppose he's right. Suppose that's all I am, this little completed thing he sees me as. I don't want to go on and on repeating what I've always thought and felt before; nothing new ever. That's not life: there's no point in it. There must be, somewhere, something to reach out for. All the time I'm with him he reminds me of what I am, what he thinks I am. I have to get away, to stretch ... Oh, you don't know how I panic. Fitting in with it all, the set pattern. It's like seeing myself a fossil.'

Joanna stood up and crossed the caravan. It dispensed with the need to answer at once if she could appear occupied in some way. She opened a drawer out of the other woman's line of vision and started riffling through as though she were hunting for something. The way Val had suddenly unburdened her mind was so entirely unexpected. It was as though she were the exact opposite of her husband, with his strong sense of privacy. Yet Val was not an easy confider, she was sure. This outburst owed something perhaps to the influence of this unbalancing place, something more to the fact that Val saw her, Joanna, as a stranger, someone she might never again come up against.

'I'm not sure I understand,' she confessed. 'You want to do something quite new, absolutely unexpected?'

'I want somehow to grow. I want to know I'm alive.'

Joanna shook her head. She was so vibrantly confident herself, so aware of life with herself its centre, that the words had no meaning.

Suddenly Val saw this. 'I don't know why I said so much. I wouldn't normally. It must sound pretty morbid.'

'Who doesn't get morbid at times? All this squelching about muddy sites and digging into the primitive can depress me frightfully. I give Donald hell then.'

'Look,' said the younger woman, 'I know everyone's busy, but I must get back to Hugh. Do you mind if I leave you? You've been very kind, and thanks for the tea.'

Joanna opened the door for her. 'If you really wanted to shock him out of his previous opinion of you, you ought to volunteer for a part in my orgy tonight. Neolithic version of a Maenad.'

Val had no idea what she meant but laughed as though it were a joke. 'It might come to that,' she agreed, and started threading her way again among the trailers in the direction of the dig.

13

Sarson hadn't been prepared for the effect of absence from the site. Even for so short a time as the visit to Farne it seemed as though separation had intensified the charge between the place and his own mind. While he had been diverted, this further revelation had occurred. The frustration of not having been a party to the find increased his stress to almost frenetic level. He wanted to move the earth away himself, get in physical contact. Concentration on any other matter had become impossible: it was as though he no longer had any outer connections. The place possessed him almost totally.

He stayed by the excavation, supervising the lifting of the heavy stone that had slipped from the horizontal to an oblique inside the pit. When it was raised he marked its edges himself with site number and date, and sketched the plan and elevations of the vault. Scrupulously the skilled volunteers filled their little plastic bags with samples of the residue found inside, recording each nuance of changing colour or texture, while he watched with fierce attention. Mainly at the base it was a fine black substance like silt or sieved wood ash, a foreign matter that had no equivalent outside the pit. He traced the shading of chalk debris that had surrounded and covered the vault as fill-in, and there was no similar dark pigment anywhere, only the soil horizons of recent years marked sandy brown in the upper inches of the trench walls.

'I was sure,' said the woman from Iran, 'we were going to strike an inhumation. I could almost tell you how it would lie.'

'Well, there isn't one,' commented another digger. 'And I don't think there ever was, because there's no sign of interference. We're the first to dig as low as this since the pit was closed. Yet it was intended for a burial chamber, I'd have sworn. What do you make of it, Dr Sarson?'

'There was the later child's body,' said Sarson vaguely. 'The cremated one with the Roman urn at the upper level. So it was known as a holy place. But the pit had a special use, and when that was done the neolithic people covered the entire hilltop over and went away, taking all their implements and ornaments with them.'

It had been no casual business. The whole site spoke of concealment, with banks thrown back in to fill the ditches, and a complete false crown to the hill built up with rubble from the lower ground. The people tried to destroy their henge and leave the place as though it had never been. Then they went elsewhere to make a fresh start and forget. That was why the site was for so long overlooked. They had covered it up too well.

'Do you think there was some terrible plague?' Val had come up to him and was staring with disgust at the black residue in the vault. Sarson barely seemed to hear, then his eyes focussed on her again, and when he spoke his lips moved stiffly.

'Something very bad, over and done with. Finished. Perhaps we do wrong to uncover it now. I wish I knew.'

'That's about it,' said Pengelly, brushing soil off his hands. 'The sides are squared up enough now. Where do you want us to leave the capstone?'

'Almost close the opening,' Sarson directed. 'It will show off the skilful fitting together of the cell, but leave a space for looking into the interior. Stack the waterproof covers close by so that they can go back on if the rain starts again.' He watched them lower the heavy stone across, leaving a ten inch gap of blackness. It settled smoothly considering its bulk.

Everyone began packing up the tools and tackle, ready to knock off for the day. Val touched her husband lightly on the arm and he became aware of her again.

'Right then, I'll just lock these papers away, then I'll join you at Peter's trailer. I'll show you where it is.'

They slid and scrambled down to the lower level, crossing on boards above the trench dug on the circumference.

'What's that other pit?' Val asked, pointing.

'A base to support a megalith. There are twenty-eight like that all round the site.'

'And the megaliths?'

'Removed. Perhaps to use elsewhere.'

'By recent people, you mean? For their houses or barns?'

'No. Not long after they were set up, I think. Carbon dating of the fill-in debris will fix it more accurately, but I doubt if the stones were here for more than one generation.'

'So the whole place was a sort of huge experiment that didn't come off?' Her voice came across with a hint of pathos that stopped him in his tracks.

He frowned. 'I don't...' He covered his eyes with one hand and she put her arm about him, thinking he was going to fall. They stood a moment like this, the wind whipping the plastic bunting beside them and making little sticky clicking sounds. Beyond that there was only the far cry of a bird across the downs and the hum of a dynamo in camp.

'A failure?' asked Hugh, looking blindly about him.

'No. No, it ... Not a failure.' But he frowned again at the sanctuary so deliberately concealed from the future. He gazed back to where tons of earth had been carried up to create a natural-looking hill over the remaining stone slabs of the sacred place, and it seemed then only a question of remembering some little detail that lay between his present ignorance and understanding of the enigma.

'I don't . . .' he began again. 'I feel I should *know*.'

'Don't strain at it,' she pleaded. 'Maybe it will come, in its own time.'

He slowly moved his hand away and looked down at her from a great distance. 'In its *own time?*' he repeated. 'Woman, you don't know what you say.'

Until then she had been anxious for him, but something in his voice at that moment froze her. She watched him move away with a quite untypical posture, in a kind of tall glide, so unlike his normal, rather diffident way of moving. She could not say what the difference in him was, whether it existed physically at all, or was only some warning instinct inside herself that made her think *zombie*. He didn't stumble now as he had done with her arm about him. He walked straight, perhaps too straight, unnaturally controlled. There was no invitation to her to follow.

Biting her lips she went up the steps of Peter Kent's trailer and knocked on the glass of the door. He was alone and she was thankful for the chance to speak with him. The main difficulty was to know where to begin.

'What can I do for Hugh?' she demanded when he let her in.

He pointed to a low chair and she sank on to it, sitting crouched, knees close under her chest.

'Oh, no. Relax.'

'I can't. He's worse here than a few hours back at Farne. All the time, every hour, he seems to get stranger and farther from me. I'm scared for him.'

'Scared *of* him?'

She thought. 'I don't know. I thought that here, near his work, he'd be more natural; that we'd be able to talk things over together. I swear I didn't mention our personal situation. I was just ready to let him tell me what was on his mind.'

Peter nodded. 'The conflict is closer to him here. And

it's no longer a question of you versus his work, as he thought at first, but of his own time polarity at this place. I think the present demands of him a voluntary and conscious concentration which is totally at war with his natural awareness of the place.'

'He seems to half-remember things. But how can he? He's only guessing, isn't he, because he's absorbed so much of the period in his studies? Dr Kent, he is fooling himself, surely?'

Kent moved away from her line of sight, but she twisted in the chair, following him with her eyes, begging him to reassure her that the rational explanation she offered could cover the case.

Kent was silent a while, his face in shadow. Her words went on echoing in his mind and he admitted they were themselves only a repetition of what he had been insisting to himself for so long. Well, he could interminably defer the reply to his own demands, but not to this woman sick with worry. She was appealing to him. Now was the moment of confronting the truth. What then did he believe?

'I can't answer,' he said at last, 'without involving my own personal beliefs. Which you may find distasteful.'

She stared back fixedly. 'Alan warned me,' she said in a low voice. 'You believe in something like reincarnation. I don't know how you can, in your profession. I can't, anyway. Since he mentioned it, I've tried to see Hugh's trouble like that, a sort of memory from a past life; but it's too unlikely. Other explanations come more easily. There's too great a coincidence that he should recur at the same place, with an archaeological interest in his original period. And if it happens to him, why not to others? Why shouldn't I remember my past lives, if any?'

'We're all different,' he said slowly. 'Some are more directly pegged to the life they're presently in; others have stronger psychic endowments, with experience outside spacetime. When they have, there is always this disturbing half-involvement, and they will readily follow pre-reincarnation tastes which lead them to study that part of the past that still matters vitally to them.'

It was as though he was answering himself, and he had

reached some point critical in his own personal loss. 'In this way – surely you can see? – it is possible for individuals to meet up again in more than one life, and to be drawn towards some common soil.'

'You are just believing what you want to believe,' she challenged, too angry to care how far she hurt him.

He came out of his corner then and looked down on her, quite calm. 'We all do. Ultimately we all believe what we wish to believe. It is the only way to be at peace with ourselves. But you want a rational answer, from a doctor, so I'll try again and we'll see where it takes us. I think it will be to the same conclusion, because I have been all this way myself before.

'So then, as a textbook case: your husband has many of the qualities (symptoms, if you insist) I expect to find in certain subjects. Alan has listed some of the physical signs: the obsessional syndrome manifested in early nervous ailments – infantile asthma; later eczema; the frequent so-called virus infections, which often denote a strong cosmic sense resisting a too tightly circumscribed identity. Such disturbances are frequently a physical alternative to a mental working outward of psychic stress. But the origins of both can be the same, in the polarity of absolutes, the conceptual war of good and evil, in the stress of a creature from outside time finding its timeplace too restrictive.

'As a child your husband was a solitary who suffered in this way. A perfectionist, he complained of night horrors. During adolescence he walked in his sleep. While at college with Alan he once submitted to hypnosis and talked in detail of countries and times he could never have seen. And he is a meticulously truthful man. Why should he pick on such an occasion for suddenly lying? I believe that if I were to sedate him now he might return to his former life and try to continue where he left off.'

Val turned her head away. 'It's horrible. I can't believe it. Life can be harsh enough once round. To go on and on, for ever repeating your mistakes through the ages, would be diabolically cruel.'

'Why repeating mistakes? One life can never be the same as another. Imagine, there may even be progress.

For some people there have been lifetimes that were just not enough – people perhaps whose essence was too great for personal extinction. Suppose immortality depended on caring enough about life? Moments of unutterable joy can wipe out years of suffering and live on strong in the mind. Even perhaps through the great trauma of death. We manage certain transitions of mind through space-time, while we live. Why not in a more dynamic way in the concentrated power of new freedom in bodilessness? Do you really find life as it is enough? Or do you too have immortal longings?'

He watched her face steadily, and at last he smiled. 'Where then do they come from?'

She sat on, staring at him while his words circled in her mind, but it was less the things he said than some state of mind in herself that she listened to. It reverberated with an awakening insistence.

'Sometimes I get a dream,' she heard herself admitting, 'and it has come so many times now that I think of it as part of me. After all, I made it, didn't I – with my own mind? It starts with me flying, and everything is quite normal, all the controls are there and responsive, only I can't seem to see. It's not really dark, but more as if I can't find the way to open my eyes. As soon as I think that, they come open and I find I'm not in a glider at all but suspended in air, sometimes from my shoulders in a sort of parachute harness. At other times I'm sitting on a trapeze bar hung from long, long wires; and each time I'm slowly swinging. Then I look around me and find I'm imprisoned inside a tall cylinder of perspex that seems to have neither top nor bottom, and outside there's un-limited space and light. I can't reach up to get over the top nor get down to go underneath. My only chance is to swing and swing until my feet reach the sides of the cylinder and I can kick it over and spill myself out. But how-ever I thrust my legs out and arch my back to drive myself forward, I can't force the swing to go far enough. My toes always miss the cylinder wall. I can't strike through to make it fall. It seems I shall have to go on for ever, never still and never free but always straining and longing and at every move defeated.'

'And is that real?' asked Kent gently.

'At times the most real thing in my life.'

'Yes. Then believe Hugh's dreams,' he begged her. 'Believe him whatever he says.'

'I'll try to do that. Where are you going? You're not going to leave me alone with him?'

'Why not? You're his wife. You know as much about his condition now as I do, probably much more. And anyway I have to look in at Farne hospital. Make him some coffee. Get him to talk, about his present lifetime; but if he resists, go with him into the other one. Only, stay in sympathy.'

She watched Peter Kent walk away to his car, then she turned back to the trailer and began to look out cups and the coffee things on a tray.

I can't accept his ideas, she repeated silently, and then caught up with herself, reasoning – I don't believe because I won't; that's what he'd say. And what if, unbelievably, it should happen to be true? What good can I be to Hugh then? Shall I have to accept this, against all reason? What ought I to want? Which could harm Hugh more – to believe or to refuse to believe? Perhaps that is something I shall never know. But at least I can try to hold him fast to the present.

She just had the water boiling when Hugh came back.

He stood a moment in the doorway, almost filling it, and over the black outline of his shoulders Val saw a livid sky with stark patches of storm light. The upper clouds were grotesquely castled and sagging towards earth. Every long horizontal line had been dragged into tortured knurls as though sudden gusts had rushed amok about the sky and then instantly been struck into an awful calm. A violet light rippled past him through the door, but nothing stirred.

'Hugh?' she appealed to him. 'I'm making coffee. You'll have some?'

He nodded heavily and went to sit on the bed he used at night. 'It's sultry,' he said.

'Tricky for gliding. Andy will have called them all in.'

He looked puzzled a moment, then nodded. 'Ah yes. That's why you're here.'

'Not really. I came to see you.'

He sat looking dully at her, and she thought that if she could get his interest then, while he was so inactive, he might well turn away from this morbid preoccupation with the past.

'I thought we might perhaps have a talk. I've been thinking a lot lately, about you and me. Has it ever struck you how little we really know about each other's lives? Sometimes there can be too much privacy. Then you begin to wonder if it's really out of respect, or indifference.' His silence did not discourage her. 'Do you realise I've never heard about you as a little boy? It's just as though you were born adult. No anecdotes, no family jokes, no visits back to old haunts. Perhaps that's because you've no close relatives. Alan's one of the few people I've met who knew you in your teens.'

He looked at her gravely. 'You want to know what sort of child I was? How can I tell? I must have been rather as I am now, I suppose.'

At least he had spoken. If she tried she might recall to him some vital memory that would fix him emotionally within his own identity and so repel the shadow life that seemed to be encroaching.

'Yes, but what sort of tricks did you get up to? Did you go about with any one friend in particular? Or were you in a group?'

He thought for a moment. 'I had one or two good friends. But never for long because we moved about so, and boys aren't good correspondents. Once or twice I've called on ones I remembered, when I've been travelling near their homes. But there was never reason enough to keep up with anyone.'

'I met your father, of course,' said Val when his voice died away, 'and he was kind to me, but he never had much to say, and he never mentioned your mother.' Her hands were busy with the percolator and she couldn't watch him in his silence. When she had the flask set back on the lowered gas jet she flashed him a quick, apprehensive glance. His face was quite expressionless, the eyes distant again.

He didn't remember his mother. It had struck him before that there was a sinister gap there. When he tried to think back to her a quite different picture came. He had a close-up view of rigid metal netting painted dark green, the mesh wide enough for his baby fingers to hook through as he clung on hoping, breaking his heart, to see the peacock spread its glorious tail. The wonder of it possessed him; this dowdy, bundled bird pecking at the sanded floor, smelling so sour, so chickenish, but quite suddenly a shake of the head, coronet rising and then, but only occasionally, the wonder of transformation. The longing and the doubt and the rare miracle; that was childhood itself.

He didn't recall whether on that occasion the wonderful thing had happened, or if it was a day when they'd had to tear his fingers from the wire and haul him protesting through the park, hope spent and his heart unkindled. He only knew the words whispered above his head when he'd reached home. 'Take the child away. She's gone, poor thing.'

Not her face, nor her voice, only others' words: and the bitter-smelling green paint peeling on the cage; wire mesh cutting into his soft, clawing fingers. And sickly never again wanting peacocks, or parks or afternoon walks, for the fear of coming home; for the shame of breaking his heart over a spread fan of bright feathers, and killing his mother stone dead in his mind.

He moved one hand over his face. 'I was very young when she died. Too young to remember her.'

And then his father; he had not been close to him. At some point in growing up he had entered a different cell and they were no longer able to communicate. Words meant quite other things to the old man from how Hugh intended them, and so, except of the simplest physical things, they had given up talking. When his father died Hugh had been troubled. In obedience to the final requests he ordered cremation, which personally he found repugnant, but he attended the service, forcing himself to think throughout 'this was not my father but a phase somebody had to go through.' He could not endure the hypocrisy of flowers. In early times animals had been slaughtered in funerary rites so that man should not enter death entirely alone. Mawkishly now, it seemed to him, we substituted plant forms and camouflaged the motives to look like aestheticism. He could not do this. The coffin slid away bare to the flames. Instead he bought a single shrub on the day of the cremation, a blood-red azalea, and set it in the garden. It had gradually died, beginning to go brown and shrivelled almost from the first day, although a second one he bought a week later for symmetry had flourished under the same conditions. This he had seen as a failure of love.

'I have no roots,' he said aloud.

Val handed him the cup and it chattered in its saucer. 'You're tired, Hugh,' she said at length. 'Why not get some rest now? It's going to be a hectic evening.'

'Perhaps. When you've gone.'

She had thought she could sit there and watch him fall asleep, but she saw it was an intimacy he wouldn't permit. Despite his silence of the winter months she was so used to his following after her that she found it hard to accept his present apartness.

'I'll see you at dinner then, at Farne, with the others.'

He smiled and with a sense of defeat she left him sitting on the side of the bunk, beginning to peel off his shirt. He looked among his things for one of the tablets Kent had given him, but they were left at The Plough. However, the doctor's chest was there and he helped himself to one from a bottle in it, washing it down with the last of the coffee. Then he stood in the open doorway looking up at the lurid sky. The upper digging was deserted now and he wanted to take a last look before settling down, but tiredness came washing over him like a wave and pulling him over and over as it receded. With the sensation he remembered the shipwreck and Whergh taking him to the shoreman's cave. He remembered the slow journey inland and how The Watcher had almost reached the end of his quest. He lay down on the bunk and as his head sank into the pillow the dreams of the past days were suddenly assembled and fitted together, so that he recalled in detail the whole sequence until the final night before arrival.

For a single stilled moment in time he knew he hung

precariously between two lives, then he stretched himself to full length, inhaled deeply and closed his eyes. He felt the confined space of the trailer expanding limitlessly and simultaneous with it there was a lifting of all the petty cares that had filled his past day. The intrusive personalities, the details of organisation, the physical aspects of the dig, ceased to exist. Eagerly he waited for the other world to assemble in the dark behind his eyelids, and with a slow filling of joy he heard the fine blowing of young grass close by, smelled woodsmoke and knew that at last he was almost home.

14

The evening had become still. He felt the difference even before he drew back the skins they had hung to shade him while he slept. The sun, as he had known it would be, was low and hugely orange over a blue-black rim of trees. The same dark denseness of forest stretched on every side, and the open ground they had set the litter on was a narrow, stony ridge shaped like the back of a flayed boar. It still led northwards but now curved a little to the west, and he could clearly distinguish ahead, central in the lower bowl of mixed woodland and clearing, a slight eminence where double circles of stark whiteness marked a settlement's bounds. Nearby, fires were burning, and there were long strips of cultivated hill and cattle penned behind the habitations: small figures moved between round and wedge-shaped huts.

The bearers had withdrawn a little. He saw they spoke

together in a group, and there were now almost three times as many men as in the original band. It seemed that a second party had been sent out to escort them in, and the baggages were being redivided so that the travellers might enter with ceremony, bearing nothing but their spears.

Without being himself observed, he watched them posture and prance as they retold the journey. And then he saw the other man who stood alone and watched them, even as he did himself. Whergh, not one of the storytellers, not central in the bragging and the strutting, but quite alone at some distance and displaying a fine scorn for the others.

Of the woman there was at first no sign, but as he turned upon his litter he sensed a slighter movement close behind and saw her pale wrists bound to the shaft ends. She half knelt, half crouched alongside, with a coarse cloth still covering head and shoulders, barely recognisable as human at all. They had not understood the manner in which he had set her apart. But if they treated her as a pariah, at least she was free of their attentions. He drew the knife again from his pouch and cut through her thongs where they bound the litter. Her hands, still joined, fell heavily to the ground and her body slumped upon them. She made no sound but a small grunt as if in recognition, and as she lay recovering, cautiously she resettled her cheek, inside its coarse cloth, against the ground. A woman who would endure much, he observed: one who submitted and knew how to wait.

Now Whergh stepped forward, breaking into the childlike chatter of the others, and stood, legs planted wide, before them in authority. What did he read in the faces turned towards him? Uncertainty, reluctant obedience, still a brief flash of that quick, mischievous familiarity with which they had greeted each other. So he presented himself to them as a superior, a guise they were not yet ready to accept. Not their overall leader, yet he saw himself as such; but not an upstart, for he carried his authority with assurance. He was a master then, but the men who greeted him were sent by a higher lord than the man they came to meet. He began to question them with a curt tenseness, turning from one to another and selecting them by name. Their smiles slid away, the spoken sentences lagged, died on the air. The silence afterwards was strained, and an unasked question lay between the group.

This did not concern himself, The Watcher accepted, for when Whergh had thought a moment he reset his shoulders before turning to indicate the litter, and now the new men's faces relit with animation. In curiosity they began cautiously to approach and fix him with their round, bright eyes.

Unblinking and straight-backed he faced them, legs crossed before him, priestlike hands clasped loosely on his chest. He gazed through them until their movements ceased and their bodies became translucent as moth wings, then transparent as water, in essence no more than shadowy air, and briefly through them he glimpsed eternity. They stood then as though time stopped for them and the sun and the wind hung stilled. When he knew they had been touched by a knowledge of the design of which he was a part he let them move again, withdrawing his eyes from time to come back through them, returning to them their substance, their solidity, their movement. And when he threw a skin to them they knew what he wished them to do, for one spread it on the woman as she lay, and folded her within it and two lifted her between them to carry her in privacy to their settlement.

Intently Whergh gazed on all they did, and upon the strange man who commanded them without speech; and while his blood heated with resentment, yet his hunter's brain counselled him to bide his time, for through this man might his will eventually be done. Now was a time, if any ever had been, when he must walk silently downwind and disturb no creature: this was the moment of sensing the prey and of stalking for the kill.

As the procession wound down again among dark trees, so the sun too descended, and the moon already risen became less like a small white cloud against the blue, and more a lamp steadily burning to lead them in; and the sky went harebell, rosy, primrose, silver, and finally was curtained for night, gauzy dark with a single light gilding the earth, and pale stars pricking through so that The Watcher felt them like pins upon his flesh, changing his consciousness from the mortal to something other. He knew then what he must do when at last they should lay his litter down.

Through cleared strips of pasture and tilled land they came to the settlement, climbing once more to pass over the causeways above the ditches and between the gleaming double banks of chalk. Denuded of trees the incline rose, a downturned platter contained within a deeper bowl; then, as he rounded it – like a misshapen line of crones hauling each other hand in hand up the side of the hill – a coven of twisted thorns, black and contorted, sprang into view upon the skyline. *Evil*, he thought: there is evil too here, and only I to contain it.

Then they were at the centre, and the litter was lowered to the ground. A great silence followed, but not an absence of life, for in the shadows he sensed the presence of a gathering and it seemed all waited for what he should do.

Smoothly he rose to full height and raised his arms obliquely to the sky. Then he moved forward off the hurdle, and stepped for the first time upon the bare soil of this land. Immediately a great power entered him, an irresistible uniting of the heavens and the earth, with himself their channel, and he found himself singing, his face upturned to the stars, and all the knowledge of his mind and the values of his heart were pouring themselves out in music while a wind strummed over the forest and a deep murmur passed through the listening people, swaying them together, pulsing through to the roots of their being. And their feet answered him, striking at the soil so that the vibrations came back into him, their source; and all were a part of the same whole and no man separate from any other or any thing he touched or beheld. And the great music went on echoing and echoing and all the people moved with it. With their outflung arms and their arching backs and the stoop and flow of their shoulders they told him of their life and their labours and their longings. They danced for him their fears, their birth and their dying.

144

All save three in the centre were dancing. One was too old and stricken, but his eyes moved brightly and the colour that came and went upon his cheeks owed little to the firelight's flickering. The tall woman, white-haired, who stooped over the old chief's couch moved not a finger, but within was totally a-dance. Her motionless attitude was all remembered cradling and voluptuous delight. And close by The Watcher's litter the woman from the shore lay, still wrapped as they had carried her, upon the soil, inert as if dead.

Even Whergh – who wished to remain apart – swayed like a drunkard, moved his weight heavily from foot to unwilling foot, balled his strong hands and shook his head as though to free himself from bonds. Beside him was piled his part of the hunting spoils, and topping them a fine span of deer antlers. The Watcher lifted these and with his girdle bound them to the shuddering young man's head, passing the linen band twice about his jaw and round the temples, making all firm. And then the jerkiness ceased and a long, smooth movement rippled through the man and he sped among the dancers, leapt and bucked, exulting in his strength and freedom, the physical delight of flesh and untamed senses; a wild thing and simultaneously a creature of disciplined cunning, being both hunter and hunted.

The dance and the song continued while the night sky swung slowly over and pointed towards day, the dancers lying at last where they fell, exhausted, embracing each other into sleep; and their voices, raucous with laughter and weeping and song, many times slaked from pitchers and water pans, were at last silenced. The stillness of dark forests came again upon the place, with not a fox, nor wolf, nor owl to pierce it, so sated with sound and movement was everything that lived.

Only The Watcher remained awake, cross-legged again upon the litter they had borne him on. His face was turned to the sky and his shoulders east as he awaited the sun. On the earth's rim the forest seemed to flow apart, horizontal bands of darkness rising irrigated with silver; then these became distinguishable not as the tops of trees but as islands of cloud freely afloat from the solid

145

world below. The Spring air breathed with the sweetness of young grass in full flower. Then a small brown bird, gold-chested, awoke and the silence was shot through with beauty.

The young hunter came who brought him water each morning. He knelt at The Watcher's side and looked into his eyes so that he might learn, from mind to mind, what special thing he had to do. And before the sun appeared he ran almost to the inner bank of chalk with his spear, and where The Watcher signalled he thrust its point into the stony earth. And so the sun rose behind as though out of its shaft.

This was the mark of the first morning of The Watcher's coming, and in the same manner, viewed from the same point, were all other days recorded. The sun's setting and the sun's rising were the beginning and the end of The Watcher's vigil, and during the hours of light he slept, or walked among the men as they built, or cleared the trees, or tended the beasts, and with the women who worked upon the soil. Often too he would sit and listen to them as they sang, breaking down grain into powder, mixing the flour into paste, turning the cakes upon the hot stones.

And later in the year he would come upon them as they gathered fruit, and the stems and leaves that they used to dye the grey wool left by sheep on the thorn and the bramble. And he marvelled at the care they lavished, washing and carding, setting the colours with mordants sifted from powders ground from the rocks. They favoured the bright, warm tones that came from cherry bark and walnut leaves, fiery oranges and tawny brown; but for him, and for the young woman he sent to the Maidens' House, they dyed other hues – all moon shades – from white to palest lemon, from the pods of vetch; and silver greys from berberis leaves. And they made him a cloak of woven wool which they soaked in a ditch of water filled with crushed blackberries so that it was mauvey grey like a bank of cloud low on the earth when the sun has just sunk, and all along the border they sewed teeth of wolves, taking him for their magician; and around the neck a collar of split boar-tusks, each pale and luminous as the young crescent moon.

All these things they delighted in doing for love of him, and the months were like days and the days were like hours in their speeding. Yet at night he knew in numbers the passing of time. He recorded the settings and risings of the sun, as it zig-zagged across the heavens, and he marked too the more mysterious wanderings of the moon, learning to fear the portents of their meeting.

At each rising of the sun the old chief, Luth, was brought out on his couch and the two men spoke together, acting their thoughts and the chief speaking the words until The Watcher had also mastered the speech of his new people. And when the days came that the old man lay silent, the white-haired woman continued the dialogues, but then the two men spoke direct, mind to mind without the use of sound. And again later, when Luth's eyes were heavy with death and he could not make out The Watcher's shadow against the sun nor raise a hand to clasp the other's, The Watcher would make a cone of his hand and place the prongs of his three longest fingers on the sick man's forehead to pass peace in for his coming journey.

The old chief had no sons. Three daughters had babies of their own and one was still in the House of Maidens, which had been given into The Watcher's charge, but both his sons had died in childhood. Whergh was not his own but his wife's and had come with her as a suckling, in alliance, from the dead chief of a neighbouring tribe. This widow, Erghlaun, was one of the ancient people of the land and not, like Luth's family, from across the grey water.

They were a mixed people at Brevaryn, and although the chief was feeble they were not restive under him, for all was done in his name for them all, and this they understood. If they were fearful of what would befall them when his days were completed, they forgot this in their joy at The Watcher's coming, confident that he would be able to contain the dead leader's spirit and pour it again upon them. Only a few looked sideways as if to assess who might be his successor, and fewer still were ambitious. When they met in The Dance, their passions flowed together and there were no secrets from The Watcher. They lived for the joy in their fingers and their loins, for the surge of the heart and the satisfaction of the belly. They were a people quick to laughter and their angers were open and soon spent. All save one, and he was an apple with a maggot at the core.

Still Whergh was loath to dance. His golden brows a single line, heavy over brooding eyes, he clutched his secret like a craven hunter covering his fear. And the image was wrong, wounding to The Watcher, for Whergh was the bravest, the first to spring in defence, the steadiest in attack, the gentlest in despatching the kill, beautiful in his youth and generosity, an eager lover and begetter of sturdy infants. He was all a people should desire, except that within he was sick of a malodorous spirit.

No longer willing to accept the antlers bound upon his brow, nor the boar's tusks jutting by the mouth, he elected instead to stand behind his mother, spear in hand like some phantom guard vigilant against an assassin that should never come. The watchfires of The Dance, burning crimson with flame and billowing black smoke upon the chalk ramparts of the Gathering Place, flared beyond him, and though he stood still as though the evil in him were an enchantment, yet his shadow danced, twisted and black, savaging the aged man who lay helpless on the couch.

'Dance,' said his mother. 'Be merry, be one with the people. You have no need to stand aside with me.'

But Whergh shook his head, again heavily moving his weight from foot to foot as though the bonds his mind had tethered them by were loaded with stones.

It is as well he stays apart, thought The Watcher. He might otherwise communicate the uneasiness of his mind, while spirit flows freely among the dancers.

So he waited for such time as the woman was preoccupied with her lord and then sternly he spoke to the young man so rigid behind them.

'Behold,' he said, pointing to the obscenely offending shadow, 'how the dark side of your body dances!'

Whergh gave a thin cry of discovery and horror, gazing

where it ravaged the dying chief upon his couch. Vehemently he shook his head and clenched his fist upon his breast. 'No! No, not I! It is some trick. It is an evil magic.'

'There *is* an evil magic,' agreed The Watcher quietly. Beware how it enchants you.' But the young man would not stay to listen. Abruptly he tore himself away and went striding out of the firelight, beyond the circle of the dancing, to the very edge of the Gathering Place. There he stood, in terrible division of purpose, while the sound of the dance was all about him in the chants and the howls and the drumming and the liquid voice of the pipes. His body demanded and would not be stilled, but he dared not reveal his heart because of its dark places. No longer could he leap and buck in the rippling movement of the deer or rush and thunder in guise of the boar. Nor would his arms any more extend and bear him on the wind while his predatory beak curved earthwards in his eagle flight. The beautiful and innocent mystery of the hunt had left him. He was a creature apart, that was unclean among men. For it was man his heart hunted, and no enemy he might seek out in honour, but one of his own that he should cherish and serve, the special one. And even among enemies does a young man in his strength pick an adversary among the half-dead?

So much treacherous emotion, thought The Watcher, must surely burst his heart unless he finds release. And silently he commanded the tortured man, 'Dance!'

Despite himself Whergh began to stamp, head low and body curled in a womb of agony; and then his spine slowly grew straight and, the great chest outthrown, he beat on the air with his flailing arms, threatened the stars with his fists. The cords of his neck writhed and knotted, like the trunk of some monstrous oak wound about with serpents. His was all the power of the bison in unspeakable anger. And The Watcher was deeply disturbed, for he loved the man; and the man had only hate for him who had discerned his mortal secret.

So, apart from the others, Whergh danced his anger out, and in place of it came a quieter hate, and, slowing as the night wore on, his body was all arrogance, and he worshipped himself as one should worship a lord, and pitied himself as one would pity a child that has neither father nor tribe. But he did not any longer hate himself as one hates a coward or a traitor. He had passed beyond that for a time, and on the morrow and for many years yet he would reveal a new impatience and an irritation with other men who had not learnt what he had learnt, or suffered as he had done on that night of The Dance.

'I fear for him,' whispered his mother. 'The Fierce One. That is how we called him, and laughed, when he was a baby. But now he is terrible.'

'He will be better soon,' The Watcher promised. 'It is good that he can dance himself open once more.' But he spoke with sorrow, for it is evil when a man goes apart and dances to himself. Then indeed he has a sickness of the soul.

'I have offended you,' Whergh told The Watcher when they came face to face again three days later. Closing his eyes, The Watcher listened to the voices of the young man. One voice questioned and seemed to ask pardon, another was indifferent, another barely stopped short of defiance: all three the voice of Whergh, and in the man's face the truth was covered over.

'Have you done wrong?' asked The Watcher cautiously.

Whergh laughed, a short dog-yap of mockery. 'What is "wrong"? How do we know the rightness of our actions?'

'There are things permitted and things not permitted,' answered The Watcher soberly. 'You know as well as any.'

'Permitted. Ah, yes. And who is to permit? Again, how am I to know what is permitted? I am a simple hunter, not forever lying upon couches musing like a seer. I do as my heart tells me. The heart does not lie, I have heard you say.'

'It is true, the heart does not lie. One opens one's heart in The Dance: all that comes from it is the truth. But there are permitted truths and truths that are not permitted.'

'But you have not said who is to permit, or to make

taboo.'

'The voice of the tribe. What is good for the life of the people, that is permitted. What does not seek their benefit is not good. I have seen lands where the souls of the dead are balanced by the gods against the weight of a feather. Whose heart is heavy with bad living is not acceptable. But here we do not wait to be dead. In The Dance each man may weigh his own heart. If we are with our people in The Dance we know it, for The Dance is a mystery of commitment. If we can dance as a part of the whole, then we are not at fault, we have not endangered our people by violating any taboo.

'There is danger when a man holds back from The Dance, for he will soon be apart from his tribe and will end by fighting even himself.'

'Our lord, my father, does not dance, and you do not dance, Night-gazer.'

'In memory, our lord, your mother's husband, dances with all his people, living and vanished. And it is through my still body and my heart that a power comes, making great music, moving all things together. No man – no worthy man – is quite apart from The Dance, for that would be death.'

'I have danced. Do you imagine I am not of my tribe? Am I not the most skilled hunter who brings home their meat? Does not my father love me above all?'

'You are much loved, but not content. Yourself must love more, and you may yet be blessed.'

'Ah, I have brought down too many nimble beasts to have practised long with the twisting of words. You have mastered it well, even in a tongue that is foreign to you. I do as poorly with argument as you would with a real man's spear.'

And Whergh had stalked away but did not cease to wrangle, returning again and again after days and weeks to demand, '*Who* permits? *Who* is to decide what is taboo? Can a grown man not walk alone?' Always the thorn that tore his flesh was the principle of authority, and at each rubbing of the wound the sharp point drove more deeply in, taking soil and base elements to accumulate and spread the hurt.

'Only the gods permit and forbid,' said The Watcher, seeing black danger opening ahead. 'I am, as you said, no more than a voice, a passageway between perils.'

'Apart,' said Whergh in a dead voice, 'from the people. A stranger who has set himself over us as though a chief. Even our lord is one of us, born to us. But not you. You are outside. You are alone.'

And later, when he had given up speaking openly of such things with The Watcher, he continued the dialogues in the darkness of his mind, so that when the time came, in the days of frost, that he gathered the people to hear him, his own poison was in the speech he uttered.

The Watcher said nothing, but gazed on the scene of accusation as though it happened to some other man. He saw that the people could not distinguish between magic, that was a man's thing – held inside the hand – and the gods' will, that grew in the earth, blew in the wind, lay mute in the great stones of the plains. So there was no easy way to teach them, when Whergh had made them distrustful and afraid.

'Ever since he came among us,' said the princeling, 'Our lord, my father, has grown weaker. Now I fear to see the white flower of death lie on his lips. His spirit can no longer speak. His eyes open, but they do not behold. From his mouth come poisonous vapours, witnessing to the magic potions that have eaten him away within. And behold this Day-sleeper, how he has changed while he counted his moons. He came here as a weakling. When I took him from the sea he was all but dead. We gave him life, nourished him and set him in a place of honour. And like a feeding spider he has sucked all sustenance from us, his flies. Look on these two: the great man laid low, and the weakling grown tall and mighty. See what foul magic has been done. How long must we tolerate this monster preying upon us?'

From a great distance of time, it seemed, The Watcher heard a wave of voices break upon him, and he seemed to feel again the bruising and the broken limbs. Once more, he thought, the deck of the ship fell apart beneath him as he was tossed from side to side in a storm of dissidence.

There were some voices spoke for him, but fear shouted

more loudly. And at last Whergh sprang lithely on to the chalk bank of the inner circle, weight balanced on lower foot, the other heroically set upon a boulder. 'My people,' he cried, his voice swelling warmly on the words, 'my own people, how often have you heard this man declare, "Men who have killed are themselves not wholly live men: *they shall be killed*."? What then must we do with him? For he has sought the death of our great lord.'

They could not stone him instantly there, for women were among them and they remembered the babes who lay waiting for day in their bellies, and how they might be born with stones for heads and with all their blood spilt. So they sent the women away inside the houses, all save the white-haired woman of the chief who lay across his couch, weeping alternately for The Watcher and her lord. And by this time the gathered men had cooled their madness enough to recall that the silent man they threatened was a wizard such as none had ever seen before. Against his magic they could do nothing, unless he would condemn himself before them.

'Tell us,' demanded one more bold than the rest, 'why we should not do to you as Whergh has said.'

But The Watcher said not a word, seeming to listen to the silence. It had happened before, he told himself; just such confrontation, accusation, sentence. The place had been different, under a hot night sky, with a changed tilt to the stars, but on a High Place he had been condemned to death, tortured and – killed? Surely he remembered the knife and the pain, *the crackling flames*? But if so, how was he alive now? Or had he, falling into death, dreamed another lifetime between? Was it only now to happen? Faced with the supreme mystery, how could he find words to waste on men?

'He has drawn apart,' said a woman's voice. 'He is communing with the gods.' And the Moon Priestess was among them, the woman who had come from the shore when The Watcher was first brought here by Whergh. She looked remote and terrible in a silvery robe hung with annular pebbles and small petrified creatures set in rock. Beneath it her child, almost at term, distended her form like a monstrous jar, and the bright hair was bound flat beneath coils fashioned from its severed ends.

'Of course,' said Whergh, slowly relinquishing his stance upon the bank, 'he is a holy man, one that at times must draw apart. Let us aid him then. Is that not how he receives his messages? We will leave him in peace to commune with the overall spirit, quite alone. And we have ready at hand an underground chamber that will serve our hermit. Close by is the tomb we have prepared to receive our lord's body. But his spirit is delayed by a spell. Let us place The Stargazer in this, for while he is in occupation he will surely not let our lord Luth's spirit leave him, or else the tomb will be required again. So we shall ensure our lord's recovery, fulfil this hermit's needs and raise our hand against no man's life.

'Let it be done well. We will prepare the place fitly, and fast until next evening. Then, with wine and feasting and music of the ram's horn, let us bear him there in all honour and seal him away.'

15

Kent leaned over the bunk. 'Sarson! Wake up, man.'

There was no answering movement. There seemed in fact to be no movement at all. Sarson lay extended on his back, hands crossed at the base of his throat, as though dead. If he breathed, there was no visible lifting of the chest.

Kent reached for his wrist, feeling for the pulse. At first there seemed to be none, but then he found it, faint and slow. He lifted one of the drooped eyelids, grunted at sight of the upturned pupil, opened the man's jaws and smelt his breath.

'Come on, man,' he insisted, more to himself than the sleeper, and began opening the windows, reheating coffee, checking through his chest of medicines. It had been moved, he saw, and one of the drawers was not quite closed, but the bottle of tablets like those prescribed for Sarson wasn't notably more empty. He thought he knew then what had happened: deprived of his own supply, Sarson had gone to the chest for his normal dose. The state of suspended animation he lay in had been partly induced by the tranquillising drug but was sustained now by the workings of his own mind. Bringing him back would be quite dodgy.

He pulled the blanket over Sarson's cold hands and went over to the site hut, tapped on the door and brought Pengelly back to lend a hand. With a hypo, coffee and massage, they got Sarson propped up against pillows, glazed and abstracted. Then they pulled him to his feet and started walking him up and down the cramped floor of the trailer until Kent's continuous hail of words began to touch him. Yet still the doctor was conscious of Sarson's unnatural drawing away, almost certainly a question of the complicated mechanics of fear, but with an element of will, he thought: a sort of philosophic fortitude. It was as though Sarson walled himself up inside some concrete barrier, deliberately negating himself.

Pengelly was openly disturbed by Sarson's condition and puzzled by the treatment which must surely suggest measures against alcoholic poisoning.

'Doctor, has he taken an overdose?' he whispered during a pause in their labours.

'Not exactly, though he's in a state when almost anything would constitute an overdose, even a couple of aspirins. Not to worry, though, he's coming on all right.'

They had done all they physically could. It was now a matter of persuasion, of pitting Kent's will and the present against Sarson's subconscious clinging to the past.

'Fine,' repeated Kent, grinning at Pengelly. 'Thanks for all you've done. I can manage now.'

The Site Assistant looked down at Sarson sitting stirring his cup with mechanical monotony. His eyes, heavy-lidded, were fixed on something dead ahead, and he stared unblinking as Pengelly took leave of them.

'Now,' Kent accused Sarson evenly, 'you've been dreaming again, haven't you? Tell me about it. Did you continue travelling? On the sea?' He thought at first that the other man hadn't heard him, but then Sarson turned his head and seemed to look through him.

'I came to Brevaryn,' he said tonelessly. 'I came to this place and was joined with my people.'

'A good place?'

'A most beautiful place, dense with trees and running with sweet water. Great grasses grow and nourishing herbs. There are fruits and grain and succulent roots. The sun is gentle and the winds cool.'

'And the people welcomed you?'

'The people are good, full of laughter and quick to action. They love easily but anger fast.'

'There is no danger there?'

Sarson hesitated. After a moment's silence he spoke in a changed tone, as though he wrestled in his mind. 'There is always danger. There is good and evil in every place. Evil cannot be destroyed, only drawn off.'

'Drawn off?'

'Absorbed. Absorbed by a greater good it becomes powerless. Yes, evil within greater good, that is how it can be overcome.'

'Sarson, whose evil? Your own?' But they had lost contact again.

It was the same, continuous dream, Kent told himself, and now it had reached a new phase. Sarson claimed that he had 'arrived', and that meant he was deeper committed, recognised his own situation in it as fitting. He had given the place a name and spoken of its beauty and wholesomeness, of its people, and then of abstract evil counterbalanced against good.

So now the crisis was within sight, a crisis of absolutes. And Sarson's function in it? To 'draw off the evil' as he'd said? That had a most sinister ring; such absolutes in the mind led almost inevitably to destruction. If at professional level Kent regarded this dream as no more than the creation of Sarson's sick mind, then that sickness was about to reach its dangerous limit. But if, as his intuition insisted, the past was actually reaching out to reclaim the man, disaster was even more certain, for unless the present reasserted itself then Sarson might be utterly overpowered and swept away, leaving some mindless wreck in

157

his place. Kent had to prevent this, get Sarson firmly linked again with outer reality.

'Look, drink up. We'll take a walk outside, blow some of the cobwebs away. Where's your dressing-gown?'

Obediently Sarson sipped at the coffee. 'Dressing-gown,' he repeated after a moment. 'Somewhere here.' And now he spoke more normally, although still with a curious languor.

'Val was with you,' Kent reminded him, trying to peg him down to the present. 'What became of her?'

Sarson thought for a moment. 'She went back to the hotel. I was tired. I said I'd come on later, after a rest.'

'To Farne? I see. I've just come from there. I had a call from the hospital. About the PM on that old gypsy.'

'The post mortem? What was it killed him?' At last he seemed to have caught Sarson's interest.

'The old man's heart finally gave out. Which isn't surprising at that age. But he was under-nourished too. They thought he was well over ninety years old; very fit, for all that.'

'You said before he'd been embalmed. Who would have done that?'

'Appearances were deceptive. It was the effect, they thought, of a pretty unusual diet. He must have been a brewer and stewer of local remedies. Whatever it was he used as his main food, it had the effect of dehydrating him. It's possible he went for long periods asleep, without food, and then had short periods of activity.'

'Hibernating, you mean?'

'Something like that. Unfortunately his stomach was quite empty when they examined him, so there's no clue to what he lived on. The police examined the caravan, of course, but not for that sort of thing. They'd have spotted conventional drugs, but his food cupboard wouldn't have interested them. I'm going across to have a look myself later.'

'Odd,' said Sarson. 'He'd kept apple twigs in a pot.' He shrugged the dressing-gown on and slowly tied the cord. 'The apple's an ancient symbol of immortality.'

'Well, ultimately it didn't work. Do you feel up to going out? You won't be seen. The site's practically deserted.'

Sarson rubbed a hand through his hair. 'I took one of those tablets. It's still left me hazy.'

'If you were tired already, why take them?'

They started walking through the camp, Kent a little ahead and alert for guy ropes barely visible in the gathering dark. Sarson mumbled some answer and he turned back, asking him sharply to repeat it.

'I wanted to be sure,' Sarson said again.

'Sure you'd dream?'

'I have to go on,' said the archaeologist doggedly. 'I feel it matters. There's a parallel life.'

'Experiments you feel obliged to continue? Is that it?' Kent spoke hesitantly, aware how precarious was the man's balance. 'What are you trying to find out?'

'The truth.'

'About what?'

Sarson trudged on uphill, disturbed because although they spoke of the same things, their minds were on widely separated tracks. Then he encountered a smooth current of patience within himself, and he turned back to the other man. He smiled.

'Not truth *about* anything. Truth itself. We've lost it; we no longer know from direct experience, but look for proofs. And so we are for ever moving farther away, with little left but cynicism and the self-inflicted jest of "What *is* truth?" But truth exists of itself, and when we are in unity with all existence we are a part of it, and it of us. We have it, and so, being involved in it, cannot be apart to test it. We can only test the validity of others' approach to truth, or guess the degree of our separation when we are without it. Before ever reason was, there was truth.'

'But you can't override reason, it's part of the human scheme.'

'Reason is there to be used. But what abysmal dangers it opens, once a man dares to stand alone and question. Dangers of fragmentation for the community – and so he violates taboo; and for himself some similar kind of disintegration. We modern men are of so many layers that it is almost impossible to exist equally at all levels. Most

often a man will find it easy to use one argument outward to others and hold another secret dialogue in his
heart. If reason could penetrate our whole being we
would arrive again where we began, at truth; locked on
to what has always been, changeless and unsubjected to
time.'

'And that is how you find yourself now?' Kent questioned softly, afraid to break the almost trancelike calm of
the man, and yet feeling about for some clue to his recall.
'Locked on? Completely penetrated? Obsessed?'

Again Sarson smiled, tranquilly. 'Possessed. Perfectly in
balance. Centred.'

Kent went on looking at him, and briefly something of
what Sarson experienced came through to him. Physically
the man was planted there, motionless and dark against
the paler sky, his heavy dressing-gown making him tower,
ominous and monolithic. It was as though he seemed capable of the same resistance to weathering and time as
Stone Age monuments themselves. Kent felt then that he
was seeing, not the twentieth-century man he had roused
from heavy sleep, but the other person he had once been,
in such a distant past, but perhaps at this selfsame place.
Had this priestlike philosopher come from four thousand
years ago, from a society of near savages?

'You want me to say,' Sarson pronounced slowly, 'that I
feel in balance because I have in fact returned. You believe that I had a former life in this place, and that across
a fold in time I am remembering experiences of that
former person. Think that if you wish. The idea may
have some irradiation of the truth, but to my mind what
happens is a little different.'

He turned and paused so that he faced the dropping
moon, poised huge over the west horizon.

'These things that I have experienced, once happened.
These people I have seen and spoken with, lived here.
They were not like us, all facets, but had a single surface.
Their worship was of such overwhelming, elemental
power that a soul-force was created. You know what mir-
acles of faith even we moderns can achieve by will; imagine this greater concentration of power, with no dissent,
no doubt even; a massive upsurge of willed spirit fed into

this little space, bounded by ditch of water and bank of flame. Like all denser matter, spirit cannot be destroyed, only dissipated or dispersed. It passed in this concentrated essence into the mute stones that circled the gathering, facing in and for ever reflecting to each other all that was significant in the minds of men. And the air above, and the living sky from which they derived inspiration, and the earth from which they drew life, echoed back the integrity of unfragmented creation.

'Within this circle was safety, holiness, and all acceptable passions. Outside it, destructive chaos. While this is remembered, survival is ensured. I have to go and make certain that my people stay mindful of these matters.'

Kent scarcely dared to breathe, so precarious now was the passage of this strange man before him, suspended between two worlds four thousand years apart, yet with his feet upon their common, ancient fabric. He leaned forward, trying despite the darkness to see the other man's features and the detail of his dress, but the moon's face was obscured for a moment and it was quite impossible to tell what manner of man stood there before him. He put out a hand. 'Who ... are you?' he whispered.

There was no answer.

Sarson heard his question, but the thread that had existed between the two men was becoming attenuated, and the words were in some way drawn out, so that they seemed to be echoing on as sounds, but losing all meaning on the way. While he was yet in touch with Kent a part of him wished to answer that each of the three words was false, since it was only word and not the pure thought it was meant to represent. Identity itself was an illusion in the face of the true nature of existence.

'Who – are – you?' The words began to float like mist, condense, fluctuating with luminescence, expanding and contracting, undergoing vast changes like the phases of a star – gas; condensing to solid; pressure and heat increasing to burn up its core; helium flash; expanding to red giant, swallowing all surrounding matter; then, spent, shrinking to white dwarf; dwindling; cooling over millions of years. He saw the words at last suspended in space, a ball of dead ash perpetually rotating. And through that emptiness and awful silence came three other words, and the language was not the same.

'All is one,' Sarson repeated, and watching the moon he saw her change in phase, and his own shadow, that had lain behind, swing across the grass and lie ahead, before his left shoulder, hugely oblong and straight like the shadow of a megalith. And he knew by its path that the season too was changed and the moon, which had been setting in Spring was now rising in midwinter. And when all else was duly changed and waiting, the moon herself, unhurriedly, passed up the sky, going backwards, and he turned, The Watcher, to face her arrival on the northeast horizon.

'Who ... are you?' Kent insisted, and there was not a flicker of response. His hand touched the other's which seemed to have suffered a rigor, being deadly chill and unmoving.

'Sarson!' he shouted at him, within a few inches of the wide-staring eyes, but the man was incapable of being reached. Kent shuddered in the sudden wind that had come whipping up out of the bowl of the plain, but Sarson stood there untouched, not a fold stirring in the heavy dressing-gown, the outline of his head as clear and smooth as though it were shaved of all hair. He might have been hewn from stone.

And as he moved, pivotting, his hands lifting sideways to meet and clasp loosely before his chest, the mild, meditative face, which should have been in black shadow, caught now some cool, reflected light whose source was not visible to the doctor. It gave the smooth features a texture of alabaster, accentuating the dominance of the wide, dark eyes. 'Alsleth,' breathed The Watcher.

Kent held his breath. He no longer felt required to treat this as a professional case. He was encountering the shadow of incalculable mystery. Yet there was a compulsion on him to know what substance cast this shadow.

Across the henge there seemed now to be another figure dimly visible. On the outer rim, against the white chalk that the dig had exposed, rose the insubstantial form of a woman, facing in towards Sarson. Kent caught his breath, for he could not swear that she was there at all. The flickering shape of a woman, yet not wholly real. He could almost believe she was some projection of Sarson's mind. Which she must be; as all other strange phenomena here at this moment were. And then, as Sarson's hands again extended, the shadowy figure made the same answering movement, like a priestess, and Kent knew himself caught in some field of force between two poles.

He was suddenly sure of the phantom's identity, impossible though it must be, for Josie was fifty miles away in Bristol. 'Josie?' he whispered.

The wind blew the sound away.

The priest of Ishtar bowed from the waist; a smile of joy lit the serene face and he began to speak, quietly but with mounting passion until the speech was almost song; and not a syllable was comprehensible to the transfixed man who watched him across the gulf of time.

16

The child had been completely quiet for about twenty minutes now, but she wasn't asleep. Her aunt slowed the car before the crossroads and threw a quick glance over her shoulder. Josie lay hunched in her corner, eyes wild and wide-staring, her mouth slightly open, wispy hair sticking damp and tangled on her forehead.

'Not far now,' said Irene coolly. 'We're nearly home.'

The child could tell this herself, of course; she would be recognising familiar cottages, farms, road-ends. If she saw them, that was. She wasn't looking out, but staring, sight unfocused, at some spot in the car's interior.

The moment that Irene had given up the trip and turned back from the Bristol road, Josie had started to calm. It was as though her sense of security was tightly tied in with her innate sense of direction.

Such an appalling display of fury and panic; Irene

couldn't remember when the child had approached anything like this passion before, even in the earliest days
after the tragedy. Perhaps this was some new phase connected with adolescence; if this was only its beginning,
how would it be at peak? Irene didn't know that she
could go on very long at such a pitch. She had made a
habit of this calm, cool response, always offering, as the
doctors had advised, at least one infallible haven of
reasonableness and tranquillity to the tortured child –
but it wasn't natural to her. She too suffered, both with
Josie and because of her. She too had the family tempera-
ment and her own personal need to scream.

The weekend at Bristol had seemed such a good idea,
and Josie's state secure enough to allay any doubts. In
fact, both from Mrs Pyke's evidence and her own observation, Irene had been quite sure that recently Josie had
been more contented and equable. She had herself heard
the child making those heart-aching little attempts at
singing that escaped her when she knew her brief moments of happiness. But the instant she had headed the
car westward, with Josie and their cases inside, there had
been trouble.

'There's Alice and her donkey,' she pointed out, but
there was no response. She wondered how soon Dr Curry
would get over to them. She had phoned back from Bath,
warning the housekeeper how things were and asking her
to make sure Curry could see her before she settled down
for the night.

They were approaching The Plough, and Irene unconsciously increased speed, fearing the child might make a
fuss when she failed to stop there. Recently the pub had
seemed more of a home to her than the house where she
had been born and grown up. If there were things that
she treasured left in her room there, they could be brought
over later tonight. But when Irene thought of this it
struck her again as curious that the child had no favourite cuddly toy, nor even any more a familiar piece of
cloth to hold in her hand as she went off to sleep. These
habits she had lost when younger and she had never
found a substitute. She did not even suck her thumb.

This time The Plough had passed without causing any

reaction, although the lurid pink of the lights that
flooded its mock-Tudor face leapt from the dark and
shrieked for attention. But there were fewer cars than of
late on the forecourt, so the dig people must have dispersed or moved all the transport over to the site. Was it
they, Irene wondered, who had unknowingly upset the
child's delicate equilibrium?

And now, a little late, came the new protest that Irene
had wished to avoid. The child was mouthing, leaning
over to claw at her as she drove. Pray God she'd not go for
the door handle. Better to cut speed, for fear she should
try to get out.

'There,' she breathed in relief, 'the drive-way lamp.
We're home, Josie, and everything's all right.'

She pointed ahead and to the left, but Josie went on
with her terrible little shuddering gasps, pressing her face
against the other side of the car in an effort to penetrate
the blank darkness over the plain. Oh God, what did she
think she saw out there? For mile upon mile there was
nothing at all.

As soon as the car stopped Irene was out and round to
get Josie. Mrs Watts, the housekeeper, opened the front
door and warm golden light welcomed them from inside.
Irene herself felt an impulse to rush straight in and
throw herself down by her old winged armchair, hide her
face in its cushions and sob out her tensions from the
maddening drive.

Not so Josie. She stood hesitant on the threshold, with
the old servant's arms about her, her chin lifted as though
she half detected some slight sound and wished to follow
it to source. But there was no sound, Irene thought,
checking herself to listen: only the stalking tread of the
grandfather clock across the hall, utterly regular but for
the longer, gathering stroke as it moved on the hand at
the end of its minute. Beyond that and behind it, the
whole house was as empty of movement as the dark outside.

The girl went forward a pace or two to disengage herself and then listened again. The expectancy, momentarily glimpsed, left her eyes, and again her face quivered.
She began to shake her head slowly from side to side as

though to push away some unbearable memory, denying its truth. With hunched shoulders and balled fists she endured the staircase, but at its top she stopped, refused her own bedroom and went on up again to the loft where she'd played as a small child on rainy days. She still had a desk there and tables where she sometimes drew or modelled clay. In one corner she kept a miscellaneous assortment of china and metal objects that she would play on with an old kitchen spoon, and along one of the exposed beams hung weird fluffs of sheep's wool, gathered off brambles, that she had tried dyeing with onion skins or damson juice or walnut bark. They and the dried grasses and wild herbs, strung up and whispering in the draught from a broken window, matched something almost formless that was emerging from her mind. Now she let herself sink down in the middle of the bare wooden floor, first to her knees and then crouched foetus-like, but with neck twisted and her cheek bruising against the dust-smelling, splintered boards.

She fixed her mind on the darkness outside, heard the low, vibrant sound that never ceased over the upper downland and felt herself balanced, erect on the rim of the henge, reaching out, out ... But there was nothing there beyond her now. There had been, a few minutes ago, while she was still cramped in the car. Something had happened then and she'd been able to get completely free in some way. Now the ability had gone, and she couldn't remember what it was she'd so desperately wanted. It was like suddenly learning to fly and then, suddenly again, never more being able to.

Even the picture book in her mind had shut again. She had to remain where she was, inside her body, on the floor here, quite alone.

Despite the one glaring electric bulb, she felt blackness around her as she stared out, defying the dim shapes of the room to change and bring instead worse pictures. The good images and the music were quite gone away; she couldn't reach them now, but every effort she could make was centred on the blackness remaining. Just black. So long as the red didn't come. Oh, not the red and the terrible running away. No. Just black, black, black.

Dr Curry sat on his heels, looking at the child. Normally there would have been no question. They would have carried her, by force if need be, to bed, kept her warm, given a tranquillising injection. There was no possibility of pouring anything between those tightly clenched teeth. Poor little Josie, she had seemed so much happier, easier in her mind, of late. Wasn't it love, not a hypodermic syringe, she had need of now? Briefly he touched the rigid, chill hand, covered her with the thick patchwork quilt Mrs Watts had given him to bring up, and went quietly down to interview her aunt.

Hesitantly, because already she had spent a fortune on specialists and there'd been little improvement to show for any of it, he mentioned the man the archaeologists had with them, what a sound reputation he had, how he'd already met Josie at the inn when she waited at table. 'I can settle her physically,' he told Irene, 'as a temporary measure, but if Dr Kent saw her as she now is, he might make some valuable suggestion.' He stressed for her the man's standing as an experimental psychiatrist, but for himself he valued him for his evident gentleness, for the fact that Kent too had intimate knowledge of grief.

Irene was desperate enough to agree to almost anything and offered to sit on watch in the upstairs corridor, where she could keep an eye on the room where Josie had gone for refuge, while Curry went out to try and contact the London man.

All the bumpy way out to the camp site the doctor was turning in his mind the girl's recent improved condition and the suddenness of this reversal. He had a country practitioner's normal reservations about theoretical psychiatry, the jargon, and the prefabricated case-history that the patient was often, he thought, too readily slotted into. He mistrusted airy references to positive and negative transference. If a patient took an immediate dislike to a doctor that was positive enough for him, and whose failure it was didn't concern him. But Kent had already met Josie when she served his party at The Plough, and he had himself asked Curry about her when they'd had dealings together at the hospital. It seemed too great an opportunity to miss. Kent could always decline, after all, the request to call him in.

There appeared to be some special preparations going on out at the camp. Two large generator vans had been drawn up between the living quarters and the dig itself, and cables ran up to where floodlights were being tested. Camera crews were checking equipment or drifting about the canteen marquee, while a small army of props men were busy setting up canvas and lath 'megaliths', plastic boulders and strangely distorted tree trunks mounted on wooden bases and painted with emblems of supposed totemic significance. The whole activity had an air at once professional and cheerfully spurious. Dr Curry, who had never seen so much as an amateur play from the participating side of the footlights, was fascinated. All signs of serious archaeological interest seemed to have disappeared and a completely different cast of characters taken over. With some difficulty he found his way to the site office and there enquired for the Medical Officer's quarters.

He found Kent with his shirt sleeves rolled up, washing socks in the galley end of his trailer. One of the archaeologists, wearing a dark dressing-gown, was asleep on a bunk at the near end and a transistorised radio was emitting a quiet but tinny version of a Haydn symphony. Kent switched off the sound and invited Curry in.

'Sorry I can't offer coffee. The gas cylinder has run out. I guess they're too busy to bring round my refill.' He sounded a little distrait.

Dr Curry perched on the end of the free bunk and explained that he wasn't there for refreshment but advice, and launched into an account of Josie's new development. At the end of it, Kent sat silent, the towel still screwed between his hands. Finally he went over to look down at the sleeping man and seemed to be considering him.

'If you could only see her, poor child,' Curry repeated. 'A terrible state. I'll have to get back and sedate her, but I thought if you would come you ought to see her at her worst.'

'Yes,' said Kent impassively.

'Even if you can't see your way to taking her on as a

case, well, I mean, she is used to you, seeing you at The Plough every day and so on. She'd not be afraid of you as she might be of a stranger.'

'I'll come,' Kent told him at last. 'I'm sorry the week-end her aunt arranged didn't come off. I'd feel happier with her away from here at present. She's become too involved, far too close. It's bad for her and for others.'

'I've left my car up on the track.'

'Thanks. I'll collect mine and follow you back. Which direction, in case I miss you on the main road?'

'Right. But I'll wait for you again at The Plough. Thank you, doctor.' He rose and went to the door, looking down curiously at the sleeping man as he passed, but Kent offered him no explanation.

While he was groping among the tent guys he heard Kent come out after him, lock the door with a key and come lightly down the steel steps. With so much on his mind, it didn't strike Curry at the time that the sleeping man was left a virtual prisoner.

The Watcher awoke late, for it was already evening. The moon had barely risen but the stars showed fitfully behind a massing darkness of cloud. Afar off there were sudden flashes of violet light and a distant roll of thunder. The humid air seemed to crackle as he moved, and when he rose, his feet at each step tingled as though pierced by a thousand fine bone needles.

After he had washed, and shaved his head, they brought him a mess of fungus to eat, mixed with hares' liver and certain roots that had been bruised into tenderness, but this could not change the harshness of their taste, that continued strangely burning within him long after he had eaten. He affected not to notice how all watched him, but even when he lowered his eyes to his hands, loosely clasped on his chest, he could still read their hearts as clearly as though each spoke with a voice of treachery, of faith, of greed or malice, of fearfulness or courage.

Their emotions entered him, but over all he felt compassion for the two women who loved him. The young priestess, who had been Alsleth, was terrible in her cold, contained anger. She was sure of his ability to overcome, but that he should submit to suffering filled her with rage against the men who sought to destroy him.

'Guard your anger,' he counselled her softly, when she brought him the potion he had directed her to prepare. 'You will require all of it and more to achieve the near impossible. Anger begets a magic of its own, when fully come to term.'

At his words she placed a hand on her swollen belly, feeling the child dance. 'Tonight,' she told him, 'before you woke, I watched for you, and there was a new star where none had ever been before. It is large and unbelievably bright, and it still burns, for when the cloud parted a while ago I saw it again. Brighter than any star before. Surely it is a good thing.'

'Continue to watch for me. Be steadfast.' And he blessed her before all the people, so that no one should doubt who had his authority when he should no longer be there.

Erghlaun did not approach him. She stayed at the couch of her lord Luth, and although he lay close by the high-heaped fire of burning alders, they had now draped skins about him on willow branches against the chill airs he fancied touched upon him. He did not recognise the cold hands of his fathers-before-him, plucking at him to loosen his bonds of flesh.

There was a great moving together of the people when The Watcher knelt beside Luth; and some of the young men, allies of Whergh, murmured together, suspecting The Watcher might attempt to do some damage to the dying man in the hope of surviving himself. But The Watcher raised both hands with the fingers open and the palms towards the assembly, and he took his leave of Luth with his face lifted to the blinded sky, knowing, without seeing, where the lord's star was in juxtaposition to the sign of death, with his own star across from it, exactly in balance. He did not speak aloud because Luth's ears of the body were already severed from his spirit, but he spoke directly, mind to mind, saying that these man-forms of theirs would not meet again, but their spirits would come together once more and would know each other as one recognises in a dream.

Again Erghlaun wept, and none but he knew how much she wept for her lord and how much for The Watcher. Nothing could comfort her, for she feared for them both and could not spare either for the tomb.

'I too have seen the white flower,' she whispered through her dishevelled pale hair. 'It lies upon his lips. I dread to look upon you, for fear to see it there as well. What if I care for him so well that he lives on long enough to make you die?'

'Cherish our lord Luth,' he told her sternly. 'May his spirit stay long with him among his people. For myself, I have a task to perform and a proving to undergo. Let the ritual fires be lit and see that the ditches run with water. Drive the maidens away to their compound and the children after them. And then let all the men and women come and stand between the pit and the moon. Let all be made ready as if for a great Dance, with fire and wine and music. And The Watcher shall withdraw a while from you, and all that is unacceptable among you shall go with him. And in time, as Ishtar-Inanna wills, there shall be a great chief over you.'

He looked a last time over the people assembled there and it seemed that this had all been before, across a great chasm of time. Just so had the people massed, in fear, and some with evil in their hearts, seeking destruction; and just so had the horns wailed and the young men screamed their chants and horses reared with terrible cries. And there was a great clashing of sticks and rocks upon the stretched hides of cattle so that it sounded as though vast armies met and did battle. Over it all eddied and rolled the black smoke of the ritual fires, burning green herbs; and the flash of orange and red flame, as tongues of fire exploded from the billowing smoke, was an echo of the storm that now rolled nearer in the heavens.

The Watcher felt the potion reach a new part of his labyrinth and it was as though he was becoming white ice, white flame, a Messenger of Death himself. Then was the moment, with the Priestess on the upper bank before him and the people all concentrated between, that he raised his arms to Ishtar and began the unmentionable hymn. He sang of An, Enlil and Enki and of the council of gods when they condemned the evils of earth. He sang of the overthrow of the Highest Place and of Ishtar weeping for the loss of her children, men. Then his voice changed and he sang of his priesthood desecrated and of Ishtar's goodness in offering a passage of redemption across many seas to a far, fair land of pale light.

His voice went on of itself, and only now did he remember the incidents of which he sang.

'Here then I came, as a babe with a caul upon my mind,
Knowing neither my name nor the place of my springing,
But only the cause of my coming and the reason for all life.
And now I see the shape of the past
Like a shadow cast upon the present.
Lo, I am The Watcher of the Heavens and the counter of stars;
Measuring the earth, a shadow of the sky.
I am the Singer of Songs of the ways of men,
A glad sacrifice, and the servant of my people.
I am the lover of my mistress the moon,
Whom she pleases to lead and to prove
Over countless journeys and immeasurable time.
So, safe am I come, and willingly bloodied,
For over all tides and the ways of man for ever
Ishtar is holy,
Ishtartu, Queen!'

As from a great distance he heard his own voice cease, and all energy slowly drained from his body so that he was becoming nothing, a growing void that must be filled. Then the voice of the Priestess answering, passing through the assembled people, bending them like full grain before a tempest. And between them there was made a great magic, searing hearts and sweeping in all the anger and malice, so that even Whergh, who might have gloried in this moment of power felt an awful loss, and doubt, and then agonising sorrow for the death of this strange man, his brother.

And The Watcher lifted his arms once more and drew

on himself the evil of his people. In one instant, like a strike of holy lightning The Watcher was utterly filled, and fell, wounding his head upon the capstone of the chamber. At once there rose from him a stench of such foulness that all turned away, and his young men, who night and morning had brought him the water to wash in, lifted him gently and lowered him into the tomb on a bed of heather and young hazel twigs.

Then the elders came, in order of lordship, and the sons of the elders, with Whergh among them, weeping, with rollers to replace the capstone and make it secure against wolves and birds of prey. And the holes between were covered. First were little stones poured through the gaping spaces, and after them they rolled boulders to lean in and hold the structure fast. Last of all they covered the pit with soil in the name of Luth their lord, that he might wax strong and live as The Watcher began to fail.

So was the inhumation completed, and all this The Watcher saw, as a person unseen, from a great distance. Then he closed his spirit eyes and returned to the body in the pit, and all the people stole away, most fearful, and weary past all knowing.

No moon showed again that night, and the stars remained covered, but The Priestess stayed watching until the sun was twice its own height above the rim of the outer bank, and then the child that had strained within her all these hours could no longer be held back but burst forth and roared lustily at sight of the light and at taste of the chill air.

Erghlaun heard the baby crying and came up to where Alsleth lay. She rolled the boy child in the hem of her own warm robe, and when the woman was recovered she led her to her own couch and cared for her by day. But by night Alsleth was again The Priestess whom The Watcher had appointed, and she sat in his place and counted the stars and had the young men plant new sapling rods at every place where the sun and the moon rose and set.

And the lord Luth lived on and was seen to smile in his sleep.

17

'What the devil's got hold of you?' Beaumont demanded
testily.

Laughter from the rear of the car, following some private joke, covered any answer Joanna made. In fact she
had only curled the corner of her mouth and settled her
shoulders more firmly against the back of her seat. She
knew too well the bickering routine to wish to launch on
it now. To deny the fault and reverse the question on
him was useless. She knew in any case what devil had
hold of Donald. The fear of being intellectually out of
his depth made him need to reduce all others about him,
and to sustain his scorn he'd had recourse to the bottle.
Now not he but the drink was talking. He'd taken either
too little or too much to appear consistently brilliant,
and the threadbare patches of spite were reserved for
familiars he considered outside his viewing public. At

present this meant only herself.

'What do you think can have happened to Hugh?' she asked, to divert him.

'Sarson?' he grunted. 'He's breaking up. Can't stand the pace. These Museum types are all overprotected.'

'Or playing hard to get?' Joanna wondered aloud. 'I thought it was Val who's supposed to have left him. Now I'm not so sure.'

'Well, he stood her up all right tonight.' Beaumont slammed on the brakes and swore under his breath at a homing tractor that filled the lane ahead. As they dribbled along in its wake his mood changed as abruptly as the gear. He gave a little gasping laugh, reached out a hand to lay on Joanna's thigh and squeezed it. 'I wouldn't have disappointed her myself. She should come to me. That fellow's more likely to bed down with a theodolite.'

'I shouldn't have thought so, since you told me his version of some of the henge's uses. As an expert on fertility rites he's displaying a new facet.'

'Theory,' said Beaumont, gesturing widely and raising his voice so that the couple in the back might not lose the flow of erudition. 'There's a damn' big gulf between the theory and practice of sex.' He grinned tightly to himself, behind the pop-star moustache. 'It takes a Colossus to bestride it.'

Cue for appreciative glance, secretive smile, look of provocation, thought Joanna viciously. God, how automatic and tinny it all sounds. Like doing it to numbers. One might as well be a whore. What's the difference – courtesan, dutiful wife, payday pickup? All the same, once pretence takes over; what a hell technique is. Shall I ever feel *involved* again? If he comes mauling me tonight, I swear I'll kill him. I could, by God, I believe I really could do that.

It was frightening, the depth of passion that suddenly raked her. Her hands were sticky and trembling as she groped about in her purse for the case of cigarillos. Donald unplugged the lighter from the dashboard and held it for her, leaning across and breathing close on her face as he opened the quarterlight window.

I will not think of him, she determined. Who then? Hugh Sarson? Peter Kent? Better not; wife of public figure. Caesar's wife: though, selecting one's Roman regnum with care, that left more than adequate scope.

Donald had little faith in her grasp of ancient history, no doubt thinking she'd have her neolithic virgins robed like some chorus for Sophocles on Ice. He was vulnerable on a professional front, couldn't afford schoolboy howlers of that sort. Well, she'd done her homework well enough. The girls had been supplied with authentic-looking skins; though later, she guessed, they'd dance better without them, in and out among the phoney megaliths; and although much of that film would have to be cut, yet with the long-haired wigs and the smoke fanned in from the ritual fires some was sure to be superb material for the projected TV feature. Later they would add studio shots using real clay and stone vessels, if Donald could obtain them on loan. There were some beakers he coveted in Devizes Museum but wasn't sure of getting. They were genuine field archaeologists down there, and she privately suspected they'd consider Donald as pseudo as his plastic henge décor. Still, Hugh Sarson could probably get permission to have the relics copied.

'A penny for them,' said her husband intimately, and she was glad to be able to reply, truthfully, 'It's a pity we've not better props. I'd like something more fitting than canteen china for the filming.'

'Oh, Rudi will manage,' he said airily. 'I've great faith in his ability to make things appear what they're not.'

Without warning the tractor ahead swung right and into a farm track, and when Beaumont had eased round its bulky backside they skirted a wooded corner that brought them on to the open plain, and ahead they could see the floodlights of the site projecting the scene from a distance and reflecting weirdly in a low ceiling of dark cloud that hung locally over the sulky fires.

'Splendid,' pronounced Beaumont's backer from the rear seat.

Perhaps it won't be too bad after all, Joanna told herself. At least Donald will be involved with arrangements and his guests.

'You'll have to put me in the picture with the rites,' said the newspaper baron. 'Prehistory was a little before my time.'

They laughed politely. Then, 'But of course,' said Beaumont with zest, 'that's exactly what we'll do. Right *in* the picture, false beard, loincloth, the lot. How would you like to be the Maker of Fire? Rudi can get a shot over your shoulder while you use a tinder drill. How about it? Attended by suitable neolithic lovelies, of course.'

'I don't know. I was never much of a boy scout.' But they recognised the barely disguised delight in his voice.

Got him, Donald's smirk said to her and he tapped her hand under cover of changing gear for the descent.

'Joanna will take care of you; won't you, love? She'll show you where you can change. Make free with our caravan.'

Fenwick looked over towards her, a question in his eyes. 'My pleasure,' said Joanna.

That too, she accused her husband silently. My body on a platter, if so it suits your purpose. Damn you, Donald Beaumont, for a stinking fake.

'Well now, the rites,' he was beginning. 'You must understand the fertility cult's all bound up with the sun-moon dominance of the tribe. One can't be dogmatic, because there's no writing to check our theories by, but the community's needs were supreme, a man's individual life only a shadow of the real life that was the tribe's, centred upon survival through plenty and procreation. The communities had become agricultural by this time, and favourable seasons were ensured by a sort of renewable contract between the people, their gods and the heavenly bodies the gods were identified with.'

He darted a glance through the driving mirror and checked the effect his lecture was creating, then quickly ran through in his mind the other points Sarson had made to him that morning to introduce the fertility theme.

'Hence the need for some reliable sort of observatory. Of course, we must forget our present expert knowledge, and must see the earth as fixed, with the heavenly bodies performing intricate movements of communication with it. Within this relationship Stone Age man came to look upon the sun, moon and stars as actual gods, more powerful than man because independent of his influence. But he formed his gods in his own image, pictured them feasting, quarrelling, copulating, giving birth...'

And so on and so forth, thought Joanna drearily; words without end amen.

At the Plough, Val had caught up with Peter Kent. He had come there after visiting Josie at home, and he wanted to be alone and think. Val, he saw at once, was ready to do battle. Into the reflective mood that the child's predicament evoked, she irrupted tiresomely, for all he had such sympathy for her anxiety over Hugh.

'I think,' he told her, 'we shall have to show enormous patience. Your husband is sleeping again. If that's the only way he can face up to his problems and live them out, then that's what he has to do.'

Tension sharpened her voice, making her questions pertly challenging. 'Haven't you suddenly changed your views? You're speaking purely as a doctor now: "sleep the great healer", "living it out". We're back with a case of clinical neurosis then? What has happened to your other opinion – that he is re-encountering his past in this dream that overtakes him? Aren't you any more afraid he'll find this other life more satisfactory and want to stay there in it? What will happen then to him when he has to wake? Or will he perhaps lose the ability to wake, and remain from choice in a sort of frozen sleep?'

She turned from him, as though contemptuously. He saw her shoulders rigid with resentment as she moved stiffly away. Then she stopped, lifted her hands outwards in a little hopeless gesture and turned back. Her whole body seemed to have shrunk in an instant.

'I'm sorry, I'm sorry. That doesn't help. But what am I to believe when you speak with two voices? When you use reason I feel now you're concealing a part of the truth. This dream. It's real to him; he makes it, so it's his reality. Yes, I can follow that. But to me, to you, to anyone else outside it – it's imagination, surely. It can't *happen* like that. Can it? Tell me! I'm not an imbecile, I can try to understand. It's hard for me, but don't pretend, please. Don't *reassure* me. I'm frightened, and I know I ought to be.'

Kent looked down at his hands and was silent. At length he risked facing her eyes and asked quietly, 'Mrs Sarson, do you care which way it is? Does anything really matter, so long as he finds what he wants? Isn't Hugh's happiness the paramount consideration, whichever life it may be found in?'

For a moment she looked as though he had struck her, then she fought back at him with renewed anger. 'Of course I care. I want Hugh back, Dr Kent. I know you'll think I've changed my mind, but really I've just discovered it. I love him. I think he loves me, in his strangely insulated, perfectionist way. I wasn't ready to fit in with all that before. I resented the sort of shutter between us. But now I'm willing to try. If it's not too late. Can't we get through to him so that he'll break with this nightmare?'

'I don't know how,' he said simply. 'If only I understood the points of contact between past and present...'

'The henge.' He felt her impatience pushing him ahead. She so desperately wanted help, but above all some plan of action she could be involved in. He was reminded of a woman sitting at her husband's deathbed, willing his life to go on, refusing to let him slip away. Well, in this strange case there might well be a place for such psychic force. He was tempted to confide his suspicions to her, however alien they might at first appear to her rational mind. She had love and she had a strong will to life. Were they enough to help her reach understanding?

Kent still hesitated. 'There's something else you may not have heard about. I don't know whether he's mentioned to you – there's a girl, little more than a child...'

'She's in this dream with him?'

'No, she's here, in the present. But in some way there's a connection. Each time they're together he becomes further committed. As though she's his catalyst. But not quite that, because she's affected too. It is as though their polarity exerts a special force.'

'Where is she? Let me speak to her, please. There must be some more normal explanation. Perhaps she would be more open to a woman. Youngsters can so easily pretend themselves into emotional entanglements, especially with an innocent like Hugh. Let me have a word with her, Dr Kent.'

'I wouldn't dare. You see, Mrs Sarson, it could do harm. I don't think she has any idea what effects she produces. As I said, she's little more than a child.' He watched her carefully. 'And an autistic child at that.'

He saw the horror in her face. She began to speak again, then stopped, turning up her hands hopelessly. 'I can't believe it,' she said at last. 'This is the twentieth century. How can we get caught up in this – this mumbo-jumbo black magic?'

He let her walk about the room, knowing she would recognise for herself how useless it was to think in this way. From all that Alan had told him, he believed she would face up to the menace; but she had to take her own time, believe fully in what she was doing, and reach her own choices alone.

She stopped at last behind him as he stood by the blank window. 'Dr Kent,' she appealed, 'can you tell me about this child?'

'Come and sit down,' he said, taking her hand. 'I'll explain how I see it,' and briefly he told her of Josie's crisis, and how she seemed mentally linked with Sarson in some way. They could know nothing for certain because the child couldn't tell them, but as he slept in the trailer Sarson had murmured of a young priestess who served The Watcher. In confusion he had called her by two separate names – Alsleth, and once Josie. It wasn't difficult to follow that he saw himself linked with the child, as The Watcher was linked to the priestess.

Kent himself had seen how, with Sarson's increasing involvement in the past, the child's own stability had become at risk. Now while Sarson slept she seemed to be experiencing sights and sounds that did not exist for other people, things superimposed on her mind so as to be more vivid and more real than the circumstances she was actually in. She had tried to get away from her aunt and go across the plain towards the camp. He believed her sensitive mind was open to Sarson's dream.

'I'm sure she senses the danger he's in. She wants to be with him,' said Kent soberly, 'but I'm not sure we dare let them come together again. Two perceptive minds in so critical a state might well create some terrible force that could destroy them both.

'But then won't he try to get to her, if there's this symbiosis?'

'He can't at present, but I'd be happier if you'd watch over him. Can you come back to the site with me now?'

'Don't you have to look after Josie?'

'Dr Curry's on call, and she fell into a natural sleep about half an hour back. They don't need me.'

'Both asleep,' said Val, turning on him fearfully. 'If what you think is true, maybe that's all they need for meeting. Perhaps they're already together.'

The dog paused in his scratching at the loose board and cocked his head. A car was starting up in the forecourt, then another. The first pulled slowly out and the second followed.

They were not important. He had caught a known scent off the man as he passed near the side of the shed, but the one with him was a woman who'd not been here before. Something about the sound of their steps was wrong, a lack of springiness that added to his own unease. The car sounds died slowly, but not along the main road, and the night scents of the downland pressed more urgently upon him confined in the close, black space that stung his nostrils with fumes of varnish and paraffin. Panting, he lay licking his sore paw where broken claws and a torn pad were all he had to show for his work on the loose board. Chewing through the rope on his collar had been easy, but that alone hadn't brought freedom. He whined, pressing his nose against the small space where air blew in, bringing scents of the hotel and the detestable stink of cat's urine on the nearby gravel. His hackles rose and he growled deep in his throat. He drew back, spattering through the dish of untasted scraps they'd left him, and flung his full weight suddenly forward on the leaning board. It shuddered and pivotted slightly to one side. Now there was room to push his muzzle through and this was better. Shoving from the side enlarged the hole. There was a new rush of smells: grass and leaves after rain, reaching him through petrol exhaust fumes and the nearer stale scent of leather shoe soles. He wriggled farther, lifting the board's weight on the ridge of his collar, inserting his shoulders in the new space, gathering in his forelegs to strain upwards with all the power of his narrow back. And he was through, blinking in the pink, artificial light of the forecourt, free to run and smell out the girl who hadn't come for him.

So many feet had passed and cars rolled over the gravel. He picked up her scent faintly by the kitchen door, but it was hours old and covered by others'. It seemed she wasn't here. He drooped disconsolately but went on sniffing his way among the cars, along the road's verge, until a man slamming a car door aimed a kick at his head and cursed him off.

Over the road the silent, black plain opened out under a clearing sky. That way were the grassy tracks he and the girl had made on their walks. She would be out there at this time of evening and he'd only to follow. Trailing the gnawed end of rope that hung from his disreputable collar, he shot across between two travelling cars and fled over turf towards the little grove of cherry trees.

Joanna looked down at her husband slumped in the caravan's one comfortable chair. He threw his head back and drank from the hip flask left ready on the table. In a moment he would reach out, start walking his hands down her back, drawing her hard against him.

This, she thought – her view of him startlingly unfiltered and clear-etched – this is the man I am perpetually shackled to, if marriage means anything. It's for him that I must dose myself to a lifetime's sterility, running God knows what insufficiently explored circulatory and carcinogenic risks – so that he may take his pleasures without inconvenience. And me enduring him. If he is all fake, what does that make me?

Why couldn't he be a real man and let her simply bear

children?

Her hands trembled as she bound the leather girdle on. Was that then what lay at the root of her disgust with him – the age-old Eve complex: the need to breed her young? The desire for survival in seed. How long had that resentment burned hidden under her revulsion for her husband? Was what she felt about his false professionalism only the surface aspect of her rage at this undiscussed cheating of her rights?

It had taken this place, with its lingering ghosts of ancient rites, to release the tensions, to reveal her to herself as all woman.

But she had never really thought about children. Surely she would have known if this need existed in her, however deeply covered. And yet suddenly the idea was totally acceptable, almost in an instant. It had begun, she thought, in the car when he spoke of fertility and really meant sex. As though the physical urge was all there was. To him that's how it seemed. Because he was the centre of all life, and only things impinging on himself were of importance. On outer perimeters, things and people mattered less and less. He was, she saw, his own sacred henge.

'Why couldn't you be nicer to Fenwick?' he complained. 'It wouldn't have hurt you to be a little more forthcoming. He's a very useful man to know.'

Without a word she shook out her long hair, threw on the table the combs that had held it coiled in place. 'I'm going to look after our guests,' she said, as though from a distance, and went out, carefully latching the door behind her.

After a few moments Beaumont heaved himself from the chair and followed her up the mound, stumbling in the dark on the tussocky grass. There were more people about than he had expected when they'd planned the party. News had spread fast, and at a guess he'd say nearly all the volunteers had returned from their projected weekends elsewhere, and they appeared to have brought hordes of outsiders with them. Turning back a moment on the outer bank, he could no longer see them, but looking down he had the impression that outside the official floodlit ring there was gathering a further circle, a massing of unknown people out in the dark, silently waiting.

Even the camp, as he'd passed through, had not been quite normal, crowded but unnaturally hushed, as though in watchful preparation. There had been the customary bursts of tinny music from transistorised radios, the wail of pop, and the home-made strummings of amateur guitarists, but only as dimmed background, something to fill the time of waiting. And now he realised that what had unconsciously stirred his unease was the complete absence of light at the lower level. Not a single tent or hut showed a lamp, and all the usual fires had been dowsed. Expecting the camp to be deserted, Pengelly had diverted the generators' power up here for the filming. But where were the hurricane and battery lamps the volunteers normally hung in their quarters? What were these unseen people doing out there in the dark? Did he only imagine this sense of hostility, even danger?

Black smoke drifted past him from the far side of the henge. Ten heaped bonfires, fed with all manner of filth and oil waste, gushed at various points along the bank he stood on. Heat from them had caused a wind of its own that blew suddenly on him and was followed by a complete suspension of movement and a deadly chill. He felt sweat break out on his face, then almost instantly evaporate, the scorching tightness of his skin left crawling with icy veins. He turned back to the light and warmth of the henge's centre.

Floodlit activity reassured him. From here he could appreciate the clear production setup, the placing of spotlights and scenic effects, the mobility of the camera crews, the modern party paraphernalia masked from the film-makers by a hefty megalith of stretched canvas behind which guests surged about the bowls of brandy punch. He stuffed the empty hip flask back in his pocket. He was reminded of his duties as host and began to cross the short causeway that interrupted the excavated ditch. Here the tarpaulins had been allowed to sink under the weight of the earlier rain until one side had finally pulled free, inundating the opened ditch. And there, then, was the second ritual ring of defence against evil:

first fire, then water. In its sardonic way the weather had cooperated in the traditional precautions.

From the recording area a man came staggering towards him, earphones still clamped over a white and sweating face. He rushed past Beaumont as though he were invisible and began retching horribly in the vicinity of the ditch. That augured bloodily, thought Beaumont in sour appreciation. With the technicians soused, the whole effect could flounder. Joanna would have to check the caterers weren't mistaking workers for guests. But to judge from the rising pitch of laughter and the abandoned dancing he had to thrust himself forcibly through, no one was going short on drinks.

Dammit, where was Joanna? No one here looked familiar. They were so heavily made up in their clumsy Stone Age costumes that he could recognise none of them. Hands plucked at him as he pushed against the stamping, moaning horde. A girl seized him and thrust herself upon him, her eyes rolling upwards like a madwoman's. She wore nothing but a roll of canvas about her hips and the remains of rag shoes, but her body was slippery with sweat and a heavy-scented oil. For whole minutes he let her hold him, stamping and undulating fiercely, until with horror he penetrated the make-up, that was of a kind he had never seen before, and realised that the blackened teeth were not painted over but actually broken. The stench of her breath over him was inimitably foul.

With all his strength he broke free, but the madwoman clawed out at him, her nails gouging his cheek, and as he twisted to duck away she caught his shirt by the collar and tore it from his back.

He went plunging on towards where he thought the catering table had been, but in the billowing smoke, that was now twenty times denser and ranker, there seemed nothing there. Even the canvas megaliths were impossible to find and he was brought up against a series of marker poles, like spear shafts that ringed the inner bank. Turning, so that they lay directly behind him, he started blundering in again towards the centre. Then he came to one of the stone pans round which guests were crouched to drink, and he squatted to scoop up a handful and taste whatever was having this hellish effect on them.

If there had been brandy in it once, there was no sign of it now. Something else coarse and herbal had diluted it away. The drink was not even fruity, but tasted indeterminately of something like mould yet with a sort of sweetness that he half recognised on the tip of his tongue. He dipped his hand back in the pan and tasted again, almost certain that this could not be what had produced the crazed state of the dancers, for it wasn't strong. Disappointing, really, and yet not unpleasant. It cooled his dry throat and left the tongue unsatisfied. He could no longer distinguish the mould he had first imagined. Was the sweetness honey?

It was ridiculous. He heard himself laughing, and then afterwards came the thought that seemed so amusing: that the people outside, the prowlers in the dark, had spiked the drink. But of course they hadn't, couldn't have, because they were beyond the circles. There was fire and water between. He'd even thought for a moment that they'd played a sour joke, added 'acid' – students used it because it was easily enough prepared; any lab could stew it up – He checked himself suddenly. Acid, he thought; what is this *acid*? I don't know what I . . .

There was a stirring among the people round him. He half rose to his feet to peer out at whatever was happening now. Something new, because there was a distinct change in the air. He began to shudder as the wind whipped at his bare shoulders, and he tried to move in among the others to get some shelter, but they drew back, watching him from enormous, round eyes. He had a sensation of tallness as though he stood out head and shoulders above them. But of course, he told himself, I am a big man. I am a Colossus. All the world else is pygmy. And he began to move apart from them, stamping and slapping his arms to some private rhythm of his own, whirling like a rearing horse under rein, springing light as a deer, making darting rushes like a savaging boar, feeling the dark night of forests close about him. And then he was the hunter, the man-beast, dancing the death dance with his prey; yet part of him stayed hunted and part of him was hunter, so that he marvelled at the spirit that combined him into one being.

He was fired with a wild pride, because even as he whirled and leapt, he knew he was unlike the others, that while they danced indistinguishably together he was mightily alone and revelling in himself. I am enough, I am all. See and marvel! he danced. And while he moved, with such outstanding beauty, the others became quiet and huddled closer, drawing away and away, until all around him was the space worthy of a great chief. They accorded him honour and set him apart. He was above all men, fearing no spirit of earth or of sky.

Then again, despite the leaping and the stamping, there came the cold, and he saw the terrible space about him with no man in it. He was entirely alone and every man's hand set against him.

Poor, feeble cattle, cringing together. Who were they to look sideways at him? He despised them, afraid of their own shadows and the whisperings of sorcerers, believing that the stars concerned themselves with such as they were. Did *he* cower? did *he* fear? No; he shouted aloud that he too was a star, a free being, The One who was to be Feared.

Give me a fit adversary! he shouted to the sky, and stood, naked chest heaving, arms raised to the moon. And in the silence afterwards came the howling of a wolf, and a strange jackal-hunched shape slid from the darkness, itself dark, and started to circle, slinking. Closer it came all the time, and yet never directly towards him. *Pad, pad, pad, pad,* and the slump of its ugly haunches over the trotting feet, hangdog head looking every other way but at him. Yet he wasn't deceived. He knew who it came for. Such a puny form to take on against him; it filled him with anger. He deserved some nobler creature, something horned, with hooves of stone and a breath of fire. Let it have at least great beating wings and the hooked talons of an eagle, the venomous fangs of a viper. He despised this slinking grey shape that howled and could not meet his eye, slavering the ground and tainting where his feet would pass. He loathed it with a cold anger and a bitter contempt.

188

Slowly, crouching, he too began to circle, calling to it low and softly until its pace faltered and at last it stayed still, belly close to the ground. As he went forward to it, the creature sensed his intentions and turned, its hackles rising, the grinning lips pulled back over yellow fangs. The man sprang, seeing the hot, red eyes and foam breaking from the snarling mouth. Then his strong, brown hands were at its throat, shaking and squeezing; and the beast's hind legs came lashing through at him, the broken claws slicing into the flesh of his belly with each spasm, firing him further with the pain of the red weals opening. Then the tongue lolled and the bulging eyes glazed, and a shuddering ran through the thing's rotten frame.

He lifted his thumbs, readjusted his hands and settled his fingers about muzzle and chin. When he tore the jaws apart it was like the sound of oak splintering, and the life was completely gone from the beast. He threw its body contemptuously among the scattering crowd.

It was then he thought he saw a woman standing straight and tall on the top of the outer bank, midway between two blazing fires. In a way she was Joanna and yet not, as people have sometimes more than one identity in a dream. From the distance her eyes bored into his and her arms were raised, funnel-like to the sky. He felt her penetrate his mind and he no longer knew what he did, nor even who he was supposed to be. He turned to run, and ahead on another eminence he saw a second, similar figure, but he thought this a man, bearded and with shaven head, arms raised in the same gesture. Between them he was caught up in a great force of anger, so that what he had experienced himself was as nothing in comparison. The emotion engulfed him, transfixed him for an instant, and then it seemed to be gone, dragging something out from inside him as it fled. All strength too suddenly was drawn off and he fell to the earth, covering his face with his bloody hands. He was sobbing still as they carried him back to the camp and laid him on the bunk in Kent's trailer.

Despite his misgivings over what Beaumont might already have drunk, the doctor was obliged to sedate him

189

before he could relax the curved body sufficiently to reveal the lacerated abdomen.

Outside the doorway Joanna and Val Sarson clung silently together, until Kent called for one of them to give him a hand with the dressings. Then they both went in and Val took the bowl with the swabs while Joanna stood stiffly, her arms tightly folded across her chest as though refusing to reach out and touch her husband in any way.

'Where is Hugh?' she demanded suddenly.

Peter Kent looked up with weary eyes. 'We don't know. We hoped you could tell us. He should have been here, but his bunk was empty and the door lock broken.'

'Oh my God! This place; what it's done to us. Couldn't you feel it too, up there? Indescribably evil.'

Val shook her head slowly. 'Only for a moment,' she said. 'It was terrifying, but then quite suddenly it changed. Whatever was there went away. I know Hugh's missing, but – I think it's going to be all right. In the end.'

Kent straightened and looked thoughtfully at her. 'Have you some idea where he could be, Mrs Sarson?'

'No.' She shook her head slightly again. 'But I have this feeling. Of strength. As though all I have to do is wait. Does that sound stupid?'

'Not really.'

'Do you think,' she said slowly, 'that Josie could take us where he is?'

18

They sent down for one of the contractor's men to come and bury the dog. Pengelly, when he heard about it, flatly refused to let anyone do it. There'd be hell to pay, he knew, when the poor beast's owner heard what had happened. No hope of keeping a thing like that dark, with fifty onlookers at least, and all done by floodlight in front of cameras and the press.

'He must have gone out of his mind,' Gifford marvelled, for the second time. 'My God, he was obscene.'

Pengelly looked sourly at him and bit back any comment. The dog incident wasn't the only one that he'd to take action on. There'd been another outbreak of hooliganism down in the camp and a case of near-rape. Thank God he'd taken the precaution of arranging for security men to be on watch tonight or things could have gone further. Kent had warned him there were probably hopheads among the volunteers, but either they'd made converts fast or they'd been sharing their stuff with a few unwitting innocents. Beaumont himself might have been nobbled by someone with a vicious sense of humour. It was the only thing that could even approach an explanation of the disgusting way he'd behaved with that girl dancer and then the dog.

'I can't leave here,' he said tightly. 'Take a plastic sheet up, and you'd better let me have its collar.'

'There wasn't a name tag on it,' Gifford told him. 'We looked for that. Just a scruffy collar and a piece of chewed rope. We thought he might be a gypsy's.'

Still a dog, thought Pengelly. It made no difference who owned the animal, except to affect the size of the scandal later. It was up to Mrs Beaumont to try and contain it here and now. Fenwick was the man she ought to be working on. He'd better make sure the results of Kent's examinations were freely available, always assuming Beaumont's drink had been got at.

He found her in the doctor's trailer. She seemed unusually withdrawn and he assumed she was in shock, but there was no sign of any mental aberration parallel to what Beaumont must have displayed in his fantastic behaviour up at the site.

'Excuse me, madam,' he insisted, 'but did your husband eat or drink anything you didn't have yourself?'

Kent looked up from bending over Beaumont's dressings. 'It's all right, Mr Pengelly. We've decided it must have been the hip flask. Whatever was in it, he sank the lot himself. But I've got some dregs to examine later.'

'Well sir, perhaps if Mrs Beaumont could pass the word on? There's all these people from television and the Sunday...'

'Oh, my God,' said Joanna faintly. 'You're not suggesting I ask everyone to forget what they've seen and go quietly home?'

'See them anyway,' Kent counselled. 'There's going to be talk spread of an orgy here. Satisfy them that you at least are in your right mind, and allow them to satisfy you. Point out that when they get back to town and spread the word, people are going to ask what *they* were up to at the time. See that the technical chaps still get a chance to do a good job.'

Joanna stared at him, her eyes expressionless. 'Leave a nice taste in the mouth,' she said flatly.

'You can do it.'

'I don't know why I should. Swan Song, I suppose. All right.' Still vague she went over to the door, stood there a moment looking at her hands, and then went away.

'Mr Pengelly,' said Kent, his hands still busy, 'do you happen to have seen Dr Sarson recently? Because if not I want a search made immediately. Discreet but thorough. He could fall in any of the workings, wandering about in his dazed state. There's the pond down in the wood too. Better send someone there first.'

He went across to the sink, away from the strong battery lamp under which he had worked on Beaumont, and rinsed his hands. 'Right. I think, Mrs Sarson, we'll do as you say and look in on Josie. Your husband may well be making tracks in that direction.'

But Sarson hadn't turned up at Josie's home. The child was awake again and very disturbed, Irene told them. Some three-quarters of an hour ago she had howled in her sleep, for all the world like a dog, and since she had awoken there was no calming her. She sat rocking herself and moaning, while her head turned rigidly from right to left and right again in desperate denial as though the effort of the movement itself could wipe out the hauntings of her mind. When she heard Kent's footsteps she opened her eyes that had been so tightly shut, and she gave a little cry. The wretchedness of her struck at the man and he risked a direct approach.

Gently he took her hand. 'Josie, the dog. You know he ran out, don't you?'

Her mouth hung open and she fought for breath.

'They tied him up, but he got loose and went looking for you,' he told her. 'At the camp.'

She was staring fixedly at him, waiting for more.

'Yes,' he said quietly. 'He's dead, poor old dog. He's quiet now. You've nothing more to worry over. There, there.'

'What dog?' whispered the aunt fiercely. 'You mean

that old brown dog at The Plough?'

'There was an accident,' said Kent curtly, to silence her. 'It's been killed, and somehow Josie knew.'

The woman drew back sharply. 'She dreams things,' she said shakily. 'I've thought so before, because when something happens she isn't surprised. It's almost as though she were waiting for it.'

Josie had relaxed a little, sitting in the curve of Kent's arm, her head against his jacket.

'Josie,' he said again. 'We wondered if you know something more. Where Dr Sarson is. Has he gone away somewhere?'

Her face was different now, less relaxed than withdrawn, perhaps secretive. She closed her eyes.

They waited a long moment and then he spoke again. 'Josie, is he asleep?' The child opened her eyes and smiled.

'He's all right then? But we're afraid he might get cold. He should be back in bed, don't you think? Shall we go together and find him? That would be nice, wouldn't it?'

The girl's aunt started to protest, but he held up a hand, keeping his eyes on Josie's all the while. Her face had changed again and she looked softly happy. She pushed back the blankets and made a noise, holding out her hands for the clothes that hung on the back of a chair. Val got up quietly and brought them over.

Kent turned to the child's aunt and lifted his shoulders slightly. 'To set everyone's mind at rest,' he explained. 'I'd be very grateful if you'd allow her to come with us. We'll be most careful, in every way.'

The woman sat down abruptly and bit her lips. 'I don't know. I don't understand any more. But you seem to have reassured her. If you're positive this isn't going to upset her again...'

'No one can be that sure. Come yourself, if you prefer.'

'No. I'll wait here. I should have had to sit up tonight in any case. Will she be gone long? I mean, it makes no difference, but...'

He pressed her hands. 'It will be as short as we can make it. You've been very understanding.'

194

'No,' she disagreed. 'Not that. I've given in, but I don't understand any of it at all.'

'We have to find Dr Sarson,' Kent reminded her. 'Every minute that goes by makes it less certain that he's safe.'

In the pit The Watcher held his breath. For a while there were still sounds. From afar he could just distinguish the ram horns wailing and the movement of the people processing in a chain with the slow, solemn heel beats of the ritual, but gradually this receded too and then there were only the small sounds of his own existence and the occasional settling of the close-packed boulders, followed by a little trickle of the pebbles used to fill in.

He was bound by blackness, a dark quite unknown to him, conscious as he always was of luminescence, for the sky is never without light even when stars and moon are covered. This, however, was an utter stifling of life; all hope, all contact, all sensation severed except for a mounting fear that pressed in and threatened to consume him. Surely when at last they came to open up this pit they would find him disappeared, and in his place some monstrous apparition of fear would emerge to confront them. How could he protect them then, being neither of the living nor the dead?

Yet what should I fear but my own inadequacy? he asked himself. Where else is there any enemy?

Cut off from the world of men and of gods, deep in the insensate earth, he needed light. His body was demanding air. He heard himself draw a labouring breath, and the sound was itself monstrous. His heartbeats too padded closer and closer, pursued by panic. And nothing followed after but silence.

Yet the earth was not dead. It lived, if stones lived. Older than men, their breaths were drawn more slowly. Should he not be now like them? Could he not diminish the human and exist otherwise, as earth in earth, himself a rock at the centre of these stones? How else can a toad or a snail live walled up, but by becoming itself more faintly alive? So he would reduce himself, his breath, the coursing of his blood, and slow himself to the imperceptible rhythms of the earth.

Every part of himself he commanded and subdued in sequence, each fingertip, each space between the hairs of his skin, each muscle that bound bone to bone. First he became over-conscious of each part separately striving for recognition in the whole, then he made them submissive, weightless, without sensation, lost them as though they were no more his own, had never been. Only some small, deep core retained warmth and knowledge within him; and in all this he did more than control his own body, for he overcame time.

Yet he knew that above him the stars tilted nightly over the earth that pressed on him, and that night followed day followed night incessantly. Without intentionally counting, he knew the moon had grown to full beauty and begun again to decline. So Ishtar had passed through her phases of maid and nymph to become crone, while a part of him slept and grew wise in the way of the earth his mother; but his spirit moved abroad in the sky and was untroubled. From the tight, black restriction of the grave, he possessed illimitable space and all times both forward and backward, yet not in any known order.

He could not in fact tell whether he had already been exhumed or merely thought he had, but it seemed now that he was also alive in some future time from which he remembered the interment as a searing experience. He recalled the physical sense of horror and stifling as things already endured but of everlasting effect. He drew from them still a fund of knowledge and understanding, for from the moment of his burial all life had grown a deeper significance, his sky-awareness having become sacramentally rooted to the earth, and to his physical sources. Not only was he changed in himself but also details of his environment had undergone a transformation.

A second shadow life was going on about him, in which he was barely involved, and he seemed to be visited by the ghosts of future men, strangers for ever increasingly committed to their own artefacts, seeking to live through them rather than by direct experience, and persistently creating imitations, false creatures, sights and sounds to simulate the live world he was still connected to. These phantom men did not attempt to foresee and foretell, but the things they fashioned did this on their behalf, and the men trusted them above themselves. They made false stars. They set up an artefact that took part in the solemn dance of the heavens. Instead of a holy man, emptied of guile, there towered a sterile construction that lifted skeletal bowls of some man-made substance to link itself with the heavenly bodies. Magic appeared to have been cut off from the heart and wrought into a quite separate thing, working to create and destroy irrespective of holiness or evil. And so, in some way, effects were achieved without man's involvement through love or hate, but only through his industry. It was curious how this had come about, and it saddened him because these ghost-men knew something lost without being able to name what they were without. Yet he loved them still and felt the stirrings of compassion for them, as if for his children.

The veils behind which these strangers from time to time appeared fell sometimes shut like mist swirling after brief clarities, and then he saw the sharper outline of men he seemed to recognise, but they were changed too, being older than as he had thought of them. He saw children growing up whom he had never known born, saw himself a white-bearded and spare-framed ancient whose eyes had rested on truth beyond mortality. But he knew himself by the scarred brow that had never become quite smooth, and he recognised the insignia that he had brought with him over the great seas from the temple of Ishtar. He seemed to watch himself at work through decades, dispensing knowledge, rewarding, condemning, guiding, counselling the leaders, for ever protecting wholeness against fragmentation. He watched innocence corrupted and corrupt in its turn, guilt many times purged and then embraced anew; he saw knowledge like a beacon fed by the efforts of many men, one following another, and all immolated in its service. His heart warmed to their loving and grew heavy at their despair.

Above all men it was Whergh he suffered for, for the great good in him that was ever at the mercy of his ambition and trickery. And Whergh's son – unclaimed by him, since born to the priestess Alsleth – grew tall, and he recognised in him another such as himself, one who observed and informed himself on all manner of things that concerned mankind. He caught the child once, still barely able to walk but engrossed with work, sorting leaves of ash and ivy and emmer, and making them fit one into the other to make a flat structure. Some, the child found, would combine, but others were incompatible. And he had put in the child's hand many-shaped plaques of bark fingered from felled pine trees, so that he might further ponder the forms of life, so that his spirit might learn what things were fitting and what were not, for the child found joy in completeness and pattern, and although his body was received from Whergh, yet by his nature he was the child of The Watcher.

And so he saw himself, an old man, unfolding to this growing youth the mysteries of the heavens. And in time the child dreamed good dreams and The Watcher knew that this youth would live to build great temples to which all the peoples of the most distant parts of those lands would give their best and gather there to honour the gods and keep holy the spirits of men.

But not all went well in this future life glimpsed, for from the very first, when the old lord Luth awoke suddenly from his sleeping death and his spirit cried aloud for his promised burial, Whergh watched like a jackal some chance to encompass power. And when The Watcher was taken up from the pit of stones – faintly breathing yet because of the birch-bark channels, bound with the hair of the two women, one white-haired and the other golden, so that water and air had reached him all the time that he lay in the earth – one man regretted the soft, slow heartbeat that was all of The Watcher that spoke of life. He would have stilled it if he could, but that all remembered it was through him that their holy man had been sealed away; and since at that time they did not know that it had been a good and necessary thing, they sucked their lips in when he passed and he took himself away to hunt game, because men would not breathe upon him. When he returned with gifts, The Watcher had recovered and spoken well of him, and Whergh heard his mother pronounced the Great Chief.

Whergh's spirit was again torn in two, believing that a

woman should not stand between him and his adoptive father's place, yet cautious not to offend because he was next in line to her and his succession now seemed certain. But less and less, during the wise queen's long reign, could he endure the waiting, and he feared the holy man who established a temple his feet felt strange in. At the times of the Dance he would again draw himself apart, being afraid of what men might recognise in him if he abandoned himself to frenzy.

He had heard that his mother had been born in a caul and that this had been buried secretly as was the custom, at the root of an oak tree afar in the place she had come from, and he tried by all manner of means to discover where it might lie so that he could go and tear it in two and make her spirit depart this world; but the men of magic did not dare to find out for him, because The Watcher's magic was greater, coming not from himself but from somewhere beyond him, from the sky or the sea, both of which he seemed to have sprung from.

But a man must dance or die, so Whergh took his spear and his skinning knife and went off into the forests of night, quite apart, to abandon himself to anger and dance alone; which is evil. And so it was that full of black lust he came back upon the temple one night of the Spring Fires and leaped the ditch, and cleared the bank by wriggling on his belly like a worm between the cleansing beacons. Then, seizing his moment, he fell upon a virgin of Ishtar and ravaged her to within a breath of destruction.

She did not die, but from that time her tongue was stilled, and never could she speak again, however gently the Queen and her priestess counselled her. But The Watcher remained as silent as the child, knowing that in time truth would speak with its own voice. So it was that, moons later, in the great heat of Summer, when trees hung heavy with indigo shade, and foxgloves leaning from the chalky banks hung out their purple tongues, seeming to pant with thirst, the child rose up to dance at the rising of the moon, and her dance was the story of her desecration by the Queen's son.

So the people knew that Whergh had violated taboo,

and he was brought by force to The Watcher that he might name him The Destroyer and invoke the law.

'He who has killed,' said The Watcher, 'has chosen death, so he may not live. But this man has killed in himself the law, and cannot remain more among us. He shall be utterly cast out, to go his own way, and when his spirit comes to leave him he shall not be buried in the earth to contaminate its life, nor left in the open so that the wild beasts may feed on his evil, but the carcase shall be borne away, sewn in skins bound with the slough of serpents. And, carried by four strong men towards the sea, it shall be flung from a high cliff to where the sea beneath is deep, and an incantation made to protect the shore from its encroaching waves. And into the sea shall be poured back a whole bowl of its own salt, separated from the water and completely dried, as an offering, that the destroying spirit may be salted free of evil and return no more among the spirits of men.'

And so The Watcher laid upon Whergh the triple accusation, with the look, the word and the touch; so that he was condemned. With sorrow he heard himself pronounce against his beloved shadow and the black side of his own heart.

'Forever,' he said, 'art thou named The Destroyer,' and it seemed to him then that even he did not know the full significance of those words, but their effect was as none other's, for with them he had a premonition as of the end of all that existed.

So Whergh was outlawed, and in time other men joined him who were cast out from neighbouring settlements. They bound themselves together under oath and acknowledged him their leader, outside the law but creating their own; and in their small band was the communities' life mirrored, just as a single drop of water can reflect the same image as a mere. So good and evil struggled together within them, and it was seen that The Destroyer also created. The Watcher saw that all men were subject to the same flux of forces, however they claimed they chose the way to turn their faces, and all life was a perpetual movement between the two extremes. They created, he saw, by destruction, and destroyed in creating.

And Whergh, opposed, grew strong, while his mother's people, under wise rule, continued industrious and vulnerable. A time was coming, so The Watcher read from the skies, when each would need the other, but as yet he did not see how this could come about.

Nevertheless, conditions followed the intelligence of the stars, for new peoples were moving in upon the settled tribes, warrior races with terrible weapons of bronze, and these men respected no established customs as the earlier immigrants had done, and they were not numbered among the gatherings at the great festivals. They would as soon have overthrown the camps and taken what they wanted from the ravaged plantations as parley for grain against barter of their new instruments; but they feared the brooding stones that now ringed the holy place and any magic of which warfare was no part. Yet familiarity would make them bold. It was comforting to Erghlaun's people to know that Whergh's wild men hunted between the encampments and the newcomers.

The Watcher continued to scan the skies and they held now scant comfort for him. Relentlessly nearer came the time of great risk, and each morning the heavy counting stone was lifted from its hole and rolled along the circle to its next resting place, marking off the days. So it drew ever nearer the black rock that threatened the confluence of sun and moon. And at last he knew that in seven appearances, when the moon was in her full phase of nymph, the encounter must come. If the sun once more lay over the moon then would he, their priest, spread his body upon the maiden priestess before all the people assembled and beget a child to Ishtar.

But his own star lay across from the death star, and its light was wan, forever paling. And if the sun were crossed by the moon, then it would go badly with him. If the moon lay over the sun and the sun's ring shone around to protect him, then he would sicken and recover. But if the sun were quite extinguished and the world grew dark and cold, then this time he too must release his spirit. Only then would the moon relent and move away to continue her wanderings: the sun would revive to warm the soil and light again the spirits of men.

Seven days, therefore, before the day of calamity predicted, The Watcher sent for the son of Whergh, born to the elder priestess Alsleth, and gave him instructions. The young man was entrusted with the insignia and informed how he should counterfeit them, swiftly and skilfully, carving a replica from the bark of a birch tree, to be coloured like gems with bright dyes and made shiny with the hardened slime of snails. And, white-faced, the young man heard with sorrow how his master was to be served, that the tribe might regain strength and the truth continue. Then The Watcher dressed himself in a simple skin and with a bow in his hand and flint-tipped arrows at his side, he set out to search for The Destroyer.

When they saw each other from afar, Whergh would have leapt upon him and forced him to the ground, but The Watcher raised his bow, the string tense upon an arrow. Whergh had for weapon only his spear and he feared to launch it and leave his hands defenceless. So he mocked the other man to make him loose his shaft, intending to leap aside and fling his spear after; but The Watcher did not move, knowing his cunning, and kept his arrow trained upon the other's breast.

'Hear, Oh Destroyer,' he said at length, 'how you may be made chief and rule over your people.'

So they moved close and put away their weapons and spoke with their heads close together.

'Do thus, and thus,' said The Watcher, 'and all shall come about as I have said, for it is blazoned in the sky. Come down as soon as you shall see smoke from the watchfires of Spring Festival and smell green juniper and broomwood burning. And stay beyond the outer bank until I shall call you to destroy that which the people has need to have destroyed. So shall you make your peace with them and come again within their law, through performing what no man else may do. For we have need of a Destroyer, as we need a planter and a cattleman, a breast to give suck or a hand to set light to our fire. And when you have done this service for the people, speak comfort to them. And the Queen, who is old and longs to lie at rest, shall take you and mark your brow with a burning torch, and they shall call you King and Father, and all will honour you once more.'

Whergh spoke back to the ground, though his words were for The Watcher's ears, yet he could not look upon him, so eager were the flames behind his own eyes. 'It sounds well,' he agreed. 'Perhaps too well? And what of you in all this ceremony, old man? While I do this thing you ask, what of The Watcher of The Heavens?'

'There is always a Watcher. He is for ever your priest and will tell you the will of Ishtar as written in the sky. He must read it for you and translate in stones the divine numbers, that the seasons may continue and the Sun for ever return. And I swear that, even as you shall return to be a son to the Queen your mother, so shall your priest love you as his father and his king.

'But you will have need of courage, for terrible things must occur. Though the Moon fall from the sky or the Day become Night, while you do what we spoke of, yet do it to deliver your people. If you fail, disaster will be on all men.'

'I am no coward, Man-drawn-from-the-Sea.'

'All must fear who have no gods, hollow man. Yet you have gods, and a temple to worship them; but you do not recognise that they are there. In fear you will come to know them, and you must then swear that these are your gods for ever, for only then will they be for you. What I promise comes only from them. So submit. Once you are your people's king, you become the gods' creature. You cannot escape it.'

'I do not fear magic or the threats of quavering old men.'

'You are no longer young yourself, Man-whom-the-gods-once-permitted-to-lengthen-my-days. But honour the young, for whoever treads upon your heels is the man you pass your spirit to. Go apart now, and consider what has been said. Drink and eat sparingly, guard your tongue, bid your men stand stoutly at your back beyond the outer bank, and have courage to do as I say, for you will know fear before you are king, and you will never thereafter be such a man as now.'

Then The Watcher returned to the camp and lay till evening on the capstone of the tomb in which he had so long before been immured in living death. And the man already lying beneath the stone stirred in his stifling sleep, seeming to reach out forward and backward in time, so that all times became one and there was only one man, a single experience, all contained within himself.

He knew no identity, being of so many times, and when at last Pengelly's search party lifted the capstone and took him out he was confused by the manners and the faces of apparent strangers. Only the child stumbling alongside seemed known to him, holding on to his wrists with the urgency of love. She said nothing aloud, but they communed together as he was accustomed to speak with the servants of Ishtar, directly from mind to mind. He warned her, as he had warned Whergh, of terrible things to come, but not disaster if she were brave. 'Do not flee,' said his mind, 'the loss of one you love, nor the day gone dark, nor the consuming fires, for this has to be. Of fear is born understanding, and understanding is life.'

She did not completely follow his mind, but she would. It was the fire that so spellbound her, the roaring of the flames, their awful brightness, the agony as they seized on her body ...

Josie went on looking at him as though entranced. The pictures in her mind were stirring all at once, but they made no sense to her, like the pages of a big book turning so fast under her hands that there was only a blurring of outlines. And the colours all merged, making a grey through which a hot pulse of crimson began to throb. Then the pictures started to pull apart like strips of gelatine separated, each transparent in some degree so that all were simultaneous scenes, moving, surrounding and involving her.

It was as though all the remembered fear she had ever known was still active, crammed together in her mind within these pictures, and in each fires were devouring all that was cosy and loving and lost. One moment a misty hillside and the agony of her own flesh burning, while behind her screams rose and rose and then were cut to leave a silence even more terrible. Then the downland with acrid smoke blown apart to show fire like blood. Surely it was blood, this man's blood. She had hurt him, killed him. No, how could she?

Her hands tightened on his and she sobbed, begging him with her eyes. She didn't have to hurt him, it couldn't be that. No, not feeling as she did.

And now the redness spilled out of the pictures and spread all over the trailer they'd just come into, so that everything was aflame about her and she covered her face to blot it out, then bowed head and arms into her lap and sat rocking on the floor while they laid the man on a bunk and covered him with blankets.

'Come home now, Josie,' she heard a woman say gently. 'He's quite safe, and you've been wonderful.' They were lifting her up, going to take her away. She flung out an arm and hung on to the edge of the cooker, growling in her throat and frightened for the man they were forcing her to leave. And there, on the shelf next to it, she saw through her angry tears a circle of worn brown leather and the gnawed-through trail of rope. She let go the cooker, and Kent, hesitating a moment while he watched her, picked up the dog's collar and laid it in her hand. The fingers closed over it and drew it in out of sight, the wispy blond head bowed over it. She curled up again in her secret world.

Kent found he had been holding his breath. Such a poignant reminder, with the child at crisis, might have been disastrous. But at least she was quiet now and un-bound to Sarson. She was Josie simply, with no claim on her from The Watcher.

Sarson stirred, reaching out blindly. They were taking away Alsleth. There was more to tell her. Unsure, he searched for contact, but blundered into new mists and heard himself speaking aloud. Words in a strange tongue, yet not really unknown. Forgotten perhaps. So much had been forgotten and now had to be remembered. He struggled to sit up.

'Steady, sir,' cautioned Pengelly, reaching out. 'You've had a nasty accident. You might have suffocated in that old tomb, if the little girl hadn't got us to you in time.'

19

'But who put the capstone back?' Kent demanded, when they had time for an inquest.

'That was me, sir. That's to say, I was in charge of the gear,' said Pengelly. 'It was on Dr Beaumont's orders. After he got back from dinner and just before the party was due to start. Like Dr Sarson ordered, we'd left a ten-inch gap earlier on, but the Director was afraid of some visitor falling in. We were going to film him opening it up during the party. That's why he still wore his dig clothes, instead of fancy dress like the others.'

'But didn't you check, man? That it was empty?'

'No, sir. I was directing the mobile crane. Dr Beaumont checked the pit himself. He flashed a torch in.'

There was a short silence.

'My God,' said Joanna. 'What does that mean? That some superman opened and closed it later, or that Hugh was already in there and Donald never saw him? Or that he did, and...? How horrible! No, he wouldn't have wanted the cameras to find Hugh there later, unless ... No; even Donald couldn't want publicity that badly! Not that sort, surely.'

'Don't be so macabre,' said Kent shortly. 'It's more likely the hip flask was already taking effect and he wasn't focussing too well. Sarson's dressing-gown was dark and wouldn't show up against the grey rock. Anyway, it's done now and we've got him back. It's the obvious place we should have looked for him of course, but everyone said it had been checked before closing. Thank God Josie made such a fuss about clinging to it.'

'I only opened it to calm her,' Pengelly confessed. 'You saw how she was, breaking her fingernails off trying to move the great thing on her own. Well, I'd best get back and write a report up.'

'And I'd need to have a look at Donald,' muttered Joanna.

Kent darted a swift look at her. 'Take it easy now. We all deserve some peace and quiet.'

'Come across later,' she invited, with a twist to her lips, 'and make sure I'm not doing him any mischief.'

She turned as he followed her to the door. 'I wouldn't wish any harm on him,' she added soberly. 'Especially now. It makes it harder.'

'Leaving him?'

'I'd decided before this happened. Or a part of me had, and the rest hadn't quite got the message. People will think I'm running out on him because of the scandal, but at least I'll know the truth.'

'It's your choice.'

'Entirely, because nothing he can say or do now can make me change my mind.'

'You'll survive.'

She nodded and started down the steps.

'I shall come across,' Kent told her, 'when Val gets back from taking Josie home.' He closed the door after her and went back to look at his patient. Hugh was staring up at the ceiling, a deep line scored between his brows, but the eyes were unfocused.

'Are you awake?' asked Kent quietly. 'What do you see?'

'Everything,' the man answered. 'I am enveloped in darkness and I see total light.' He smiled to himself, then went on. 'How can a man have a shadow unless there is a light? How can he have a substance without spirit?'

'True,' said Kent. 'What is your name, wise man?'

There was a little silence. 'Once I had a name,' came the reply, 'but no more. Here men call me The Watcher. I am the servant of the gods.'

'And before this place, how were you called?'

A longer pause. 'I no longer know. I have come far, by sea and sky. The past is cut from me as the cord at birth. I am myself. I am many men.'

'You are The Watcher,' Kent agreed, sitting beside him. 'Tell me how you come to be here, what you seek to do for your people.'

'I bring them Ishtar.'

'Ishtar? I do not know Ishtar.'

Hugh smiled slowly. 'Ishtar is creation. She is completeness.'

Kent waited, but the man was silent again. He was still smiling when his eyes closed and he seemed to fall alseep. Then, after a few minutes, without further questions, he began to talk, fluently and on a level tone, speaking of his shipwreck and the bargain made for possession of him, his journey to Brevaryn, and, with love, of his people there.

While the story flowed Kent listened, moving only once to let Val in at her quiet tap on the trailer door. He put a finger to his lips and she sat beside him on the second bunk, watching while Hugh, eyes closed, lips barely moving, continued to speak of The Watcher's mission. She held her breath when he came to speak of the tomb and his inhumation, questioning Kent with her eyes when she noticed the changes of tense, for one moment he spoke of it as something endured and survived, yet in the next he seemed still to be undergoing the trial of the dark and airlessness. She had the impression that the experience was one so traumatic that he carried it forever as a key to everything else that happened, and that it held for him the clue to all existence, being utterly wonderful in some way. As though the complete blackness had illumined him.

But this is Hugh, she had to remind herself, having accepted for whole minutes his version of himself as The Watcher. This is Hugh, existing in the present, and I must listen to make sure he knows he has really been taken from that pit. However his dream went after this point must surely indicate whether he knew, even subconsciously, that they had already rescued him.

She concentrated on every word, and remarked the change now in his facial expression. He was growing sterner, apprehensive, terribly *old* somehow, even as she watched him. He spoke of the near future with such grave disturbance, but she couldn't tell what this calamity was that he expected, this 'time of great risk', for the references to stones and markers meant nothing to her.

'Soon,' he breathed. 'So let it be. I have done all that may be prepared. The rest is Ishtar's.' And then his hands fell apart and he turned on one shoulder in his sleep, a lock of hair falling from his temple across his closed eyes in a way that twisted her heart, so often had he lain like that in her arms.

'Hugh,' she called, daring to think he might open his eyes, himself once more. 'Hugh!'

But he settled more deeply asleep and in a little while he began gently to snore.

'About bloody time,' Beaumont greeted his wife as she let herself into their caravan. 'What have you done about Fenwick? Sobered him and sent him home, I hope to God.'

Joanna undid the borrowed coat. She had forgotten the Stone Age costume underneath, and now she grimaced down at it before sliding on to her bunk. 'He didn't need it. What he saw up at the site must have sobered him sufficiently. He couldn't get away fast enough and issue wholesale denials. I gather he's put quite a bit of money into the project personally?'

'Some. I'd hopes for more, once we were under way.

God, what a bloody business.'

'You're beginning to repeat yourself,' Joanna warned.

He gave her a savage, sideways look and the movement pulled on his chest. He drew a sudden breath and put his hands on the adhesive taping across his abdomen.

'How do you feel now?' she asked. 'Hasn't the injection killed the pain?'

He swore under his breath.

'Peter did say you could take the tablets as well. I'll get some water.'

Beaumont followed her with his eyes, hunched over the table, his fair moustache drooping as though it too were disgruntled. Joanna brought the glass to him and stood watching assessingly while he drank, missing nothing of the petulant mouth, the thickening neck and the mottled skin that a week outdoors had made shiny and flushed. His fineness was leaving him, she thought: the bones blunting over with fat, the hair stiffening into fuzz, his wit degenerating into grunts.

'*Peter*,' he said thickly. '*Hugh*. You're damn' familiar with them.'

Oh, no, she told herself, I'm not going to be caught so easily. We don't have to fight any more. We haven't enough in common for that. I'm on my own already. No need to take anything more from this salesman of second-hand ideas.

But her silence was too sudden. Even in private they were accustomed to play at scoring points off each other. At his best he was never fond of his own unadulterated company. Now, groping at rock bottom after his fall from grace, he needed sympathy, however phoney.

'Donald,' she said, facing him, 'I'm sorry this happened. It was a filthy trick for anyone to play, but for heaven's sake forget it. That's what you want us all to do, surely?'

He swung round on her, jaw slack and eyes wild. 'Who tampered with that hip flask? I left it filled when we went to Farne. It was there, standing on the table. You did it, didn't you? Only you and Fenwick were changing in here. Or did your precious Hugh sneak in when my back was turned? It had to be one of you. Sod him, what was he trying to do? Did he say it would knock me out and leave the way clear for him? Is that what you wanted, you slut? Since when did you have to drug me to get your bit on the side? Well, he never got you, did he? You on heat, and he went missing! God, that's rich! And he's not getting my job either. You hear that? It's my project. I produce the whole thing. I'll have it *my* way, damn him and damn you!'

'Donald, you're hurting my shoulder. Let go!'

'When I've finished. And I haven't even begun yet.' His speech was becoming thick again and his face mottled with deep colour. She was afraid the tablets were serving only to stir up the demons once more. She swung about and twisted from his grasp so that he went staggering back against the boards of the bunk.

'Yes, Hugh went missing,' she said coldly. 'So he couldn't have interfered with your drink. Nor did I. I didn't need to because you're not in my way. Do you hear me? You are nothing to me, nothing! No more than I am to you. But Hugh, that's different. Ever since you met him, there's been this worm eating at you, hasn't there? Because Hugh's the real thing you only pretend to be. He's what you might have become if you hadn't been greedy and impatient – if you'd troubled to work instead of grabbing and posturing. Every day you've grown more envious, trying to discredit his achievements. But all you managed to do was devalue yourself. And then tonight. You ordered that vault closed. And you knew he was in it, didn't you? Didn't you? You meant to murder him.'

He rocked on his haunches, hands covering his face now. 'The vault? Sarson was inside it? I didn't know. There were old sacks in there. Something. I wasn't sure what I saw. That stuff I drank – everything was changing. My God, woman, can't you understand? It wasn't really me doing all that, any more than it was him in the pit. I knew I had to, that's all. Something I couldn't resist. I had to close it up, just as I had to – do what I did later. If only you could realise what I saw then, that dancing-woman's face, the terrible fires blowing from the chalk bank, that bloody wolf, slinking in on me ...'

'Some poor old dog. Josie's stray.'

'But to me it was a wolf. I had to kill it.'

'Like you had to kill Hugh.'

He shook his head, rubbing at swollen eyes with the heels of his hands. 'Not kill, no. I had to cover him over. I had to. You won't see. You don't want to...'

'It makes no difference. None at all.' She was quiet again now, picking up her belongings and rolling them in the dress she'd worn to dinner. Her husband followed her movements with unbelieving eyes.

'You're going?'

'Back to The Plough. You don't need me. Peter's coming across when he's settled Hugh. He can have my bunk.'

'You don't mean only that. It's not just tonight. You're really going. You're leaving me.'

She looked back from the door, resisting the impulse to say, 'Yes, for good. For best,' and Kent's arrival just then gave her the excuse to slip away.

The night was full of smells. She stood by the Range Rover and shivered. Acrid fumes of the fires on the chalk bank hung in the air, and the greasy, charred stench of the pig they'd roasted on the spit. But behind them the earth was giving off a mouldering scent of its own, with the added bitter green of aromatic plants. On the silhouetted bank smoke still drifted and embers showed red, breaking through where the moist undergrowth, piled on to douse them, had left the bonfires smouldering. But there seemed to be no sound, neither near nor distant, so that she had a piercing sense of isolation. Overhead the stars seemed struck into immobility, a blank statement of now, without any cloud to smudge their hard clarity. She was conscious of a pause within herself, a quite distinct break with both past and future. Yet whatever that future might be depended on this moment. She felt disinclined to continue in any way she had already set out on. It was important to prolong the moment, because it was unique. She turned her back on the car, hugged her bundle under one arm and set off to cross the plain on foot, without haste and living each instant as it came.

Back in the camp Pengelly finished his report, rubbed a hand over the bristles of his chin, grunted and went out for a final look around. He watched the glow of the damped down fires that still smouldered up at the site and knew that before dawn they would break through and flare again. But the contractor's men were gone and he couldn't hope to cover it all himself. However, the camp was to windward, as much as there was a wind at all, for it seemed to have dropped now. To be safe he'd better set his alarm for three thirty and take another look then; the watchman was good, but the best were known to nod.

Apart from his own hurricane lamp there were no other lights he could see from here but the one in the Beaumonts' caravan. He remembered then the new gas cylinder he'd promised for Dr Kent and not checked on having delivered. No, it was still there under the bench. If he coupled it on now, they'd have coffee when they woke and they could use the light for emergencies in the night. He did it quietly, crouching by the trailer's junction, intent not to disturb Sarson and his wife who slept above.

Val Sarson moved once restlessly and half awoke, listening for Hugh's breathing through the dark. It rose and fell steadily, still with a hint of that vibration at the back of the nose. She lay back, satisfied and strangely content. The steady whisper of escaping gas from the main jet of the cooker, knocked on by Josie's desperate hand, would scarcely have disturbed her if she'd heard it. She turned on her side, facing towards Hugh, and drifted again into sleep.

20

The clack of the metal-frame door as she went out: it kept coming back. Every time he slid into half-sleep it happened over again. Her cold voice, and Joanna standing there with her evening dress rolled up under one arm; leaving him.

Between himself, lying there enduring its repetition, and her, rigid at the open door, there was a confusion of movement, for which he felt half responsible. He knew he tossed restlessly on the bunk, but there seemed also other pulsing more frantic than his own. Something padded about the thin, shaking floor and came to stand over him, hotly panting. In new terror he gazed up at the wolf, its wild eyes red, slavering on to his unprotected face. He started up and it swung away, dissolved greyly among the shadowed fittings of the galley. His own heart still padded after it. His breath was soughing, the pillow drenched with saliva.

He swung his feet to the floor and, despite his buzzing head, sat resting elbows on thighs, alternately thinking back and refusing to think. Kent coming in; that was the next thing. (Think forwards, not back: that's better.) Kent waffling on about – he couldn't remember what he'd said. Only remembered shouting at him about the tests, the blood and urine samples he'd taken; Kent answering that they took time, twenty-four hours at least, but not to worry ... Not worry? Funny. And then Kent saying he couldn't smell anything wrong with the flask: it seemed just like ordinary scotch to him. Well, it had to be the flask. Because, if it wasn't, then it was himself that ...

He tried to think what he'd drunk at dinner. More than Joanna, certainly less than Fenwick; and he was a big-framed man, used to sinking it. There'd been nothing wrong with his driving. He'd handled the car all right, hadn't he? Yes, there'd been a tractor dribbling along ahead; he recalled it clearly. Well, he hadn't been impatient then. What's more, at the same time he'd been chatting old Fenwick along rather cleverly. That's when he'd put it to him to take part in the costume filming. The old fool had seen himself as a sort of Hitchcock, sneaking in on the screen at the same time as managing it all from the outside. Flattered and intrigued, just as he should have been.

Well, there'd been nothing at all wrong then. It was later. So it must have been the hip flask. That was all he'd drunk from – except those stone bowls the extras were squatting round. And Pengelly denied all knowledge, said they hadn't used anything like that; that the only drink was in bottles on the caterers' table. So, the careless sod just hadn't noticed. Fire the berk in the morning. They *had* been there, because he'd drunk from one. He recalled how the stuff tasted. Damn it, but he had it still clinging to the top of his tongue, on the inner surface of his teeth.

And then Kent hadn't seemed to understand his reactions. Just because he'd got a grip on himself soon after. Well, what does he think I am: an inexperienced kid?

No need to suspect a brainstorm, or whatever these head-shrinkers call it, just because it lets up a bit quickly. And it hadn't properly cleared; only, there were normal patches. (Normal? My God, it was all perfectly normal, of course. Moments when it felt better; that's what he meant.) Intermittent attacks. If Kent had really known his own subject he wouldn't have talked through his bloody arse like that. He'd have known straight off that that creeping zombie Sarson had fixed his drink.

He couldn't say what it was about Sarson that really put acid in his guts. Not at first, because when they'd originally met, both on their best academic behaviour, Sarson had struck him as nothing impressive. Docile, well-trained, negative: a good second in command. He'd have said he was stable enough, too. Sensible back-room boy, feet firmly on the ground. Everything that he'd subsequently proved not to be. He should have stayed cooped up in his safe little hole in the British Musuem, not come out on fieldwork with the men. *And the women.* Joanna making such a fool of herself right from the start. She'd never been a pushover, but since coming here she'd reverted to Eve. Nothing he himself could do was right for her. But *Sarson!* A bloody little tin god.

Now, if anyone's behaviour had been erratic and abnormal here, that was Sarson. Sleeping sickness, or something of the sort, with *illusions de grandeur* thrown in. Kent should have spent the night with him, not here, taking up Joanna's place. If Sarson was left alone and had another one of his attacks – *Sarson alone?* Was he, though? Beaumont fumbled with the curtain and pressed his face against the glass of the window. No lights showed from the trailer's direction. So no doubt Sarson slept. Slept . . . alone?

The Watcher drew his eyes from the midday sky and looked out across the henge. His people stood as motionless as the solar stones, so that in the long moment while his affected sight adjusted to earthlight he could not distinguish between them. But the stones circled inside the chalk bank with a regularity that was god-ordained and holy. The men and women had no such order. They were all in disarray, assembled roughly in wide circles, but some a little apart from the others in groups of family or workers, according as they felt the need for comfort or the incumbency to protect. Although none moved, their stillness revealed them as openly as The Dance, for every creature of them was shot through with fear, and this fear illumined each one's nature. Fear, thought The Watcher, is from the gods, as is anger. Both hold a magic essential to life.

He had called the people together for the Time of Decision, of which he had been speaking to them, enigmatically, for the age of this moon. Now even they could see this day that a confrontation was upon the sky, as the two great orbs, equal in size, unequal in light, moved inexorably in upon each other. A space of no more than their own dimension separated them now, and with every heartbeat this was gradually dissolving away. The wispy moon looked insubstantial, sailing into the consuming fire of the sun. She must surely be destroyed completely when their impact came. The sun, so bright that none could safely look upon it and hope to see again, burned with confidence. How could it ever be quenched? the people had demanded.

In his white robe he stood upon the capstone of the tomb in which he had, a score of years ago, once been inhumed; and he knew that the sun struck a feeble fire from the birchbark replica that hung on his breast. The true insignia of priesthood was already worn by the initiate Watcher concealed close by. Somewhere on the chalk bank, his men behind him in the hollow, stood Whergh in his sublime role of The Destroyer. The newest Alsleth, priestess of Ishtar, little more than a child, was erect behind his own shoulder, the torch of pitch ready unlit in her hands. Naked, she awaited coupling or death. Upon the capstone, at his feet, beside the green knife of sacrifice was the bowl for blood and seed.

No one knew. The Watcher saw this. Whergh's face was hidden from him but he closed his eyes and remembered the man's savage glorying once in his rival's burial alive. Whergh had been younger then, less desperate but less wise. Perhaps now he was sufficiently transfixed with fear to let a little pity mingle with his triumph in the deed to come. And even he did not know with certainty, though The Watcher had spoken more directly to him than to any except the Initiate. Nor had Whergh understood how by at last freeing himself of The Watcher he would become more bound.

So none knew but himself, The Watcher, alive now briefly in the bodies of two priests already merging. One whose star was marked with death; the other ascendant, close to Ishtar. They, *he*, knew that the moon would certainly extinguish the sun; that the end of the world of men was upon them; that only by suffering could they hope to save existence. It was right that the less should be destroyed in place of the greater, and his spirit be spread among his people, his body a torch to rekindle the sky.

And now a stirring passed through the people as the face of the solar stones seemed to alter. None dared to break taboo and scan the sky, yet all held their breaths, hearts leaping as the shadows on uneven rock softened and slowly disappeared in a soft twilight that came silently upon them and stole away even their own shadows, so that at noon with a cloudless sky their feet were severed from their dark spirits and they knew themselves half-dead. A great shudder went up, and women wailing. Then The Watcher raised his arms as he had promised Whergh, and he fell upon his knees and stared at the dying sun, and offered up his sight for the saving of the light.

He felt, rather than saw, The Destroyer appear, and reaching out blindly, eyes fixed upon the celestial coupling into death, he gave the green knife into the other's grasp. He felt a tremor pass into him and the strong, warm pressure of a loved hand. Then his beard was drawn high so that the terrible enactment of the sky wheeled over him and he felt his throat slowly cut and the blood, warm, spilling about him as the bowl was held under.

How cold the earth had become, and eerily silent. Evening at noon. How long now until complete night, extinction?

The sky ashen, violet, but not a single star. The fires

billow black smoke but there's no flame. No wind stirring, not a bird calling as the moon blackly closes over the quenched sun, and still it grows darker, with the day dying. Sky like deepest sea, rocking over me. Darker, darker. No colour any more.

Have I no more blood to give? Nothing that may yet stain with red? Only this blackening flood everywhere. My life's blood; useless? Can nothing make the light return?

His own final darkness was lapping about him, and still behind him the child priestess had not uncovered the bowl of embers to kindle the funeral torch. She waited with her eyes fixed upon the ground where the first ring of the reborn sun should halo the dying priest's shadow. And still no light, no slightest shade thrown from his body.

Ishtar cannot fail, he prayed. Now, even now, Alsleth will kindle the torch.

Irene Blaydon, although asleep, heard the child scream. 'I'm coming,' she called. 'Josie, I'm here.' She stumbled to the next room, plunging one arm into her wrapper as she went.

Josie was bolt upright in bed, quite naked, dilated eyes fixed on the shadowy wall opposite, fingers spread stiffly over her lower face, mouth agape in silent agony.

But she *was* silent, and incredibly still. No moaning or rocking or flinging her head from shoulder to shoulder. This was utterly different. She was appalled, as an adult might be at some horrific encounter, and this encounter was continuing, invisibly, even now.

'Josie,' whispered her aunt. 'What is it?'

She couldn't answer. More than anything then, the child longed to cry out what she saw. But there was no way of describing the awful world of crimson that she was in, a sort of kaleidoscope with herself at the centre feeling it all, unable to escape the blinding brightness and the terrible roar of flames.

Just as it had happened earlier in the evening, she saw overlapping scenes, herself in each of them, each moving, but still nothing clear enough for her to know what fear-

219

ful things menaced her. And then Josie felt about herself a little space, so that although the fire ringed her she was as yet untouched by the flames. They couldn't reach her until she began to move in some direction. It seemed there was a choice then.

Petrified, she dared hardly breathe, holding herself rigid and apart, yet peering to see what lay through the curtain of fire.

Then the space about her began to grow outwards and she recognised other figures with her. Before her the man they had taken from the tomb, but bleeding terribly, held up upon his knees by a wild demon brandishing a knife. And suddenly there was an abrupt change of angle and of significance, so that it ceased to be terrifying and wrong, but became utterly right. He *had* to suffer so, she saw. He was dying for them all, and they must help him to die. She held in her own hand a dead torch, and between her feet was the bowl of embers to fire it. Heaped alongside, dried shells of holly leaves to drop in and make it instantly ablaze. She had only to await the sign, when the first shadow and light touched again the megalith she stood on. All round were piled faggots for the pyre, and still the victim bled, but slowly now, suspended between life and ashes.

She heard a voice speak, and the gelatine film of the scene she was in trembled, distorting the details. The word that came through to her meant nothing, and yet from inside herself there was some response. Again, 'Josie! and the membrane wrinkling. She thought suddenly of a dog. Why such a thing, in this moment of anguish? What did a dog matter, at the end of the world?

There was a hardening of some outline beyond the membrane that held her. In the depth of the inferno, a gaunt, black structure was sticking up against the sky. *Fuselage.* What was that word? She didn't know it, but it terrified her. The object itself was the most awful thing she had ever known, and she knew it from very long ago, from before life, it seemed. It reminded her ... *Father,* was that it? Father, Mother. Dead, it meant dead!

She couldn't get away. It was fire, death. There had always been that. And nothing ever being right again.

Now she was trapped between layers of this film. It was all running together and thickening, opaquely, with herself in between. Not belonging, in some way. There was a place, though, in this chaos that she'd once come from. The rest was someone else's, this man's perhaps. She wasn't involved in it, didn't have to do what they wanted. She couldn't, in any case, ever set fire to anything, burn up the terrible, bloodsoaked body.

It was someone else with the torch, she realised. Not me, not me; see, I'm over here now. This is me, going back through the thin film towards where the plane is burning.

She could smell charred trees, blistering paint, the choking fumes of hot metal and molten plastic; cloth; human flesh. All she loved was destroyed, but she was going back to its destruction, *through the fire.* Now she was in the middle, feeling the hot wind, the pain of scattering debris clinging to her dress and limbs, eating at her. Blinding brightness and the awful viciousness of it, more real and more intense than ever before endured; and yet this was what she chose, going right through it, back to be herself.

Only once she looked round to the group at the henge and was amazed. Her link with it was quite broken. The man she had taken for Sarson was not him at all but a dark-skinned stranger, smaller and very much older, with a beard. She had to leave him behind, but he was with the others who belonged to him. They would see him to the end, not she.

She turned forward towards her own world and saw again, in the blazing aircraft, an arm thrown up in agony, that disappeared once more in flame. Fire everywhere now, and herself walking, not running any more; walking deliberately right into it and through.

Everything was slipping away. As I die – he told himself, but without regret. He seemed to see double now, as each solid object was ghosted beside itself. And then the ghosts were no longer duplicating the physical but moving independently, hardening in outline, taking over from the others. Before his eyes, people changed. Whergh wavered and began to fade into something insubstantial; and from the dark noon of eclipse, walls seemed unaccountably to grow up and enclose Sarson. He looked once more for Whergh, and now it was from a new angle, the space between them for ever lengthening as he himself receded.

Yet *The Watcher was still there,* almost lifeless in the Destroyer's grasp; and the priestess crouched over her bowl of embers, throwing in leaves and cupping her hands above it. He remembered the sun and felt, rather than saw, a ring of extraordinary brightness burst from one rim of the moon, so that he knew all these people here would be saved. And Sarson too was able to move off, someone separate, while The Watcher's blinded eyes gaped towards the heavens, and at last there was fire, like bright blood, spilt across the moon.

From behind The Watcher came answering light as the torch was lit. And the people screamed, wounding themselves with their weapons to make more blood flow and the magic be greater. So the young men howled, to make their blades strike deep as they scarred and mutilated their own limbs. Whergh himself, with the same jade knife, cut out a circle in the dark hair of his chest, and his blood ran down to mix with the dying priest's. And down on the course, where the horses and cattle were enclosed, there was a terrible stamping and whinnying and thunder of hooves as the beasts too plunged in frenzy. Everywhere a clashing and screaming like a mighty battle; and in himself The Watcher knew a confusion of pain and the sensation that this had all happened so at some earlier time and that he now relived it.

Then they were straightening his body upon the capstone and the priestess held out the torch to fire the faggots heaped about and smeared with the fat of slaughtered cattle, so that a great flame should engulf him and set his spirit free.

Beaumont continued tossing restlessly, his mind full of Sarson, picturing him in the nearby trailer, perhaps with Joanna. Now he thought back he couldn't remember the

Range Rover starting up. The engine had a distinctive sound, and Joanna always revved it extravagantly. Even with Kent coming in then, he would have heard it. But had he done so and not properly registered the fact, or was that the one odd incident that kept nearly coming back to him? – that Joanna, although she'd said she was going to The Plough, had never actually left the camp? Well, there was one way to find out.

His torch had rolled under the bunk and he didn't want to disturb Kent raking after it. He had a lighter in his dressing-gown. He put it on now and let himself quietly out into the night air. It stank of carbon and smouldering weed. Up on the ridge of the chalk bank two of the damped fires had broken through and were ablaze again. Briefly he felt a violent nausea, remembering the last time he climbed up there, but he turned his back on the site and made his way over to the cars.

The Range Rover was there. You couldn't miss its square bulk any more than you'd miss the sound of its engine starting up. Just the same, he had to make sure; had to savour every smallest particle of his fury. He flicked at the lighter and peered again. Rover all right; white; his registration. The bloody bitch! As if others beside himself couldn't put two and two together. But that, of course, was exactly what she was after. Hadn't she always mocked him over his public image? Wasn't fame where he'd always scored over Sarson, the nobody? That was what lay behind this interference with his drink – to make a fool of him in as public and wholesale way as she knew how.

Well, he'd settle it now. Not in front of anyone at all. It would be just Sarson, and Joanna and he. In the dark, and with no one there calling the rules.

He tasted sudden bile in his throat and there was a rush of answering tears smarting his eyes. He leaned an instant against the trailer door before he tried to unlatch it. He wasn't well. There was this terrible shaking coming back, and the trailer's walls weren't solid any more but billowing like sails with gusts of wind blowing through them. His fingers, in the flickering light, were distorted and out of focus; the small sounds he made produced rings of echo, like circles in a pond. He thought he saw them coming out at him, ringing him round. And then nothing was real any more but the white-hot, blood-drumming anger all through him, sweeping him up, burning him away. Not *him* any more, but just the anger itself like a possessing demon ... He wanted to destroy and destroy.

One moment anger and darkness and the feeble, scrabbling flicker of the lighter in his hand. Then the door open and all creation bursting outwards in one searing flash of agonising light.

He heard his scream but was unaware he made it. Screamed, and knew nothing more. The flames, exploding the accumulated gas, roared over his falling figure, fed on his hands, his hair, the reluctant stuff of his dressing-gown; roared on and snatched at neighbouring tents, creating their own wind and reaching out, horizontal, for more, ever more, to feed on.

Sarson, between two existences, was conscious briefly of open sky and then walls closely round him. He almost was aware of his own identity, but also of incompleteness and of something unfinished. Then, in a searing flash, everything was split apart. The walls flew open and the sky spun, night sky once more and pierced with reeling stars. And through the blazing blackness one small, pale star falling towards earth, turning and coming slowly towards him out of space, taking on form, ever increasing in size; a sandy, four-pointed star that he reached out for and held at last against him.

Beyond the living man's reach, across time, The Destroyer thrust through the fire to deal the mercy blow, yet the victim felt nothing as his skull was cleft, for Ishtar had taken him.

Irene remained kneeling beside Josie's bed, afraid to reach out in case a touch might set off the expected hysteria. But as the seconds passed she watched a quite new change at work on the child. It was as if Josie understood now what a nightmare was; as though, for the first time, she looked straight back at it and refused to be touched.

'Good, good. That's my brave girl.'

There was a little answering flicker on the child's face. She almost smiled for an instant, then the look of absorption was renewed. She was trying so hard to hold back some spectre. Irene could nearly experience it herself, so intense was her own concentration.

And gradually the strain eased, the child's back was becoming less rigid. Her hands dropped away from her face and she leaned back against the pillows.

Then Irene dared to touch her, holding her close and warm and safe. 'Dreams are only dreams,' she whispered.

Josie heard her aunt's voice, lying back and seeing, past Irene's shoulder, the ceiling of her own, old room. She felt exhausted, but the sense of achievement was something new. She held in her hand the slippery silk of Irene's nightdress, springy and soft between her fingers. It seemed familiar from a long time back.

'Is there anything I can get you? Something you want?'

The child's lips moved and Irene couldn't tell whether she tried to speak or to pucker her mouth for a kiss. She leaned close to encourage her.

'Mu ... sic.'

It was impossible then for Irene to speak in return. She couldn't trust herself. She nodded. After a few minutes, 'Shall I play something?' But the thin hands wound tighter round her own. 'No? What then? I'll put a tape on and come right back.'

All those recordings of Lucas practising. She'd left them in the music room cupboard, because she could bear neither to hear them nor to be irrevocably rid of them. She took the first that came to hand, and there were some Beethoven Bagatelles, followed by Debussy, and she sat there on Josie's bed, sharing a rug with her and listening in the half-dark, hoping and believing that everything was somehow different now.

Josie was filled with wonder. She had been able to do what The Uncle had said, trying not to be afraid of the flames; and once the decision was made, the flames were a little less real. She had stared hard at them and begun to see other things through them, and some things were so sad but they belonged to her; others hadn't belonged and she'd sent them away. They had paled and quite disappeared so that the room came out and settled solidly all round. So she was safe. Out of the dream. And next time she would know what to do, and it would be easier. Not fearing the flames, he'd said; and someone loved being lost.

The music had come back in a way she'd never expected; not for herself alone, fleeting and inside her head, but just as she remembered it once, with light spilling in round her door, making the same slice of gold across the ceiling, and someone being with her, listening together. Not pictures in her mind any more, but real.

The sounds were silver, spreading like a curtain of hair, trailed like fingers in a ripple of water. She felt the notes enter her forehead, steal down her spine, extend in slender threads throughout her limbs to her very fingertips, curling into her toes.

She looked up at her aunt's tightly closed eyes and saw the little snail trails of damp down her cheeks. She wondered why this grownup was crying and what she was thinking behind the tight, white face.

21

'Sure you want to?' Andy had asked kindly, remembering how reluctant Sarson had been before about gliding. 'I could take you both across in the chopper. No bother at all.'

'Thanks, but we'll do it Val's way.' Hugh grimaced as she helped with his harness and he slid a hand inside his jacket to make sure it didn't lie across the adhesive dressings.

Outside they were going through the cable release check, and now the all-clear was signalled.

'Take up slack.' Val settled square in her seat alongside him, right hand lightly on the stick. Ahead the cable started straightening.

All just as before, thought Hugh; but it couldn't be more different. He hadn't followed dumbly this time, from fear and inertia; he'd had time to plan it during all those weeks of hospital and recuperation, with Val always just a stage ahead never for a moment doubting he'd come through and that their life together would pick up as well. He'd looked forward to sitting here beside her like this, with the field starting to run past and the glider's nose tipping up towards the sky, rising, then at last the light pluck of release as the cable fell, and the sensation of floating free, hearing the little, soft sounds of the fabric, with the world fallen right away below.

Val looked across at him and smiled.

'No thermal this time?'

She shrugged and pointed to a slight haziness ahead. They held level for some time and then slanted in towards the uplift, circling till they felt rising air. Then the horizon swung down out of sight and they were climbing. It felt good. Hugh forgot what they'd come to see until Val touched him and pointed down. They had come out on the rim of the thermal and levelled. Below and far away was the tidy, toy camp and the white chalk scars of excavation.

It was like a textbook illustration; no more. From up here he could appreciate the overall plan of the dig, academically correct, as the findings had justified. A site opened, a piece of fieldwork closed.

'And what did it all amount to in the end?' he asked. 'There's little enough material finds to show for all we went through.'

'At least the press had their nine days' wonder, with the Curse-of-the-Sanctuary-Defiled line.'

Hugh gazed down ruminatively. 'Beaumont wanted a dig that would be remembered for a long time afterwards; our own, local Tutankhamen. Surely no dead Pharaoh ever cursed so far and wide as this? But in the long run we were lucky to get away with a few burns. It's only Beaumont who looks like losing out.'

'He was lucky too, that there wasn't a greater build up of gas at floor level, and that the wall blew out with him. He'll pull through. His sort always does. Even without Joanna, and with months of painful surgery ahead, he'll make a comeback.'

'Poor old Pengelly,' said Hugh. 'He meant well, fixing

on the new gas cylinder for the trailer. Who would have guessed the cooker tap had been left at the ON position. We were asleep by then, so we couldn't have heard or smelt the leak.'

'I've been thinking about that,' Val interrupted, 'and I remember that when Josie refused to be separated from you she reached out for something to hold on to. That must have been when the tap was knocked on, but it didn't matter then because the cylinder outside was empty.'

'So Josie would actually have cremated The Watcher, as in my dream? Horrible. Yet I feel she was somehow able ... I felt at the time that she began some process that let me emerge. I can't explain. It was as though she refused to let the dream go on. Anyway, her face was there instead of Alsleth's, then came this star thing falling and I remembered you.'

'No,' Val countered. 'It was Pengelly caused the fire and Pengelly who dragged us all clear. Utterly physical. Nothing spooky at all.'

She banked and they turned in a lazy half-circle, a little lower over the abandoned workings. Now they saw a small, fire-blackened area, but there was no sign of life. Even Pengelly had moved out since the medical team had discovered the strange fungus. They'd ordered the site's closure and had it ringfenced for safety. Their report wasn't out yet but it was possible that the mould's insidious influence had helped to produce the inexplicable. Was much of their aberrant behaviour attributable to its spores, dormant for so long without light or heat in the soil of the tomb? – some toxic mycelial organism that suddenly exploded into predaceous life on being exposed?

Was that all his experience amounted to? Sarson asked himself again. It was strange how the idea of fungus kept recurring – in the old gypsy's diet; in specimens taken from Beaumont after he went berserk; in spores among the cremated remains in the tomb; as part of a dish prepared for The Watcher before his inhumation. A substance apparently capable of reducing metabolism to survival minimum, and having hallucinogenic side effects?

Before his own possession by The Watcher's mind, Sarson himself had been treated with herbal drugs, rubbed into his bloodstream by the old gypsy at the site. Well, that explanation of the weird phenomena was no stranger than the other that Kent had offered: that Hugh had returned to an earlier incarnation.

'Why do you think those ancient people all went away?' Val asked suddenly. 'Because of the fungus then too? Or because of what they'd done to The Watcher?'

He shook his head. 'How should I know? It was after ...'

'After you died?'

Sarson rubbed at his eyes. 'No,' he said at length. 'After *he* died. I was confused with him, yes. But he wasn't me. In a way, temporarily, I was him *and* me. He seemed to have become detached from time, as I think I was briefly. We met up, overlapped. Everything he endured, shut away underground all those weeks while his mind could range freely must have had tremendous force. Such experience couldn't just disappear for ever.'

'But, Hugh, what became of his people? He was finally sacrificed, you said; and cremated to ensure the survival of the sun at eclipse. But was it to no purpose, if his people dispersed and the henge was overthrown?'

'It was deliberately concealed,' said Sarson. 'They must have moved on to a fresh site with Whergh as their new leader and his son the young, visionary Watcher. They removed the standing stones, so perhaps they built their new observatory with them. The sacrificed Watcher must have been mourned; became, I think, a legend. From its earliest reaches myths of holy things and holy men have arisen in this western part of Britain. Perhaps they had their source as far back as this. Perhaps even the legend of the Holy Grail sprang from some relic such as the bowl they caught The Watcher's blood in as he died under Whergh's knife. But one only supposes. There's no proof; not as yet.'

They were silent, immersed in their own thoughts as Val brought the glider round for the approach to run in. Hugh leaned over the side and saw the logging team down on the field, and over where the cars were parked, two small figures waving. He waved back.

Val took the glider gently down, rolled nearly to a stop against the wind and turned, dropping her port wing. Andy came over to weigh it down with an old rubber tyre. By the time they were free of their harness and out on the ground Josie had reached them, with Irene jogging behind.

'Sky,' the girl called to them excitedly. 'Sky, sky!' and then such a babble of nonsense as she tried to tell them all she'd seen. Irene protested, laughing, and tried to calm her, explaining that no one could follow unless she took her time and spoke distinctly.

It was clear the experiment had been a success. After the first tense moments of take-off, Josie had watched enchanted as the little aircraft lifted, hovered, tilted, turned, riding the air.

Another tragic memory overcome, Irene acknowledged. Every day now some new milestone of progress showed that Josie was catching up on the lost years. There might be setbacks to come, and they would need immense patience, but Josie was alive again and growing and reaching out.

Val hugged the girl who then made an effort at composure and gravely shook Hugh's hand. 'Thank ... you,' she said carefully.

Beyond her Hugh saw a familiar figure lounging by the Blaydons' car. 'Kent?' His voice had a warning edge to it.

The little doctor came forward to join the group. Irene smiled warmly on him. 'Peter's spending the weekend with us. He's been wonderful with Josie. We owe so much to him.'

'My last taste of freedom before work again,' Kent told them. 'I return to the Clinic on Monday. Back to square one and the more readily explicable. Josie has promised to come and see me there sometimes. Isn't that so?'

The child was nodding eagerly and smiling.

Hugh eyed him wryly. 'I hope you won't count on me for another of your visitors?'

Before he answered, Kent glanced over at the others who were now moving across to examine the glider's cockpit. 'I conceded defeat some time ago over you,' he admitted, 'because it wasn't a case for my profession. You took me way outside my element. But you did lead me to Josie, and there I found a challenge it's impossible to forgo. Nothing could be so worthwhile as going along with her as she comes awake.'

'She was always awake. Just terribly alone.'

'Well, now she's joining the rest of us.'

Sarson looked at him. Peter Kent too had stepped back among the fully living.

'I don't suppose we'll meet any more,' said Sarson slowly. 'So, thanks for all the coffee.'